A GRAVE
FOR
LASSITER

Also available in Large Print
by Loren Zane Grey:

Lassiter Gold
The Lassiter Luck
Lassiter and the Great Horse Race
Lassiter's Ride
Lassiter on the Texas Trail

A GRAVE FOR LASSITER

LOREN ZANE GREY

G.K. HALL & CO.
Boston, Massachusetts
1991

Copyright © 1987 by Loren Grey.

Published in Large Print by arrangement with
Pocket Books, a division of
Simon & Schuster, Inc.

G. K. Hall Large Print Book Series.

Set in 18 pt. Plantin.

Library of Congress Cataloging-in-Publication Data

Grey, Loren.
    A grave for Lassiter / Loren Zane Grey.
      p.   cm.—(G.K. Hall large print book series)
    ISBN 0-8161-5102-4
    1. Large type books. I. Title.
[PS3557.R483G7 1991]
813'.54—dc20
                                                   90-5235

A GRAVE
FOR
LASSITER

THE GUNSHOT CAME shockingly clear on the twilight, as startling as a bugler blowing "charge" in a quiet church. Everyone in downtown Rimrock looked startled.

Lassiter had gone to dicker for a replacement of their pack animal. Herm Falconer stayed at a blacksmith shop where a loose shoe on his roan needed to be nailed tight.

Herm, a large, fleshy man with coarse brown hair and a ruddy complexion, had been drinking from a bottle that was now half gone. Usually he was amiable. But last night was a full moon and he was edgy. To make it worse, the pack horse on their desperate journey had gone lame. Herm knew it was his fault. Lassiter had wanted to split the heavy load on the backs of two animals instead of one. But Herm's boy, Vance, had argued that he wanted to bring along his big bay and Herm, as was his custom, had given in.

Herm was just tipping the bottle again

when he heard Vance arguing with a runt with a hard face and stained clothing. The man wanted the smithy to put aside Herm's horse and tend to his own.

The little man's molasses drawl pried up the lid of Herm's temper even further. "You talk like you got a mouthful of grits," Herm said. It struck Vance so funny that he ha-hooed loudly and slapped his thigh.

"Ah's Southern an' damn proud of it," the little man announced, and something in his eyes made the big smithy step back and make silencing motions to Herm and Vance. Herm failed to notice.

"Ah was one of Jackson's boys," the little man snarled. He came up to stand in front of Herm, who was slightly taller sitting down on an upended keg.

"Jackson *who?*" Herm asked with a tight grin.

"Stonewall Jackson!"

"Mudwall Jackson, you mean. . . ."

And that produced the gunshot from a big Remington pistol that had the roar of a Napoleon howitzer. Herm fell off the keg and rolled in the straw, clutching his right leg. Blood poured through his fingers. His large face was twisted in pain and graying fast. His mouth hung open.

The little man sheathed his big, smoking revolver and went roaring south out of Rimrock, heading in the direction of the Mexican border.

Like everyone else, Lassiter had turned in the direction of the revolver shot. The twisting in his gut intensified when he saw Vance coming at a wild run.

"Herm's been shot!" Vance never called him Dad or Pa.

Had Vance Vanderson been the one to invite a bullet wound, Lassiter would not have been surprised in the least. Although the "kid," as Herm usually referred to him, had just celebrated his twenty-first birthday, he wasn't grown up enough to sidestep trouble.

Lassiter hurried back to the blacksmith shop.

"Shoulda kept my mouth shut," Herm was babbling.

The men made a litter of an old blanket and Lassiter helped carry Herm two blocks to the Rimrock Hospital.

A doctor named Ferguson, tall and spare, with a beak nose upon which his eyeglasses rested, made a hasty examination. Then he came to the room where Lassiter and Vance waited.

3

"You're the son?" Ferguson asked Vance.

"Stepson," Vance winced.

"The bullet splintered the femur. I'll try and save the leg, but I don't know. . . ." He spread his scrubbed hands apologetically, and allowed the men to go see Herm, who was barely conscious.

"Lassiter, you an' the kid git movin'. Leave me be. My brother Josh needs help. It was why we was ridin' hellbent in the first place. . . ."

Lassiter told the older man to save his breath. "We're not moving till we see about that leg."

"Herm's right," Vance cut in. Lassiter could have kicked him. The "kid" had clear hazel eyes in a rather handsome face. A bushy brown mustache not only made him look more mature, but fascinated the ladies, so he claimed.

"I'll be fine right here," Herm gasped. "Lassiter, you do what I'm askin'. We been friends a long time. You an' me an' my brother Josh. Do it for us."

Before Lassiter could reply, a deputy sheriff entered the room to discuss the shooting. The big, slow-moving man with a mean eye let it be known that he had been in Beauregard's command during the war and hadn't much sympathy for a man who'd malign Stonewall Jackson by calling him Mudwall. The deputy had evidently gotten his information from the smithy.

Lassiter didn't argue the matter; the war had been over for some years but wounds were still raw. He knew it would take little effort to run down the runt who had put the bullet in Herm Falconer.

Before the day was out, Lassiter agreed to continue the fast trip north to rescue Herm's older brother from financial quicksand.

"You got the money," Herm said in a feeble voice, clinging to Lassiter's hand. "Eleven thousand from me an' seven of your own. Eighteen thousand will see Josh clear."

Lassiter looked across the bed and saw Vance Vanderson watching him closely. Being reminded of the gold coins they were carrying had put a contemplative look in the hazel eyes. Lassiter told himself to sleep lightly until they reached Josh.

Lassiter chanced the suggestion that Vance stay behind. "He'll be company for you, Herm. I'll get the money to Josh and give him a hand with his freight line till you show up. . . ."

But Herm wouldn't hear of it. "Purely my fault I got in this mess. Shoulda listened to you about bringin' two pack horses 'stead of one." Herm turned his head on the pillow and looked up at his stepson. "Meanin' nothin' against you, but Lassiter's smart," which made the younger man's lips twitch. "An' if that goddamn hoss," Herm continued, "hadn't gone lame, I wouldn't be in this pickle."

When they started riding again, Vance said, "Sure glad I didn't have to stay behind. That hospital's got a stink that turns my stomach."

"Herm'll have to live with it for a spell," Lassiter reminded crisply. He was an inch under six feet and rode his black horse with all the grace of a Comanche warrior. What could be seen of his hair under a flat-crowned black hat was very dark. He had a strong nose and chin, and a pair of blue eyes that could be amiable or cold as winter rock.

"Reckon it was me laughin' so hard that made the runt mad," Vanderson said. They were pushing north through country with house-sized boulders in a sea of chapparal.

"You shouldn't have laughed."

"No reason to get uppity. Hell, I'm sorry as you that Herm had to go and open his big mouth to that runty little Reb."

"Herm was half-drunk and you should

have known better than to throw coal oil on the fire by your howling."

"Maybe. But it was a full moon, for one thing. The pack hoss giving out on us was another. I've lived with Herm since I was eleven so I can smell a drunk coming on just like sniffing a barrel of dirty clothes."

"You haven't shown a sliver of sympathy for Herm getting shot."

"I am sorry, hell." Vanderson was silent for a mile or so. Then he said musingly, "Be somethin' if Herm didn't come out of it. I'd own Northguard Freight Company along with Josh, now wouldn't I?"

Lassiter was too disgusted with the way things had turned out to say anything. It had started out as one brother going to the financial rescue of another. And because Lassiter knew them both and had some ready cash for a change, he had wanted to be a part of it. But when Herm insisted on including his stepson, Lassiter had almost backed out. It was like that pack horse that had gone lame; too late to do anything about it now.

That night he lay in his blankets with the two money sacks under his legs, Henry rifle and .44 revolver at hand. Vanderson seemed impressed and made no attempt to appropriate the gold coins. The "kid" wasn't one to take a chance when the odds were not favorable. Lassiter smiled to himself and rubbed a hand over his new lucky silver belt buckle.

Toward the end of the week, Lassiter and Vanderson pushed their jaded horses toward Bluegate, their destination. Thankfully they reached the twin columns of bluish stone that had given the town its name.

After all else that had gone wrong on the fast desperate trip, learning that an old enemy was a resident of Bluegate was the last straw.

On the late fall day on the main street in front of Dixie's Saloon, Lassiter spotted the tall, arrogant figure of Kane Farrell. At the sight of Lassiter, Farrell's jaw dropped and he nearly lost the cheroot he was smoking. Quickly recovering, he challenged, "I thought by now you'd be in your grave."

"Not quite, Farrell," Lassiter said, halting his horse and pack animal on the busy street.

Farrell pointed at Lassiter's belt. "I hear a sheriff down south wasted county funds buying you that silver belt buckle."

"In appreciation for helping him rid the

county of scum," was Lassiter's rejoinder. "I see some of it's drifted up this way."

Their voices crackled in the late afternoon. Men and women on the crowded walk looked at them in surprise.

Lassiter, his face darkened from years of sun and wind, grew taut. "You living here, Farrell, or just passing through?"

"I'm establishing myself." A light brown hat was set at a jaunty angle on Farrell's thick dark red hair. "How about you? Passing through, I trust."

"Not quite." Lassiter could see the heel-plates of a revolver under Farrell's well-tailored light brown coat. He could read hatred in the cold green eyes. "Let's go, Vance," he said, giving Vanderson a nod of the head.

They moved off down the street. Vanderson swung alongside Lassiter's weary black horse; his own chestnut was in worse shape.

"You were downright insulting to that gentleman," Vanderson said with lifted brows.

"That *gentleman* and I go back a few years."

"Obviously you hate each other."

"I've put my bootheels down on a few of his schemes. He hasn't forgotten."

They rode past a bank, a milinery shop,

9

a large building that was the Bluegate Mercantile. To the north, a notch in a purple barrier of mountains was Northguard Pass.

The town was larger than Lassiter remembered from some years before. That time he had ridden with Herm Falconer, who had just sold a cattle ranch and wanted to visit his brother Josh. They stayed around for a spell, helping Josh try to locate an elusive vein of silver in a mine tunnel. In addition to mining, Josh Falconer also ran the Northguard Freight Company, the first building of which Lassiter was now passing. He whistled at the magnificence of the stable, more than triple the size of the former one where the company mules were kept. Beyond that was a huge building of new and unpainted pine. Northguard Warehouse, so a sign proclaimed.

"Josh must've stumbled over a pot of gold," Lassiter said to Vance Vanderson.

"Josh was always rich, so Herm claimed. Just stingy."

Lassiter noticed that whenever Vanderson spoke of his step relatives, father or uncle, there always seemed to be a note of resentment in his voice. He was the son of Herm's second wife, who had died some years back. Lassiter had first seen Vanderson when the

10

kid was twelve. Even then he had thought that Herm's wife had made a career out of spoiling her offspring. When Herm took over, he tried to straighten the boy out and sometimes almost seemed to succeed.

Passing through town most recently, Lassiter had stopped by to see Herm. The stepson had given him the usual surly greeting, but Herm was overjoyed to see Lassiter. He had just received a letter from his brother Josh up at Bluegate. Josh needed financial help with his freight line.

"It'll give me somethin' to sink my teeth in, Lassiter," Herm had said, his eyes shining. "Why don't you come in with me?"

Lassiter hesitated but when he learned that Josh was in very bad shape, he agreed. Lassiter had just quit a ramrod job he hated, but he had cash and decided it might be a challenge to help get a freight line back on a sound basis.

The first hitch developed when Herm said, "I want Vance to come along. Workin' with us'll put starch in his backbone."

"But I thought he had a job as segundo out at XY?"

"He quit."

As Lassiter debated whether to back out or go ahead with it, a tearful second letter

11

arrived from Josh, saying that he was about to go under. Josh, the old reprobate, needed a hand with his freight company. Lassiter couldn't refuse.

There was more to Josh's letter that Herm discussed with Lassiter. "The girl's come out to live with Josh. Alice died last July."

"Who's the girl?" Lassiter asked.

"Our sister Alice's offspring."

Then Lassiter remembered.

"Our sister got treated shameful by me an' Josh," Herm went on dolefully. "On account of her runnin' off an' marryin' with that fella Ralph. We told her not to but she went ahead an' done it anyway. Reckon Alice was as pigheaded as me an' Josh."

Lassiter recalled meeting Alice one time when she came south from Denver and stopped in to say howdy to Josh. Alice had brought her daughter with her on the visit. A shy child, built like a trimmed cottonwood pole, he remembered somebody saying about the girl.

A sign at the end of the warehouse said OFFICE.

There were two bookkeepers, their pens scratching away in ledgers. Through the windows Lassiter could see two men rolling barrels onto a loading platform.

A pale-haired girl sat beside a large table that was being used as a desk. It was piled high with papers. Faint shadows were visible beneath her light gray eyes. She smoothed out a frown so that her delicate features seemed to relax.

"Can I help you gentlemen?"

Lassiter had heard that a few females had moved into the male province of secretary but he hadn't expected it of Josh, the traditionalist.

"I'm Lassiter. . . ."

"Oh, yes, there's a letter around here someplace from Uncle Herm. He mentioned you. . . ."

"Then you must be their niece."

"I am."

"I took you for a secretary."

"I'm that and more. I . . . I am trying to operate this freight line." She peered around Lassiter who was standing so he could keep one eye on the pack horse that carried the precious gold. "Where is Uncle Herm?"

Lassiter told her.

She slumped back in her chair and murmured, "My God, what next?"

Tears filled her eyes and she put her head down. Lassiter gently pressed a clean handkerchief into her hand. She nodded her thanks and used it to wipe her eyes.

"Where's Josh?" Lassiter asked, looking beyond the office into the vast warehouse with its scattering of crates and boxes.

"He . . . he's dead."

Lassiter gave a deep sigh. He leaned both hands on the table. "How did it happen?"

"He . . . he just up and died." She wiped her eyes again.

"You must be Melody," Vanderson said. "Herm has a daguerr of you. Of course you don't look the same. Now you're kind of . . . well, rounded out." He gave her his boyish smile. His hazel eyes acquired a glow of excitement. He rubbed slender hands together. "That means the freight line is yours, now that Josh is no longer among the living. . . ."

"It will belong to Uncle Herm, of course," she said, straightening up in her chair. "And the sooner he gets here . . ."

"And he just might not," Vanderson stated wryly.

Her head came up, the damp handkerchief clutched in one hand. "Surely he's not that badly wounded."

"He might lose a leg."

14

Lassiter gave him a hard look. "Herm'll be all right."

Lassiter noticed Vanderson's eyes locked on the shapely breasts outlined by the thin material of Melody's white dress, with its decoration of small yellow flowers. Vanderson irritated him.

"Your Uncle Josh's death must have been sudden," Lassiter said. "Herm got a letter from him about two weeks ago."

"It was because of a . . . a woman." Taking a deep breath, Melody Hale told of her late uncle and Marcina. A sorry tale of an older man infatuated by a beauty who had drifted into Bluegate. He had tried to impress her by building a new stable, a warehouse, and an office. Topping his reckless expenditures with a fine house at the north end of town. Although he tried to get her to marry him, she hesitated.

"By then he had taken all his money out of the bank to put up the buildings, so Uncle Josh told me," Melody whispered. "She demanded to see a profit from the freight line before she'd let him put a ring on her finger. He had neglected business terribly because of her."

"Go on, Melody," Lassiter urged.

"They . . . they got married. And she was

with child. She and the baby died. Uncle Josh . . . well, he wrote for me to come live with him. By the time I got here he was in terrible shape."

"We're here to help you, Melody."

"If it's not too late. So much has happened since Uncle Josh died," Melody said in despair.

"Tell me about it?"

"There's a man. He's been giving me all kinds of trouble." She wiped her eyes again, but her firm chin came up. "I'm still trying to fight him, but . . ."

"His name?"

"Kane Farrell."

Lassiter's lips tightened at the mention of a man who had been his enemy for so long. Seeing him today in Bluegate had revived old hatreds. And now their paths were interlocking once again. . . .

_____ 2

MELODY'S GRAY EYES began to fill again. Lassiter reached across the cluttered desk to grip her hands and told her about the money, eleven thousand from Uncle Herm, seven from him, hoping to make her feel better.

"That'll keep things going," he assured her. "And Herm'll be here as soon as his leg heals. . . . Vance and I will help get the company rolling again. Won't we, Vance?"

But Vanderson seemed too bewitched by the girl's figure to listen. When Lassiter repeated it, he lifted his head. "Yeah . . . sure we'll help." He beamed at her.

One of Northguard's current problems, Lassiter learned, was a shortage of rolling stock. A wagon had been wrecked, another had a broken tongue and a missing wheel. The only serviceable one was mired in mud, five miles above the town of Aspen Creek.

"And I have freight to move and I don't know what to do," she said, spreading her hands in a gesture of defeat.

"Vance, let's go get that wagon out of the mud," Lassiter said.

"The very thing I was going to suggest." Vanderson flashed his boyish smile again, his eyes merry.

But first there was the business of depositing the money. They all went down to the bank where the two sacks of gold coins were removed from the pack animal that Lassiter had led along the tree-bordered street.

The banker, Donald Edgerton, bald and pompous in a tight black suit, supervised the deposit. Melody and Lassiter affixed their signatures, then signed as witnesses under Herman Falconer's name.

Edgerton revealed small teeth smiling at Melody. "My dear, now you have fresh blood in your organization. Too bad your Uncle Josh couldn't have lived to see this glorious day. Ah, well, the good die young, as the saying goes."

Lassiter speculated on the lack of sincerity in the banker's voice.

When they were outside, Vanderson spoke to Lassiter in a low, tight voice. "Seems to me, I'm part of the family, yet I didn't get my name on anything."

Melody had gone ahead to make a purchase at the Bluegate Mercantile. The walks were crowded with ranchers and townsmen. On the streets were buggies and buckboards, farm wagons, and a stagecoach just leaving for Montclair, many miles to the north.

"You're Herm's stepson," Lassiter pointed out. "Herm will take care of you."

"I'm as much family as Melody and she gets to put her name on the bank account. . . ."

Lassiter turned on him. "Don't go building big dreams in that head of yours. Could be bad for the digestion."

When Lassiter said he and Vanderson would stay at the hotel, Melody insisted they take the spare bedrooms at the big house her Uncle Josh had built.

Staying under the same roof with a young, pretty, and unmarried female, Lassiter pointed out with a smile, might give the local gossips something to chew on.

Melody laughed, saying she had retained her uncle's housekeeper. The presence of another woman should make the arrangement acceptable, she said. Over the passing hours, she seemed to have shed her mantle of gloom, Lassiter noticed.

The next morning he and Vanderson got ready to leave for the mountains. Melody offered to draw a map of the area, but Lassiter knew it well. "I guess you've forgotten that I tried to help Josh hunt a vein of silver in his mine," he finished.

Her cheeks colored and she lowered her eyes. She needed no reminder, for young as she had been, Lassiter had fascinated her. The dark man of mystery, Uncle Josh had said with a smile, who would show up all of a sudden and then not be seen for some years. "I haven't forgotten," she said. "But it was a long time ago. . . ."

"We'll get your wagon out of the mud," Lassiter promised.

She was so confident that he would succeed where her men had failed that she suggested he pick up a team of mules at Aspen City.

Vanderson cleared his throat. "You go do the job, Lassiter. I'll stay here and keep an eye on Melody. . . ."

"We're both going to do the job. Because I've got a hunch we're the only ones Melody can trust."

"You and Dad Hornbeck," Melody cut in. "He runs the office at Aspen City. He worked for my Uncle Josh."

When they were ready to ride, Vanderson was still grumbling. "She's got men working for her and I don't see why they can't help you while I stay here and. . . ."

"Too much has gone wrong. Her men couldn't get the wagon out of the mud. We will."

They left Bluegate on a bright fall day. Lassiter wondered how Herm, down in Rimrock, was making out. He hoped to God the doctor didn't have to take off his leg. There was no telling what Herm's reaction would be. Lassiter ground his teeth. He wanted to be moving on before he got mired down in the affairs of Northguard. With Vanderson a dead weight, if something happened to Herm, and with Josh dead, things didn't look too promising. But he had given his word to Herm and he would do his damndest to save something for the niece, Melody Hale. . . .

On the same hour they had made the bank deposit the day before, Farrell came along the boardwalk, two large men flanking him. At the sight of Lassiter down the block, he grabbed both men by the arms and brought them to a halt.

"There he is now," Farrell hissed. "The gent I was talking about."

"You mean the one with the mustache?" Dutch Holzer asked, squinting out of black eyes.

"That one's about as deadly as a sick gnat. Hell, no, the other one, about your size, Dutch. . . ."

"Hell, I know Lassiter," towering Ed Kiley spoke up. "I recollect him when he used to come a visitin' Josh Falconer."

"I want him dead," Farrell hissed through his teeth. "Every time I get the money mill swinging my way, it seems that bastard horns in. But not this time."

21

"How much you pay, Farrell?" Ed Kiley asked, turning his large head to Farrell.

"The job's worth two thousand."

Dutch Holzer whistled. "A thousand each, huh?"

"Don't do it in town. Wait till he leaves —which he will. I have a hunch he'll be trying to get Northguard's wagons rolling again."

-- *3*

DAD HORNBECK, A bald and graying man, shook hands with Lassiter and said he was glad, for Melody's sake, that the freight line had two stalwarts to help out now that Josh was gone and Herm was laid up. But when the old man spoke, he gave Vanderson a slightly dubious look.

There was one fairly large bedroom in the Aspen Creek office where Hornbeck slept. He offered them the bed, but Lassiter said they'd spread their blankets on the office floor. Vanderson pointed out that they would have more comfort at the town's small hotel.

"We're trying to save every dollar," Lassiter reminded the younger man.

Early the next morning, Lassiter herded eight mules up the steep grade out of Aspen City. A grumbling Vanderson drove a light wagon that held ropes and harness for the team. It was a clear day, without a cloud to mar the azure dome of the sky. Golden aspens lined the steep road and the cottonwoods were dropping their leaves. Wild geese formed long triangles in the sky as they headed south. Nature seemed to be holding a deep breath before the first onslaught of snows that would block some of the passes till spring.

Lassiter knew there was no time to waste. A freight wagon had to be put back in service so shipments could be made before the cold months settled in.

Finally Vanderson got over his grouch long enough to speak civilly. "Tell me about Josh. I never did get to meet him. And even what I don't know about Herm would fill a barrel."

"Herm gave me one of my first jobs. He was foreman of a cattle outfit over in New Mexico. He had a nice wife, but she died young."

"Then he married my ma and she died as well." Vanderson shook his head.

"I met Josh when he came through one

time and stopped over at the ranch. The two brothers were never close in those days. But they mellowed later on."

An hour later Lassiter had his first look at the mired wagon. It rested in the center of a swiftly flowing stream, sunk in mud well above the hubs. One quick sweep of his blue eyes enabled Lassiter to get the picture. Someone had widened the creek to accommodate the whole wagon and had also dug into the creek bed to make it soft enough for the wheels to sink.

When Melody saw the wagon a week before, she had despaired of ever getting it out. The men she took along had confirmed the impossibility.

When the wagon was freed and Lassiter returned to Aspen City, he intended to look the crew over and fire those he suspected of having helped put her rolling stock out of commission. He hadn't had a chance as yet to look at the two disabled wagons higher in the mountains, but this job of miring the wagon had been done deliberately. He confirmed it by wading around it a time or two and studying the creek bed. Everywhere else the bed was solid.

Vanderson sat on the creek bank watching

24

Lassiter flounder around the wagon, the waters flowing just below his knees.

"Got a strong hunch that Kane Farrell is mixed up in this," Lassiter called to the younger man who evidently preferred not to get his boots wet.

"Why this fellow Farrell?" Vanderson wanted to know.

"The kind of stunt he likes to pull."

"Reckon you know him well."

"Too damn well. I've been able to cut him off at the pockets a few times."

Lassiter's face hardened at the memory of Farrell down near the border, rustling Mexican cattle, altering the brands then selling them in the States for half the market value. When a widow, desperate to recoup cattle losses, had purchased a herd from Farrell, Lassiter had moved in. And this just before the Mexican owner, with the help of a sheriff, was about to reclaim his cattle. Farrell had done a sloppy job with a running iron so that the Mexican brands, though blotched, were easily detected.

When Vanderson made no move to lend a hand, Lassiter said, "Get off your butt, Vance, and let's get this job done."

Flushing at the rebuke, Vanderson helped Lassiter herd the mules into the creek. Some of them were reluctant and Lassiter had to use his catch rope. Finally, with the cold water pressing at his knees, they got them harnessed. Then he told Vanderson to get in the seat of the freight wagon and use the bullwhip that had been brought along. Not to cut an animal's flesh, but to pop it above their heads to frighten them into movement.

"You must have been in the army," Vanderson said with a tight grin, "the way you like to give orders."

"I'm trying to save this outfit for Herm and his niece. Not to mention myself. . . ."

"I figured you were worried about the money you put into it."

"You must stay awake nights trying to figure out ways to rub people the wrong way."

Under the impact of Lassiter's cold blue eyes, Vanderson's rather handsome face slowly drained of color. "Didn't mean anything, Lassiter. Guess I'm still shocked that my Uncle Josh is dead. . . ."

Lassiter looked at him. Not your Uncle Josh, he wanted to tell him. You're no blood kin at all.

". . . and I'm still worried about Uncle Herm getting shot," Vanderson continued.

There was a relationship there, Lassiter

had to admit, but only because Herm had married a woman with a gangling adolescent son.

"You drive the team," Lassiter instructed. "I'll prod these bastards," meaning the mules.

He had cut off a ten-foot aspen limb with an ax he had brought along in the light wagon. He trimmed the pole, then mounted up and used it to give each mule a jab while Vanderson cracked the bullwhip. At last Lassiter got the mules lunging into their collars. After several attempts, the wheels creeped a few inches in the mud.

When Lassiter took a breather to rest the mules, he pointed downcreek some thirty yards at an opening in the long, rounded hill. "That's where I helped Josh cut timber for shoring. He had bought the claim after the owner's wife took sick and the man wanted to go back to Missouri."

Vanderson, hunched in the wagon seat, splashed from creek water, said, "Don't look like much to me."

Again they tried to dislodge the wagon. Lassiter yelled at the straining mules. But the wheels settled back into their original grooves.

Lassiter finally gave Vanderson his horse

27

and climbed into the wagon where he stood, feet wide-spread, reins in one hand, bull-whip in the other.

"Jab 'em, Vance!" Lassiter shouted as the whip cracked like rifle shots.

All of it, combined with Lassiter's authoritative roar, caused the mules to expend additional effort. Hooves dug into the well-spaded creekbed. With a creak of wagon frame and wheels, it began to move, inch by inch, Lassiter's whip popping, Vanderson jabbing with the pole. With a great sucking sound the wheels finally pulled free of the mud and reached the solid creek bottom.

Lassiter turned the wagon onto a grassy strip beside the road. Mules and wagon dripped onto the dry ground. Vanderson rode Lassiter's horse up beside the wagon and dismounted. Lassiter took the reins and looped them around the saddlehorn.

"Why'd you do that?" Vanderson accused, pointing at the reins.

"I'm training him." But by then Vanderson had lost interest.

"Well, we did it, Lassiter. I knew it would work the minute I suggested I use the pole and you handle the reins. . . ."

"I don't recollect you suggesting it."

"You never want to give anybody credit for a damn thing."

Lassiter decided to let it go. Vanderson had walked down to the mine tunnel and was peering in. After tying the mule team to a stump, Lassiter followed him.

"So this is Uncle Josh's silver mine," Vanderson mused.

"A hole in the hill is all it is now," Lassiter said, after looking into the maw. Someone had removed all the shoring he and Josh had erected with the help of a crew. Lumber pulled out to be used as firewood, perhaps. Or shoring for another mine. The nearby mountains and hills were pock marked with shafts. Lassiter glanced at the sky. It was midmorning. If they hurried, they might be able to get the wagon down to Bluegate before sundown.

"Did Josh ever get much silver out of here?" Vanderson asked.

"Not much that I know of. He gave up on it."

"When was that?"

Lassiter thought back. "Seven or eight years ago. Melody and her mother were visiting. Melody was just a bony kid."

"Not bony now," Vanderson mused, "but dimpled and rounded."

"I noticed you making sure of that."

Vanderson stared at the tunnel opening. "Be something if there was silver in there after all. I'd be rich."

"*You'd* be rich. Herm and Melody would be, maybe, but . . ."

"You always leave me out of everything." Vanderson looked petulant. "I'm family too, you know."

"Simmer down, Vance." Lassiter was getting tired of his whining. But he'd have to put up with it till Herm arrived. Because the mules had had such a hard pull out of the mud, Lassiter decided to give them a further rest. "Want to go inside and have a look?"

"Sure. You know silver ore when you see it?"

"Not always." He mentioned the lack of shoring, the network of posts and planks intended to keep walls and ceiling from falling. "Let me go first," he suggested.

They had just stepped inside the entrance when a man drawled, "You gents on a picnic?"

Lassiter spun, hand sweeping for his gun. But Vanderson gave a cry and got in the way. Besides, the man who had spoken already had the drop on him. The man was in his early thirties, with coarse wheat-colored hair

30

leaking from beneath the brim of a stained hat. He was tall and heavy through the shoulders. Lassiter recognized him now. It was Ed Kiley, whom he remembered from a previous visit. His cocked .45 wavered. Kiley seemed halfway drunk.

"Put up the gun, Kiley," Lassiter said in a hard voice.

A second man moved out of the trees. He was black-haired and about Lassiter's height. He grinned, pointing at Lassiter's belt buckle.

"I admire that there silver belt buckle." He also held a gun. Lassiter swore softly for letting the pair sneak up on them, but the sounds of the creek had covered their approach.

"The L on the buckle is for Lassiter," Kiley said with a laugh.

"I'll be damned," the second man said. "Around here they call me Dutch. But my name's really Larry. That buckle'd be fine for me, now wouldn't it? L for Larry, see?"

"Do a jig for us, Lassiter," Kiley drawled.

"Go to hell!"

Both men fired into the tunnel floor, ricochets barely missing Lassiter's feet. He gave the tunnel ceiling a nervous glance because of the concussion. By then, Vanderson

31

had crouched behind Lassiter, his face drained.

"Long as we got these two hombres penned up," Kiley said, "it's time you give me my share of the money. You been keepin' it long enough. Come on, turn it over, Dutch."

"We got to finish Lassiter first," Dutch Holzer chuckled. "That's what we're bein' paid for, ain't it?"

"You got the money in two sacks," Kiley went on, sounding faintly angry. "I seen Farrell give 'em to you, a thousand in each sack."

"Shut up about it, Ed."

"Gimme my sack an' then I'll shut up."

There were more shots, the concussion so strong in the tunnel that Lassiter thought his eardrums would burst. Holzer was enjoying himself.

"Any more shooting," Lassiter pointed out coldly, "and it might bring down the roof." He was poised on his toes, ready to make a move.

"Fall on you, not us, if it does," Holzer said and fired again. Lassiter tensed but the ceiling didn't collapse.

As the two men argued about the money there at the tunnel entrance, Lassiter began backing slowly, pushing the trembling Vanderson behind him.

"Ten feet more and the tunnel makes a bend," Lassiter hissed. "That's where we'll make a stand."

Holzer said, "Pass me the bottle, Ed."

Kiley grumbled something then removed a quart bottle from a pocket of his faded canvas jacket. He passed it to Holzer. The bottle was half full. Holzer, keeping his eyes and gun on Lassiter, took a long pull.

"Tell you what, Lassiter," Holzer said with a grin. "Toss me that shiny belt buckle an' we'll let you go."

"Farrell won't like it." Lassiter was backing slowly, in deeper shadows now so that the pair in the entrance had to bend low to squint at them.

Out in the road the mule team stood patiently, heads down. Near the wagon, Lassiter's black horse nibbled at a crop of grass that had escaped the scorching summer sun.

"Stand hitched, Lassiter," Holzer warned in his grating voice. He was hunched now, a few feet inside the tunnel, tall and with a face as dark as Lassiter's. Kiley was slightly behind him, peering over his shoulder.

"We had our fun, let's get the job done," Kiley said.

Vanderson suddenly screamed. "They're gonna kill us!"

Vance whirled so suddenly that he lost his balance when he stepped on a loose stone. He crashed into Lassiter. A bullet sang above Lassiter's head. But Lassiter was falling. He fired at Holzer and missed.

Vanderson, still screaming, went pounding out of sight around the bend in the tunnel.

Lassiter tried again for Holzer, but Kiley lunged in front and took the bullet. It sliced through the web of flesh between the thumb and forefinger of the left hand. As Kiley went to his knees, Lassiter dashed around the bend in the tunnel. Vanderson was crouched, babbling again about the pair intending to kill them.

"Here's where we make a stand, for chrissakes . . ."

But the panicked Vanderson started at a wild run deeper into the shadowed tunnel.

"Watch out for holes!" Lassiter yelled, remembering places where Josh had dug in the floor, hoping to locate the elusive vein of silver. If Vanderson fell into one of those, he could break his neck. Lassiter started to turn to run after him.

But Kiley, yelling in pain and rage, came

charging around the bend in the tunnel. He crashed into Lassiter where detritus on the floor made footing precarious. Both men fell. The force of the collision jarred Lassiter's gun from his hand. As Kiley started to aim his .45, Lassiter kneed him and twisted the gun from Kiley's grasp. Before Lassiter could get a firm grip on the weapon, Kiley smashed him in the face. The weapon clattered to the rocky floor.

Lassiter felt his head jerk back. His teeth snapped and blood spurted from a torn lip. He spun back against the tunnel wall as Holzer yelled for Kiley to get out of the way so he could get in a shot. But Kiley was like a maddened bull, intent on killing with bare hands. Kiley moved in so close that Lassiter was slammed against the wall. Stones began to fall from the pressure of Lassiter's shoulders. Above it all he could still hear the diminishing pound of Vanderson's boots, his screams of panic.

Watching his chance, Lassiter slammed a fist into Kiley's stomach with such force that it doubled the big man up. For a moment Lassiter used him as a shield against a raging Holzer who was trying to get in a shot. Throwing Kiley aside, Lassiter snatched up his gun from the floor, rolling aside as Holzer fired. But the bullet screamed off the wall. Rock chips stung Lassiter's neck.

Lunging to his feet, Lassiter was around another bend in the tunnel, sprinting after Vanderson. He could see him now, far ahead in faint daylight, poised at the edge of one of the deep holes. He was gingerly moving along an edge of floor that had been left for a pathway.

When Vanderson started running again, Lassiter yelled a warning. "There's another hole up ahead. Deeper!"

But Vanderson, in his terror, didn't seem to hear him. He was at a hard run, the slam of boots against the stone floor magnified by the narrowing tunnel.

Lassiter knew he had to make a choice, either keep charging after Herm's demoralized stepson or make a stand against Holzer and Kiley. He could hear the booming sound made by their boots as they neared the new bend on the tunnel.

Just as Lassiter started to turn, something crashed into his back. At first, as he was falling, he thought he had been struck by a slab of rock dislodged by concussion because of the gunfire.

But a split second later he heard the roar of a weapon. Then he was lying on his stom-

36

ach, unable to move. The dull, grinding pain in his back did not abate with the clenching of his teeth. Somehow he lifted his head. The tunnel seemed to be swinging from side to side before his eyes.

_____ 4

THROUGH A FILM of pain, Lassiter heard a scrape of boots.

Holzer said, "Got the son of a bitch, by gad. Keep your gun on him, Ed, in case he's got a twitch of life left in him. I want that belt."

"My gun's under a pile of rocks that fell off the ceiling. . . ."

"Take mine."

Lassiter felt himself turned over on his back. His limbs flopped like coils of rope. Despite almost unbearable pain, no sound broke from his half open mouth, stained with blood from the smashed lip. His eyes were closed.

"He sure as hell looks dead to me," said Kiley, peering down. There was a sudden grinding of stone against stone. "More of them damn rocks fallin'!" Kiley cried in alarm. Something thudded against the mine floor, shaking it. Kiley gave another cry. "I'm gettin' outa here!" He ran.

Holzer quickly reached under Lassiter's gunbelt to the belt that held up the canvas pants. Holzer unbuckled it, drew it slithering out of the pants loops.

Through a forest of dark lashes, a numbed Lassiter watched Holzer slip the new belt through the loops of his pants. He had taken off his gunrig and now buckled it back on. He drew his gun, cocked it and aimed at Lassiter's head.

Lassiter lay close enough to touch Holzer's right boot. Somehow in the moment of peril he felt a reserve of strength. Like a darting snake his hand shot out. Fingers gripped Holzer by an ankle. With all his remaining strength, Lassiter gave a hard pull. It wasn't enough to topple him, only throw him off balance so that he fired into the mine ceiling instead of Lassiter's skull.

Instantly this was followed by an intensified grinding of rock on rock. Slabs of granite worked loose and came crashing down. One landed inches from Lassiter's head.

Dazedly he got to his knees as the ground shook and a great roaring tortured his eardrums. A haze of dust as thick as river fog churned up as more rocks began to fall. Visibility was restricted because of the choking dust. He could no longer see Holzer nor hear him, but he located his own .44.

Somehow he staggered toward the rear of the mine that he knew had an opening at the far end. More rocks tumbled from the ceiling. The ground shook even harder underfoot. As he had predicted, the concussion of gunfire had caused the unstable ceiling to start giving way. Sound waves had triggered a partial collapse of the tunnel. How long before it became complete?

The possibility jarred through his pain. Fortunately, so far he had been able to evade the falling rock. But how much longer would his luck hold?

In the distance he could barely make out faint daylight. He came to the first of the deep holes and edged around it as Vanderson had done. Damn Vance. If he had stayed put instead of running like a panicked cat they could have stood off the pair near the mine entrance. But Vanderson in his mindless flight had drawn them deeper into the tunnel.

Rock was still falling when he reached the second, deeper hole. He staggered to the edge and nearly lost his balance. Then he was groping toward the gray fog of daylight through the dust, thankful he had a way out without having to fight his way back to the entrance. He was in no condition to cope with Holzer and Kiley now. He knew that Kiley had suffered a superficial wound to the left hand but was still dangerous. Because of the churning dust, he had no idea of Holzer's condition. Thankfully the mine was an extended tunnel under a long hill.

He never did know how he stayed on his feet. His back throbbed. His whole left side was wet. Blood ran down his pants leg and into his boot. It made squishing sounds as he managed to continue his staggering run.

At last warm sun touched his face. Here was thick brush and some rusted tools, shovels and picks with broken handles.

"Vance!" He thought he was yelling, but his voice was a bare whisper. Three times he tried to reach Vanderson, but with no luck. Perhaps the man was still running in his desperation to flee danger.

No longer did Lassiter hear the thud of falling rock from the tunnel. But dust in great clouds boiled out the exit.

It took concentration to form his mouth and tongue into position for a blasting whistle. His first try was a pitiful sound that could be heard for only a few feet.

Even that slight effort drained him. He fell to his knees. The shock of striking the ground brought a new spasm of pain that beat on him like a club. A great pounding threatened to pull him under into darkness. It was as if someone held a red hot poker against the jagged flesh the bullet had torn in his back. His head was a giant throbbing pulse.

He had to get away before Holzer and Kiley realized there was an exit to the mine and came around the hill to trap him. He managed somehow to pry himself into an upright position. His legs seemed made of India rubber. Faintly now he was aware of running water and saw a creek meandering along a slot between the mine hill and the one that adjoined it. Although the sun had slid under a bank of stormy clouds, he could feel himself sweat. His body was soaked with it. Beads of light danced behind his eyes.

To come all this way through a dangerous life on the frontier and turn his back—turn it just once to go after Herm's cowardly step-son . . . Once was all it took, just a shaved second of carelessness and a lucky shot from Holzer's gun. And the result? He was at the edge of oblivion. His teeth chattered as if he stood barefoot on a glacier.

Taking a deep breath, he shaped his mouth a second time around a whistle. This time the sound was shrill, born of desperation. It blasted its way along a curve in the brushy hill and through a narrow gulch with the rush of a small creek he remembered from years back. For the first time he realized he still clutched his revolver. He fumbled it into his holster and remembered that the belt that held up his pants was missing. He stood with right hand anchored against a stunted pine to keep his knees from caving.

"Vance!" he tried again but the voice was as feeble as before.

Suddenly he was aware of something crashing through the dry brush. His hand dropped to the gun, missing the butt. He had to make a second try. Then he saw that his black horse had produced the sound in the brush. It came prancing upgrade from the gully between the hills, reins still tied to the saddlehorn.

"Good boy," Lassiter said hoarsely and the animal came up to where he swayed unsteadily.

The black horse stood patiently while he tried to mount. His breath was rasping when he finally reached the saddle. There he slumped, head down. Although he knew it was only a little past noon, the world seemed to be darkening. He got the horse into motion.

Somehow he had to get help. He thought of the blonde Vanderson seemed so sweet on. What was her name? Melody. A strange name. Perhaps Vance Vanderson with his coward's heart would be with her. He and the girl would help him.

Desperately he tried to think where he could find the girl. Oh, yes, she ran a freight line with headquarters in Bluegate.

As he rode the horse at a walk, he wondered if Melody knew that Vance Vanderson was yellow. From the crown of his head to his big toe. He started to laugh as he pictured the handsome boyish Vanderson lowered into a vat of bright yellow and pulled up at the end of chain, dripping paint. Laughter sent a knife of pain into his body. For a moment the day seemed to darken even more. He squeezed his eyes shut in the hope of steadying himself in the saddle. When he opened them the world seemed out of shape.

His mind moved sluggishly like an overloaded wagon being pulled up a steep grade. It dawned on him that possibly Vanderson, in fleeing, now lay under the tons of ceiling rock that Lassiter had escaped by sheer luck.

He rode on and on, the horse travelling at a patient pace.

Lassiter's head bobbed at each step of the horse on the rough terrain. After a time he tried to figure out where he might be. Behind him mountain peaks were lost in a great sea of clouds. He was going away from the mountains, not toward them. And at the same time he realized he was on a road of sorts, a path paved with wheel tracks through the wilderness. But the road had to lead somewhere; to a town, a ranch or an isolated mine.

As this was sliding through his fuzzy mind, he felt himself falling. Instinctively he flung a forearm across his face. His arm took the brunt of the fall. It was a few minutes before he realized he lay with his head against the primitive road, his left leg straight out and elevated. His foot was jammed in the stirrup. When he tried to work it loose, he lacked the strength. The slight exertion brought the warmth of fresh blood from his wound.

If that horse runs, he thought, I'm a goner. How ignominious an end for Lassiter whose early demise had been predicted for years, as shot to death in a gunfight or hanged at the end of a vigilante rope. Instead, to be dragged to death by his own horse.

Lassiter wanted to laugh at the incongruity, but he swam in pain and it was useless to try.

He still had his gun. Could he kill the horse and thus eliminate any danger of his skull disintegrating against rocks or stiff underbrush if the animal panicked for some reason and broke into a blind gallop?

No, he could never cold-bloodedly dispose of such a devoted friend. Not even to save his own life. Somehow he would survive. Someone would come along and find him.

"Easy, boy," he heard himself say. The black ears twitched.

It was the last he remembered. The earth just seemed to float out from under, leaving him suspended in midair.

5

ED KILEY WAS still frightened after his miraculous escape from the mine. He had hung around the entrance for an hour, waiting for Holzer to emerge out of the dust. When Holzer failed to appear, he went into a narrow canyon where they had left their horses. His roan was still there, but edgy and showing the whites of its eyes. Probably the roar of falling rock next door had set it on edge. Where Holzer's horse had been tied there was only six inches of rein still tied to a stump.

"Son of a bitch!" Kiley snarled. "In such a damn hurry he didn't even take time to untie his hoss!"

Holzer had run off with the two thousand dollars Farrell had paid them, after disposing of Lassiter.

Kiley, a man more brawn than brain and given to impetuous decisions, started at a hard run for Bluegate. Every mile or so he halted long enough to take a pull at his bottle.

He half killed his mount on the pounding run back. Luckily, at this time of day he could usually find Farrell in a low-stakes poker game. The high stakes came at Dixie's Saloon after midnight.

Farrell was playing with two drummers and one of his friends, Rip Tolliver. A few hangers-on were watching the game. The cadaverous Dixie was at one end of his bar reading a newspaper. A fat bartender served customers.

Kiley edged up to the table. "Got news

46

for you, Mr. Farrell." He mouthed a word, *Lassiter!*

Farrell's green eyes lighted up. He allowed one of the drummers to win the pot then stepped out to an alley with Kiley, who quickly told his version of what had happened. It was he, not Holzer, who brought Lassiter down.

"So you got the bastard." Farrell was elated. "Where is he? I want to look at him!"

It hadn't been Kiley's purpose to make the long ride to town just to backtrack so Farrell could take a look at the body. Kiley had crept back in himself and verified the fact that Lassiter was dead, crushed under a chunk of ceiling rock.

"Tell you why I come in, Mr. Farrell. Dutch, he was holdin' the two thousand dollars you was givin' us for nailin' Lassiter. An' . . . an' he never did split the money, even when I kept askin' him for my half. . . ."

"You think Holzer ran off with your share?"

"I sure do, Mr. Farrell. He's gone an' so is his hoss."

"But you did get Lassiter. You're sure of that."

"He put up a helluva fight, but I got him. Put a bullet in his back, then. . . ."

"*You* got him, not Holzer?" Farrell arched a dark red brow.

"Sure it was me." Kiley dug a boottoe into the alley dust and said awkwardly, "Was wonderin' if you could pay me a little somethin' till I git my hands on Dutch."

Farrell studied the man. Kiley's eyes were reddened and his gait none too steady when he had left the saloon. He smelled as if he'd bathed in a whiskey vat.

"You nipped on a bottle all the way back to town," Farrell said, not accusingly but just stating a fact.

"Dutch runnin' out on me was some upsettin', Mr. Farrell."

"Describe the place where I can see Lassiter's body."

"It's where we sunk the gal's wagon in the mud." He described the mine tunnel.

"I remember it. We'll ride up and have a look."

Kiley groaned, then when Farrell frowned, he laid it on his hand wound. "That goddamn Lassiter done it to me afore I got him."

"When we get back have Doc Overmeyer fix it up. I'll pay the bill. Now forget about

Dutch. You're a good man and I need you. I'll give you the thousand you say Dutch got away with. I'll have Sheriff Dancur keep an eye open for him. He'll turn up."

Farrell rode out of town with Kiley and one of the men who had been in the poker game. Rip Tolliver was tall, angular, in his mid-twenties, with sly brown eyes. A shock of dark brown hair was always tumbling over his forehead.

There was no way Farrell could quell his excitement. To look upon Lassiter's dead face would give him one of the greatest pleasures of life.

Up on the high road a pair of drifters came across a big sorrel that was brush scratched and hung up by the reins in a big clump of thornbush. It was pretty well marked up. One rein had been torn loose as if the animal might have been tied and then panicked for one reason or another and bolted into the brush.

One of the men, rotund in shabby clothing, cocked an eye at the horse. "Would bring a good price."

"An' be hung for a hoss thief?" grunted his bearded companion.

"This fella's carryin' a 77 brand. Wouldn't

take but a few minutes of heatin' up your harness ring an' turning 77 into a double hour glass."

The bearded one gave a short laugh. "Let's us go somewhere an' heat up that harness ring."

They led the horse on up the mountain.

Early next morning Melody started for Aspen Creek. She was worried about Vance, after what she had recently heard concerning Lassiter. Lena Overmeyer, who was the doctor's sister, and working as Melody's housekeeper, had been on the street when the visit had been made to the bank.

"I was with Ruth Simmons and she saw that man Lassiter and literally froze. The things she told me about him. And I can say, Melody, that some of my brother's patients confirmed it."

Melody, already overwrought by all that had happened, was badly shaken at the disclosure. It had come right after she told Lena Overmeyer that a housekeeper could no longer be afforded. From then on, Melody would have to take care of her own house.

Among other things Lena had said was that Lassiter, a known killer, was also a swindler. It was very upsetting when she thought of how her two uncles had apparently been taken in by the man.

Now she mainly worried about Herm's stepson. Vance seemed friendly but she had noticed an undercurrent of tension whenever Lassiter was around. Perhaps Vance was aware of Lassiter's reputation, yet he had gone blindly off to the mountains with him. Only to do her a favor; to help get the freight wagon out of the mud. But in the company of a man of Lassiter's reputation, anything could happen.

After reaching Aspen Creek, Dad Hornbeck told her Lassiter and Vance Vanderson had gone north to the wagon. She and Hornbeck arrived there shortly before noon.

She was surprised to find her wagon and the mule team off the road. The mules were muddied as were the wagon wheels. But there was no sign of Lassiter or Vance. What in the world had happened to them? she asked herself. She called their names until she was hoarse, but got no response.

Dad Hornbeck drove the mule team down the mountain grade, Melody riding her saddler. Lassiter had taken a light wagon, Hornbeck had told her, but it was gone. It worried her. However, when she got back to the Aspen Creek office, it was standing in front.

51

Beside it stood Vance Vanderson, looking a little pale but unharmed. In relief, she ran to him, seized both of his hands and beamed up into his face.

"Oh, I'm so thankful you're all right," she cried.

A warm smile broke across his face. Before realizing what happened, she was being enfolded in his arms. She couldn't decide whether she liked his sudden boldness or not.

Pushing away from him, she asked, "Where's Lassiter?"

"Dead."

A hand flew to her mouth. She hated it when anyone passed over the line, as her mother used to say. Even a renegade like Lassiter.

Two men had tried to jump them, Vanderson said sincerely. Lassiter had panicked and run into a mine tunnel. There was shooting. Somehow parts of the tunnel ceiling were jarred loose by concussion and came down.

"Anyway, I drove off the two men, but Lassiter failed to come out of the tunnel. I went back to look for him. I found him on the floor, on his back. A chunk of rock had bashed in his face. He was wearing his belt so I knew for sure it was him.

"What happened to the two men?" Melody asked tensely.

"I kept up such a stream of gunfire they decided to run for it."

Dad Hornbeck who had come to stand at Melody's side looked skeptical. "You said Lassiter got scared and ran off and *left* you?"

"He certainly did," Vanderson said, with a sad shake of his head. "And I'd heard such stories about bravery. He certainly fooled my father. And me. And I expect Melody."

"It don't sound to me like Lassiter," Hornbeck said firmly.

"Well, it does to me," Melody countered. "From all the things I've heard about the man.

Hornbeck's wrinkled face reflected complete surprise.

Vanderson smiled at Melody. "I guess it's up to us to run the company till my dad gets back on his feet."

Melody frowned at "dad." Always before Vance had referred to him as Herm.

Melody learned that Lassiter's funeral was to be within two days. Kane Farrell had sent some men into the mountains, so she learned, to return the body for burial. She wondered how Farrell had known where to find the body, but didn't give it more than passing thought.

Melody attended the services out of courtesy. Despite the man's unsavory reputation, there was no denying his association with her uncles.

There was quite a turnout for the funeral. One thing puzzled her. Many of those attending the ceremony seemed choked with grief at what they termed the death of a fine man. Only a rather small group, she realized, seemed pleased at Lassiter's passing. Among them was Kane Farrell.

She lingered while answering questions concerning the health of her Uncle Herm, who was recovering from his leg wound many miles to the south. When the crowd began to thin, she noticed Farrell walk over to the fresh mound of earth and spit on Lassiter's grave. To her it was obscene, no matter what Lassiter might have been in life.

A greater obscenity occurred after dark when half-drunk cowhands on their way out to the Twin Horn ranch stopped by the graveyard to "run a little water where they got the bastard planted."

In the passing weeks, fall crawled into winter's ice and many of the high passes were blocked by heavy drifts. Even when spring was finally only a breath away, the snows still clung.

During that time, the fortunes of Northguard Freight Company, which had been on shaky ground, deteriorated badly.

6

NEARLY THREE HUNDRED miles to the south a man with a full beard tried out his gun, firing at bottles and cans.

"This time you hit every one of them!" cried a black-eyed girl. She clapped her hands. "You are well at last."

"Almost . . . thanks to you."

"Now you shave off the beard so I can feel your soft cheek against mine?"

"I'm supposed to be dead, so I heard. I want to stay that way a little longer. The beard stays."

He had felt the gun kick against his hand, but it was a good feeling. For two weeks now he had been practicing his draw and his marksmanship. Sometimes Roma brought lunch and he'd shoot and then they'd eat and he'd shoot some more.

That night as usual it was hard to sleep

because memories like jagged glass filled his mind. Memories of the mine tunnel, of the terrible pain in his back, chunks of rock smashing to the floor from walls and ceiling.

He remembered falling from his horse, left foot wedged in the stirrup. He remembered a girl saying, "We can't go off and leave him here."

"We'll pull his foot out of the stirrup and carry him to the trees. There he can die in peace. He's finished."

It was a male voice, cultured, middle-aged.

"Doc, we can't let him die!" The girl again, sounding tearful.

"As an expert in the matter of bullet wounds, I can tell this one is doomed. If we fiddle around with him, we'll be late for out date in Rowleyville."

"If you and Rex think you can do without me, then . . . you just go on ahead!" the girl stormed. "I'm staying here. I intend getting that bullet out of him."

Another man said, "Roma's got her back bowed, Elihu. Give in to her."

"Rex, I suppose you're right, as usual."

"One of you build me a fire," the girl instructed. "I want boiling water. . . ."

That was the last Lassiter remembered

until someone thrust the folded edge of a gunnysack into his mouth and told him to bite down hard on it.

He lay on his stomach, reasonably conscious until something sharp probed into his wound. Then he fainted.

Consciousness came floating back in a jolting wagon. He lay in the wagon bed on a pile of blankets. He lay on his stomach. By turning his head he could look out the open back of a canvas cover and see a patch of blue sky.

A young woman of about twenty years crawled into the wagon and looked at him closely. Her eyes were intensely black. "You're awake," she said, and smiled.

"Yeah," he managed.

"I got the bullet out."

"Thanks."

"You'll be all right now." She gave him some water and he slept.

For supper he had broth from a stewed rabbit. Two days later he felt a small nudge of returning strength. For the first time he was able to assess his surroundings. He lay under a canvas lean-to. Nearby was a wagon decorated with fire-belching dragons against a background of yellow flames. DOCTOR ELIHU DEWITT AND HIS ELIXIR FROM ANCIENT

CATHAY was painted in black letters on the side of the wagon.

There was more that mentioned a long life, free from illness and pain.

It was obvious that he had been picked up by a medicine show. He started to laugh, but contracting muscles for the effort brought a stab of pain.

Roma was dancing in the center of a crowd. The audience was appreciative. Men stood with eyes wide, mouths agape. There were a few women, most of them buxom and jealous of Roma's youth and beauty.

Roma's long black hair swung out from her body as she pivoted and dipped, eyes and white teeth flashing. She danced in time to a tom-tom a tall and slender man was beating. He had an aristocratic face and thinning hair. He wore a red tunic with yellow buttons.

Roma tossed her head saucily, rolled her eyes and did a series of high kicks that revealed petticoats and pantaloons of a vivid red, as was her ruffled skirt. Dragons done in yellow thread decorated skirt and blouse. Long blue-black hair was drawn severely back from a high cheek-boned face and tied with a yellow ribbon.

At the completion of the dance, Doc

58

DeWitt, wearing a voluminous costume of faded red silk, stepped to a small platform at the rear of a wagon. In the tones of an elocutionist, he extolled the virtues of his elixir, lulling Lassiter to sleep.

Then they were on the move again, from one town to another. One evening DeWitt brewed up another batch of his elixir, a concoction of roots and herbs he found along the way and carried in gunnysacks to dry.

After a few more days, Lassiter got Roma aside. "I've got to go back."

She brushed aside her long hair. "You're not strong enough."

"I'll show you."

He started toward his horse that stood with the other animals of the troupe. But he took no more than three bold steps when the ground slid out from under him.

"I need to fatten you up," Roma whispered, helping him to her tent. The snow fell against a fall moon. Roma's smile was wicked as she kissed him. "Other things I need to do for you also."

That night for the first time her soft breasts warmed his face. Later he wondered why Doc and Rex seemed to take no offense at the affection their star attraction had for a total stranger, but she explained that the three of them were just good friends.

Days passed swiftly. He got so he could help assemble the small platform where Doc sold his elixir. But he tired easily. Patience, he warned himself. When he returned to Bluegate he had to be strong and have a clear mind. Among other things, he didn't intend to forget the seven thousand dollars he had invested in the freight line owned by Herm Falconer and his niece. By now, Herm should have recovered from his leg wound and be able to take over. But Herm would need help against Kane Farrell—a gentleman Lassiter intended to settle with. He couldn't forget Dutch Holzer mentioning that Farrell had paid two thousand dollars to have him killed.

Not to mention the least of it, Vance Vanderson, who had run off to leave Lassiter alone to face a pair of killers.

There was no hurry, he kept reminding himself. There was plenty of time.

With the coming of winter, they headed south where the sun was warm. Doc owned a rather spacious adobe house that he used when not on the road. There was a smaller house on the property. This was Roma's.

After a few days, Doc and Rex left. They

would do their show in saloons and stores. They wanted Roma to go with them, but she said it was her place to stay with her patient and see him get well.

At the first sign of spring, Lassiter began practicing with his gun. A lot of the money he had with him went for shells.

More than once, when Lassiter grew discouraged over his slow recovery, Roma would bring him to life at night. At first they had to be inventive because of his wound, but finally he was able to lock her in his arms in a normal embrace. Afterward they would lie together and he would stroke her long, silky hair. One name would beat through his brain like the tom-tom Rex used for Roma's dance. Kane Farrell, Kane Farrell, Kane Farrell . . .

Roma received a letter from Doc. They were on their way back and expected Roma to go on the road with them as usual.

"I'd rather go with you, Lassiter."

"Too dangerous."

"What could be so dangerous about a town with a pretty name like Bluegate?"

"How did you know about Bluegate?"

"You talked when you were out of your head. I learned many things about you, darling Lassiter."

Her black eyes were shining, the red mouth curved in a sensual smile. "So, you take me with you," she said.

Their parting was not easy, but he was adamant. Roma screamed at him and pretended she wanted to claw his face with her sharp nails. But in the end they fell into each other's arms in a warm embrace.

And after kissing her for one last time, he rode north. How he hated to leave her. She had done so much for him. But it was impossible to take her back to the turmoil he would face. Soon Rex and Doc would return and she would forget all about him when she returned to the old routine. At least that was what he told himself on the chill spring morning as his trail climbed through cactus and stretches of high desert, with a backdrop of purple mountains.

One night in a tavern where he was eating supper he heard his name mentioned. Some men were drinking at a short bar. They were comparing gunfighters.

"Lassiter was the best," said a man in fringed buckskin.

"Not as good as Kane Farrell," another man said. "He took down the Texas Kid right on the main street of Bluegate just last month."

"Lassiter an' Farrell shoulda faced up. Now that would've been a gunfight."

A thin mustached man spoke for the first time. "Fact is, Lassiter couldn't be so goddamn good. He ended up dead, like the Kid. I was at his funeral. I seen him buried."

None of the customers paid any attention to the slender man in worn range clothing, who sported a bushy beard and ate a lonely supper.

7

MELODY RODE INTO Bluegate on a windy spring morning. Tumbleweeds rolled along the street and frightened chickens and set dogs to barking. On this bleak morning Bluegate seemed the most forlorn town, set out in the loneliest corner of God's green earth. At one time she had found peace here with the shaded streets, the yards filled with bright spring flowers. Everyone seemed friendly, but now there was tension so strong one could see it on the faces that no longer smiled but were tight with suspicion. Could one man—Kane Farrell—cause such a change in a town?

She came to the big warehouse they used

to own, and shuddered at the memory of things gone wrong. Behind the warehouse was Black Arrow Road that led to the mine of the same name. Straight up the mountain it went without even so much as a slight bend or curve. The mine owner, a man named Dingell, had asked her to the school dance. He was a pleasant looking man of thirty or so who worked industriously on his property. But she had been forced to decline his invitation. It would be unseemly for her, as a married woman, to accept.

She was just tying her horse to a rack when Kane Farrell stepped from the saloon and came strutting along the walk in a fine gray suit. The sight of him turned her stomach for more reasons than one.

She would never forget the day she and Vance had come to town for supplies and seen the crowd along Pine Street. A gangly buck-toothed man in his early twenties was berating Farrell about something. They stepped to the middle of the street.

"That's the Texas Kid," she overheard a man say. "It'll be the end of Farrell." God, she hoped so.

But it wasn't. Farrell's first shot knocked the kid down. Farrell wasn't satisfied and walked up and pumped three more bullets into the man writhing in the street.

Such a display sickened her, not that she wasn't already heartily sick of Kane Farrell.

She realized with a sinking heart that on this blustery morning, Farrell was coming toward her. She already felt the impact of his green eyes. She had half a mind to ride back home and forget her business here, but she was determined to stay and brazen it out.

She was standing in front of the sheriff's office when Farrell hurried up. His hat came off so she could see the wavy dark red hair that was said to fascinate some women. Well, certainly not her, nor was she impressed by his ingratiating smile.

"I suggest we have a cup of coffee together," Farrell was saying smoothly, "and talk a little business like good friends. . . ."

"Good friends," she snapped, remembering the ugly wound in Dad Hornbeck's shoulder.

He put a hand on her elbow, but she pulled away. His eyes turned her cold, as if ice had touched her bare flesh.

She quickly marched toward the tall oak doors with "Sheriff's Office" etched in the thick glass, which was done at a time the town was seeking to make an impression when there had been talk of a railroad. But that dream had become as dead as yesterday when the rail line was built nearly a hundred miles north of Bluegate. All the townsmen had to show for the brief flirtation with power was a rather ornate headquarters for the law on the first floor, and a six-cell jail on the second.

Sheriff Bo Dancur was in shirtsleeves chewing a cold cigar. His round face that always seemed oily, looked faintly annoyed when Melody walked in. He got ponderously to his feet and put on a coat.

"From the look on your face," the sheriff said, "it 'pears you got important business." His chuckle disturbed rolls of fat that he tried to cover by buttoning a brown coat. He waved her to a chair, then turned to the door. "Be with you in a minute, Kane."

Melody whipped around, her earlobes burning. Farrell, completely unruffled, a smile on his rather handsome face, was taking a chair by the door.

"As long as Mr. Farrell apparently wants to listen to my complaint, let him." Melody's eyes snapped.

"Melody, Melody," Farrell said with an exaggerated shake of the head.

"Sheriff, I'm being harassed. A certain

person is trying to drive me out of business. And that party is sitting right over there," she said, pointing at Kane.

When Farrell started to speak, the sheriff said, "Let the lady have her say, Kane. It's best that way."

Anger gushed out of Melody, as she recited all the sneaky tricks that Farrell had played on her. She spoke of the wagons put out of commission and how when they were put back in service, something else was bound to happen. She talked about the employees she thought were disloyal and had fired. But the mischief didn't abate. Hay had burned, some of her mules had come up lame.

Dancur lifted bushy brows. "You got proof of all this?"

"Of one vile act, I do have proof. Dad Hornbeck was set upon by some men. He was shot by one of them. The assailant was Ed Kiley."

"Kiley works for Mr. Farrell," the sheriff said quickly, "and Mr. Farrell wouldn't allow such a thing."

"Dad Hornbeck saw him plain as day. I want Kiley arrested." Melody's jaw trembled.

"Wa'al now . . ."

"It's a wonder he wasn't killed."

"Kiley hasn't worked for me in some weeks," Farrell said smoothly. "I doubt if he's turned to holding up freight outfits. But anything is possible, I suppose."

Dancur looked grave. "I'll keep an eye open for Kiley, ma'am. Is there anything else?"

"I thought perhaps I'd get some satisfaction today. But I see I won't." Melody got stiffly to her feet.

Bo Dancur stood up out of politeness to a lady. "Was I you, ma'am, if you ever have reason to make another complaint, I figure it's your husband who oughta do it."

Melody's face started to redden. "He . . . he . . . well, it doesn't matter," she finished in embarrassment. A lock of golden hair fell across her brow. She blew it away with a puff of air.

"Far as that goes," the sheriff continued, "You oughta put the runnin' of your freight line into your husband's hands."

"My hands are as capable as his."

"You oughta put on an apron an' stay to home, Mrs. Vanderson."

"I agree to that," Farrell chimed in. "Running a freight line in the mountains can

68

be a tough way to make a dollar. Especially for a woman."

"You're right, Kane. Too dangerous for a female."

"I even offered to take the company off her hands," Farrell said, standing up, "so she could move to civilization and live like a white woman."

"Steal it from me, you mean." Melody's voice was on edge. "And because I refused to sell, you're trying to drive me out of business."

"Now, now, Mrs. Vanderson," Dancur objected. "You shouldn't go around accusin' a fine, upstanding citizen of our county like Kane Farrell."

"Three thousand dollars he offered." Tears of anger glistened in the light gray eyes. "If that isn't stealing, I don't know the meaning of the word."

"Seems to me, three thousand dollars is better'n nothin'," said the sheriff, but Melody had stormed out, slamming the door.

"You better keep Kiley outa sight a few days," Dancur suggested. "Till the little lady cools down."

"Cooling her down is what I'd like to do in my bed."

"She's got a husband, don't forget," Dancur reminded.

"I know for a fact he's run out on her. Gone up to Denver."

"Likely couldn't stand her sharp tongue."

Through the window Farrell watched Melody ride off down the street. A fine figure of a female. "I'll make an obedient filly out of her before I'm through," Farrell said lightly, smoothed down the dark red wavy hair and put on his hat.

8

FOR SOME MINUTES that evening Lassiter struck matches so he could study the names on gravestones and headboards in the Bluegate Cemetery. Finally it came to him that he would not lie among the upstanding citizens of the area. He searched and found that section known as boot hill, apart from the rest, where the notorious lay buried.

A wry smile struck his lips when at last he found what he was looking for. His name had been carved on a plank of wood. They hadn't known the date of his birth, so had left it blank. But the date of his death, October of last year, was inscribed on the rough board.

Curiosity had prompted him to have a look at his own grave. Down at Rio Bueno he had heard talk of the Lassiter grave. He very well knew the risks. Those who wanted him dead would try and make sure of the job next time.

A man called sharply from the road, some twenty yards away. "What you doin' in there?"

Lassiter straightened up and saw two mounted men, blobs of shadow in the moonlight. They had come up silently along the road, hooves of their horses muffled by mud from the evening shower.

"Just passing through, amigo," Lassiter replied in Spanish.

"Only a damn Mex." It was a heavier voice than the first one. "Let's get on out to the ranch."

"Not so fast, Barney. That's Lassiter's grave, sure as hell."

"How can you tell . . . ?"

"It's away from the others. I oughta know. I give Kiley a hand when he was diggin' it. Go take a look. I'll cover you."

"Oh, for crissakes, Pete. Farrell expects us out to the ranch."

Lassiter wondered what ranch? as he eased

71

a hand toward his gun. Six months ago Farrell had owned no spread. But his greedy hands had evidently acquired one in the interim.

Lassiter swore at himself. He should have been more careful about lighting matches out here. But it was a lonely stretch of road leading only to Borodenker's Twin Horn outfit, some eleven miles distant. And Borodenker kept a tight rein on his crew; they were seldom in town.

As the two horsemen argued, Lassiter stood very still, a faint breeze rustling his full beard.

"You mean you figure he's alive?" the man called Barney said incredulously. "Lassiter *alive?*"

"Drifter come through the other day. I never said nothin', but he claimed he seen Lassiter down at Rio Bueno. I figured he was crazy, but now I dunno. . . ."

"Lassiter's dead," Barney said.

"Might be Lassiter there wantin' a look at his own grave."

Lassiter recognized one of the voices now. Barney Cole, a gunhand who had been hanging around Bluegate six months back.

"Go take a look," Pete said. Lassiter felt

the short hairs twitch at the back of his neck, as Barney dismounted.

Barney Cole opened the cemetery gate and came tramping in Lassiter's direction. Of all times, Lassiter wanted no confrontations. But he was trapped in the open, in the moonlight.

Cole halted by a large gravestone some fifteen feet away. "Step over here, Mex. Wanta look at you."

"No unnerstan'," Lassiter muttered and started to back away slowly.

"He don't speak English, I reckon," Barney Cole shouted back to Pete who still sat in his saddle. "He's no more Lassiter than I am."

"Bring him down here!"

Cole swore. He threw a large shadow partly because of a bulky blanket coat. "All right, you, git down by the road." Cole jerked a thumb in that direction.

And then he seemed to realize Lassiter had been easing away from him. He lunged and got a firm grip on Lassiter's left arm. But Lassiter pulled it away. At the same time he drove a powerful right against Cole's jaw. Cole's knees started to sag.

Believing that escape was the smartest move under the circumstances, Lassiter

73

turned to run toward the spot where he had left his black horse. At that moment the moon chose to slip behind thick clouds. It was suddenly as black as a stormy midnight. In his pounding run, Lassiter failed to see the crumbling upper half of a fancy tombstone lying in the path. His right foot cleared it, but the left caught a corner of an angel's wing. He sprawled headlong, jarring the breath from his body.

A gun roared at his back. He cringed, for it was such a shot that had taken him down in the mine tunnel. This one missed. It smashed into the angel's wing. A bit of plaster stung Lassiter's cheek.

"Bastard sneaked a punch on me!" Cole roared. "But I got him!"

Before Barney Cole could get set for another shot, Lassiter flung himself aside. His .44 roared just a shade before Cole's second shot. Lassiter aimed for one of the thick legs, but the man had had the bad judgement to lean over as he lunged. His scream knifed above the thunder of the two guns—a scream that reminded Lassiter of a wolf in pain.

A carbine opened up from the road. Because of the sudden lack of moonlight, all Lassiter had to go on was the muzzle flash.

He fired as a second bullet from Pete's rifle struck a headboard to Lassiter's left.

Suddenly Pete spun his horse and put it to a hard gallop along the road. Just like Kane Farrell, Lassiter was thinking as he tried to spot the fleeing rider in the dark, refusing to buck odds not strongly in his favor. Sounds of hoofbeats were fading in the still night air as Lassiter walked toward Cole. The man was trying to reach out for the gun he had dropped.

"Don't make me put another hole in you, Barney," Lassiter warned.

Cole, lying on the ground, jerked back his head. "You ain't no Mex."

"You and Pete alone out here?"

"Yeah." Cole's chest was heaving as he fought for breath. "Who . . . who are you?" he managed to get out.

"Lassiter."

"But he's dead!"

"Not quite!" Lassiter picked up Cole's gun and stuck it in his own waistband. Then he looked closely at the man. The front of the blanket coat was soggy with blood. The bullet had splintered Cole's collarbone, from what Lassiter could tell in the dim light. In the bent position Cole had assumed, the bullet had been deflected into the chest.

"Where you been all this time?" Cole gasped. "Hell, it was back last fall when you was. . . ."

"Killed," Lassiter supplied when Cole ran out of wind. The night brightened as the moon left the cloudbank.

"Who . . . who the hell got buried instead of you?"

"Ed Kiley still around?"

"Big a blowhard as ever. Why?"

"How about Dutch Holzer?"

"He . . . he ain't been seen since the day you . . . you got it."

"Likely it's Holzer in my grave."

"Naw," Cole gasped. "Kiley claims Holzer run out on him. With Kiley's half of the money Farrell . . ." Cole broke off.

"Paid them to kill me? Is that what you were going to say?"

"What . . . what you aim to do with me, Lassiter?"

"Use your shirt for a bandage. Tie you to the saddle, then ride you to Doc Overmeyer's."

"You're a white man, Lassiter." There was a gurgling in Cole's voice. Blood in the throat, Lassiter guessed. He was straining to hear any sound of hoofbeats in case Pete returned with reinforcements. Even though

Pete had ridden off in the direction of Twin Horn, to the west and south, he might have doubled back to town after a mile or so.

Cole had a sudden surge of energy. "Let's you an' me dig up Holzer. If he's really in your grave, he's got the gold on him . . ."

"No hombre ever got buried with money in his pocket. Somebody got it before then."

"Two thousand dollars, so Kiley claims. We'll split it, then you git me to the doc. . . ."

"Two thousand is what Farrell figured my scalp was worth?"

"He'll likely pay more'n that to git you next time." Cole's voice was growing weaker.

"Who's this Pete you were with?" Lassiter wanted to know.

"Works with me out at Farrell's Twin Horn."

"Old man Borodenker owned Twin Horn. How'd Farrell get it?"

But the question went unanswered. Barney Cole was dead.

Lassiter had a sour taste in his mouth. On his first night back he'd been forced to kill a man. Only because he'd been curious about his own grave. He left Cole where he lay, but did unsaddle the man's horse down on the road and turn it loose. The animal, in Lassiter's judgement, was more deserving than its late, renegade owner.

As he rode toward the haze of Bluegate lights, he wondered what Roma was doing this night. Perhaps by now she was back on the road with Doc and Rex. He hadn't wanted to leave her behind, but it couldn't be helped. Returning to Bluegate was like entering a cave filled with rattlesnakes. No matter where you stepped, there was danger. Above all, after what she had done for him over the past months, he couldn't end it all by risking her life.

A gentle breeze was blowing down from Northguard Pass as he entered town, carrying with it the perfume of spring flowers, the tang of chaparral. The boardwalks were crowded and the streets choked with wagons, buggies, and saddlehorses. Small boys hooted and hollered in games of their own. The three-quarter moon was unblemished at last by clouds. It gilded the rocks high on a mountain known as Las Casitas, crowned with boulders the size of small houses, named by the Spanish early in the last century.

Voices were everywhere, boots and women's slippers scraped on the walks. Doors slammed at business establishments. A woman's trilling laughter, a man's shout as a high-stepping saddler nearly ran him down, the creak of wagon wheels all filled the air.

In his hurried trip north, Lassiter had lost all track of time, but he guessed it must be Saturday night because of all the activity. An unlucky night for one Barney Cole, who hadn't wanted to investigate a transient in the town cemetery, but who had been talked into it by Pete Bromley. Such were the narrow margins between the living and the dead on the frontier.

Lassiter shivered. He had witnessed so much killing in his lifetime. It was the reason he shied from marriage, not wanting a widow left behind because of the way he lived, always on the threshold of danger. Nor would he allow himself a lasting relationship with a woman, even without marriage. If left alone, her tears would be as copious as any grieving widow's. Some people thought him callous. Some, like Kane Farrell, hated him because he spoiled their game.

By now, Herm Falconer should be running the freight line, his leg wound finally healed. At least his niece would be relieved of that responsibility. With Herm to watch over her, Lassiter was sure the girl could resist Vance Vanderson's charms.

Thinking of Vance made him clench his teeth. Vanderson deserved a good punch in the nose for fleeing like a coward that day up at the mine. Perhaps by now Herm had gotten a tighter rein on his stepson.

After the business out at the graveyard, he needed a drink. He left his horse at the crowded rack in front of the Bluegate Mercantile. Perhaps less conspicuous than if he tied it at the saloon hitchrack, he was thinking.

As he angled across the busy street, he would probably be taken for a drifter, with his flat-crowned black hat pulled low, his faded wool shirt, canvas jacket and pants. The full beard hid most of his face. The eyes, however, were not those of a drifter. They were alert and penetrating. He neared the saloon.

A tinny piano accompanied drunken voices in a rendition of "Tenting Tonight."

A large new sign was displayed on the saloon building: SHANAGAN'S TO REPLACE DIXIE'S. It had been owned by a Southerner who had come out of the Confederate Army with a bad arm and a dragging foot.

A familiar wash of warm air hit Lassiter when he stepped through swing doors and stood with his back to the wall. Mingled odors of beer, whisky, and tobacco smoke struck his nostrils. The smell of coal oil from the lamps floated along the ceilings.

Not seeing any familiar faces, Lassiter edged up to the long bar. "Tenting Tonight" was just concluding. Even though the war had been over for some years, enough old timers remained to reminisce and sing the old camp songs. Some were blubbering.

Lassiter found himself standing next to a lanky middle-aged man, fairly drunk and with moist eyes. " 'Scuse me, friend," he said, turning to Lassiter, "but when I hear them songs I remember ol' Ned. Lost him at First Manassas."

"A lot of men were lost," Lassiter put in.

"Even though that's a blue belly song, it still stirs me up," the stranger confided. "Me, I was Reb. Reckon you can tell by my voice."

Lassiter nodded and finally got the attention of a perspiring barkeep, who set out bottle and glass. Lassiter fluffed out his beard. He doubted if anyone would recognize him with the beard in the dim light.

The first drink of whiskey hit his stomach like a clenched fist.

Lassiter took a deep breath, then poured for the drunk who had been overcome by the wartime ballad. The man thanked him profusely, doffing his hat to reveal a few hairs plastered to a pink scalp. Bushy sideburns seemed to give width to a narrow face.

"Do you know a man named Herm Falconer?" Lassiter asked, seeking information.

"Knowed a Josh Falconer, but he up an' died last year."

Lassiter frowned. Hadn't Herm put in an appearance yet? He asked about Vance Vanderson, which brought a sour look to the stranger's long face.

"Vanderson! Good riddance, I say."

"He dead?" Lassiter asked narrowly.

"The world ain't that lucky. He lit out for Denver, so I hear."

That meant Melody was running things alone. He wasn't surprised that Vanderson would run out on her when the going got tough. Lassiter's eyes roamed up and down the busy bar. Everyone seemed engaged in conversation. Many Saturday night red eyes were in evidence. The tinny piano, played by a fat man in a checkered vest, was thumping again.

"Northguard Freight Company still operate out of Bluegate?" Lassiter asked the former Rebel. The man was making him nervous by the way he stared in the backbar mirror. He turned to study Lassiter more closely.

"Ain't called Northguard here in town," the man said. "Called Farrell now."

Lassiter's bearded lips tightened. His eyes skipped around the big smoky room, hoping Farrell might have entered while he was talking. Then he cautioned himself to move slowly. Although he had emptied many boxes of ammunition down at El Puente, shooting at rocks with Roma looking on wasn't the real test. It was one thing to face a row of rocks on a dirt shelf. Quite something else to face up to a man. Especially one as ruthless and tricky as Kane Farrell.

He couldn't afford to make some damn fool play ahead of time and risk having his head blown off. Tonight at the graveyard had been close enough.

The stranger was peering into Lassiter's eyes. Then he slapped the bartop a whack with his open hand and gave a hoot of laughte:. "I knew I knowed you, by gad. I'd know them eyes anywhere, beard or not. . . ."

Lassiter felt his mouth go dry. Several men nearby were looking on, startled by the Southerner's slap on the bartop and his strident laughter.

"Wait a minute . . ." Lassiter started to caution him.

"I'm Bert Oliver. An' you are . . ." Oliver was squinting up at Lassiter. Here the light was reasonably good, for they stood under one of the copper-sheathed overhead lamps.

"And I'm . . ." Lassiter grabbed a name out of the air. "I'm Bill Jasper."

"Hell fire, you're *Lassiter!*"

The name cracked like a whip at that end of the crowded bar. Men stood stiffly, eyes widened. "Don't use his name on me!" Lassiter's voice was harsh. "That renegade's dead!"

Oliver seemed embarrassed by the reaction, the staring drinkers, the sudden stillness. Men had started to edge away.

"I only meant that I remember seein' this Lassiter once. Was down at the border. The sheriff there made a big to-do about givin' him a belt with his initial on the silver buckle. You kinda reminded me of this fella Lassiter is all." Oliver gave a nervous glance

84

around. Some of the customers had resumed their conversations, but others still stared as if unable to make up their minds.

"That ain't Lassiter," said a little man in a brown suit. "I oughta know. I buried Lassiter myself." He winked and laughed. He belched and swayed back to the bar where he picked up a full glass of whiskey and drank from it.

When the room seemed back to normal, Oliver leaned close. "Sorry I spoke up like that," he whispered. "Reckon I had too much whiskey in my gullet." Then in a louder voice, "Thanks for the whiskey, Bill Jasper."

He lurched toward the doors. Some men watched him with puzzled frowns. Others studied the bearded Lassiter.

By then Lassiter had finished his whiskey and he tossed a coin on the bar to pay for the drinks. Trying to remain calm, he saw a heavyset man with bright eyes pick up the coin. " Ol' Bert's all right, but he gets kinda mixed in the head when he drinks too much," the man commented.

"I guess we all do at times," Lassiter said carefully.

"I'm Shanagan," the man said, with a smile that revealed two gold incisors. "If

Milo Miegs says he buried Lassiter, then that's the final word. He's the local undertaker."

"Seems like it," Lassiter responded.

Shanagan slid Lassiter's change across the bar. "Hope you get to be a regular here . . ." Shanagan broke off. "What was your name again? Oh yeah, Jasper. Bill Jasper I recollect hearin' you say."

Lassiter gave the man a nod, then stepped sideways to the doors. Just in case one of the customers decided to probe deeper into his identity.

Lassiter was sitting at the counter of a small cafe, eating a bowl of beef stew, when Bert Oliver slipped onto the adjoining stool. "Made a fool outa myself in Shanagan's," he said in a low voice. "I . . . I didn't even know you was s'posed to be dead till somebody just told me up at the livery barn."

"Forget it. I only hope I can count on you keeping your mouth shut."

"Sure can," Oliver assured him. "I don't look it mebby, but I'm a good hand with a gun. In case you be needin' one."

"What'd they say at the livery barn?"

"Only that you got kilt in the mountains late last year. An' that you an' Kane Farrell never had no love for each other. You hatin' Farrell I like."

"How you feel about him?"

"The same as you. Hate the bastard."

Lassiter sat where he could watch the door. The stew was tasty and filling. Oliver slurped coffee next to him.

"Guess the beard hasn't fooled too many," Lassiter mused. "It sure didn't fool you."

"I used to see you when you was segundo for the XT outfit outa Tucson. An' then I remember you when the sheriff made his long-winded speech before giving you the belt with your initial on the silver buckle." Oliver glanced at Lassiter's waist. "What happened to the belt?"

Lassiter gave a short laugh. "Only the good Lord knows."

Although Oliver had only been in town a few weeks, he seemed to have a good idea of the lay of the land. Oliver said that Farrell had started a freight line under his own name.

"What happened to Josh Falconer's niece?" Lassiter probed. "Name of Melody. She was running things last I knew."

"She moved what's left of her outfit up to Aspen Creek," Oliver said that Farrell had taken over not only the freight line here in town, but also the stable, warehouse, and the big house that Josh had built for his wife.

"Melody must be having a hard time," Lassiter said above the rattle of crockery and voices of other customers.

"Everybody figures this spring she'll be makin' her last freight run." Oliver cleared his throat. "You aim to do somethin' about it?"

"I aim."

Lassiter paid for his meal and Oliver's coffee. Outside on the crowded walk, Lassiter ran a hand over his beard. "Wonder if the barber shop's still open."

Oliver nodded. It was Saturday night, Oliver pointed out. "An' payday at the ranches an' mines. The boys come in once a month to git a trimmin', them that don't cut their own hair." Oliver's voice hardened. "Or trimmed at Shanagan's."

"So he runs crooked games."

"Not him. But he lets Farrell sit at his tables."

"Seems Farrell hasn't lost his touch."

"Seems like you know the bastard down to his toenails."

"I've twisted his tail a few times."

"I ain't forgettin' he euchred me outta five thousand Yankee dollars."

Lassiter looked at the long face with the bushy sideburns. "You ever accuse him of it?"

"If I had, I wouldn't be here talkin' with you this night." Lassiter agreed. "There are times for a man to keep his mouth shut, for sure," Oliver went on. "Like I didn't with mine tonight. Sayin' your name right out, like a fool. Minute I seen how everybody around me was lookin' kinda shocked-like, I knew I'd done wrong."

"If I do need a hand, where can I get hold of you?"

Oliver said he was living at the hotel as long as his money held out. "I'm tryin' to git a small stake so's I can trick Farrell into a game. Next time, by gad, I'll keep my eyes open. An' I won't touch one drop of whiskey."

"The only way to play cards."

"'Course that night Farrell had a little help. I heard later he paid Vanderson to slip him cards. He was setting right next to Farrell, he was, but I never paid no attention . . ."

"Vance Vanderson, you mean?"

"The slimy, no-good."

Oliver drifted away into the shadows. Lassiter took a roundabout way to the barber shop so that he had to pass the big stables built by Josh Falconer and also the oversize warehouse. On both buildings was a sign: FARRELL FREIGHT LINES.

Farrell was up to his old tricks, trimming the innocent, such as Oliver, and fighting a defenseless young woman like Melody.

A final customer was just leaving the barber shop. The barber was about to close up. Lassiter offered him five dollars to shave off his beard, with three stipulations. He was to lock the front door, pull down the blind, and have no objection to Lassiter holding a gun on his lap.

9

SHANAGAN WAS RELIEVED to learn that Farrell was home, not out at Twin Horn. It saved an eleven-mile round trip. Even so, it was quite a walk to Farrell's house, out past the warehouse and stables. All three structures were built by Josh Falconer shortly before his marriage, so Shanagan had learned. Showing off his money for a lady's benefit —a woman one-third his age. Those who told the story got that pitying smile on their faces, as men do who think one of their peers has made a damned fool of himself.

Josh Falconer's married bliss hadn't lasted long enough to spit, as one man put it.

Shenagan knew the problems that can torment a man. He'd had his own. He had been drifting since a bloody night back in Kansas when he was supposed to be in Omaha. He had sneaked home to find his wife entertaining two of the town dandies. His intention was to kill his wife as well as her suspected lover, but he hadn't counted on a pair of them. When one of them jumped him, he killed both men with his double barreled shotgun and fled. He changed his name from Buelton to Shanagan, the name of his late aunt's husband. For a time he barely outran the uproar over the double murder. But soon memory of it faded, as did the trail he left.

After gambling his way West, he reached Bluegate where he recognized a fellow thief, Kane Farrell. He had watched with amusement as Farrell fleeced some of the important men of the area at cards. Only a few, like Bert Oliver, seemed to realize they had been cheated.

Shanagan was lucky. The saloon owner suffered from war wounds and wanted to get

91

out. Shanagan bought him out, cheap. He decided to wait until an opportunity presented itself so he could declare himself Farrell's partner.

Farrell, driven by an insatiable ambition, was headed for the heights and Shanagan intended to go right along with him. And if the time ever came when there was room for only one of them at the top, he considered himself clever enough and ruthless enough to deal with that eventuality.

Farrell himself answered Shanagan's knock on the tall oak door. He invited him into a spacious parlor with a large stone fireplace, leather sofas and chairs. "Surprised you'd leave your place on a Saturday night," Farrell said, closing the door.

"Lassiter's back."

Farrell's head came up. He had been pouring them whiskey. He spilled some. "Lassiter back? Back where?" Farrell's voice was hoarse. A sudden sheen of moisture was at the hairline.

"Here in town. At my place tonight."

Shanagan told how he had been behind his bar, close enough to overhear Bert Oliver accuse a bearded man of being Lassiter.

Farrell was beginning to calm down. They sat and sipped good whiskey in silence.

Finally Farrell said, "I think you're mistaken. When Oliver gets a gut full of whiskey he doesn't even know where he is, let alone recognize anyone."

"You oughta know that," Shanagan said with his glass to his lips. "The way you slickered him in my place."

"The game was honest," Farrell said stiffly. "Oliver's just not much of a card player."

"You had your friend Vance Vanderson feed you extra aces. . . ."

"That's the same as calling me a card cheat."

Shanagan waved both hands defensively. "I've done plenty of it myself, Farrell. I admire the way you work. I admire your nerve."

Farrell smoothed the waves in his dark red hair. "Why are you telling me all this?" he demanded softly.

"Because I'd like us to work together. Me keeping my ears open in the saloon. Like I did tonight."

"Well, you're wrong about Lassiter."

"You'll find out I'm right. I'll bank on it."

"I saw Lassiter buried. The day of his funeral my friends and I celebrated by drinking whiskey and running plenty of water onto his grave. If you know what I mean."

"Somebody else got buried in his place, then."

Farrell rubbed his classic jaw, then said thoughtfully, "Dutch Holzer disappeared and Kiley always claimed he ran out with the money I'd paid them for . . . Well, never mind what I paid them to do. But it's sheer nonsense to claim Lassiter has returned from the dead."

"I'll bet you a hundred that I'm right."

"I'll take that wager." They shook hands on it.

Suddenly there was a pound of hoofbeats in the yard, then heavy boots thundered on veranda steps. It was Pete Bromley, Farrell's segundo; he hadn't gotten around to hiring a foreman yet.

"Just figured you oughta know about Barney Cole. . . ."

"Calm down, for crissakes. What about him?" They stood in the doorway together.

Bromley explained that he and Cole were on their way back to the ranch. "I seen somebody lightin' matches in the graveyard." Bromley went on to say that he told Cole to go and see who was lighting matches. "Barney did like I said, but this fella who said he was a Mex started shootin'. I got the hell out, not knowin' how many friends the Mex might have with him. I waited till the moon got real strong. I went back an' I found Barney dead."

"So some Mex drifter shot him. Look, I have a very important appointment . . . with a lady and I . . ."

"When I got to Shanagan's lookin' for you, Sam the barber was there. He swears to gawd he just shaved off Lassiter's beard. Sam recognized him, but was scared white till Lassiter left."

Shanagan laughed. "Farrell, looks like you owe me a hundred."

Farrell ignored him. With a stiff face, he drew Bromley aside and whispered in his ear. He finished with, "And tell the lady I'm sorry for being late. I'll be there in an hour."

"What then, boss?"

"Get back to the ranch. See that the boys are ready to ride at a moment's notice. I may need them."

When Bromley had gone, Farrell got into a buggy that had been left at the side of the house. He and Shanagan started toward the saloon, the chestnut in the shafts prancing smartly. Stars shone brightly through trees that bordered the street.

"With Lassiter's guts," Farrell said angrily, "he just might show up again at your place tonight."

"I'll be at your back, just in case."

Farrell turned in the buggy seat, staring at Shanagan's rugged profile in the glow of night lanterns from the stable entrance they were passing. "You do that, Shanagan."

"Come to think of it, you don't owe me that hundred dollars," Shanagan said smoothly when they were nearing his saloon and could see the knots of excited men along the street and occasionally hear a repeated name. *Lassiter!* "Seems like we're in this together, Farrell. An' one partner shouldn't owe the other."

Farrell was getting out of the buggy and taking long-legged strides toward the saloon. "You're a slick one, Shanagan. You moved right in without me hardly noticing."

"Tonight gave me the chance," Shanagan said with a tight grin.

"I hope to Christ he shows up tonight. I'd like to finish the dirty business before there's another sunrise."

After three hours in the saloon, Farrell knew no more than he had before. Men shouted questions that he couldn't answer. Speculation was rife as to where Lassiter had been all this time. Miegs, the undertaker, drank more than usual and still insisted he had buried the real Lassiter. This new one was an imposter.

It was after midnight before Farrell reached Letitia Clayfield's house and the widow refused him admittance. Even the following morning she had her nose in the air while waiting to board the eastbound stage. He had lost his chance to have her appoint him manager of her business holdings in Bluegate. In time, with most of a continent separating them, these would have come under his complete control.

"In the years I was married to Donald Clayfield," said the comely widow, as she gathered skirts to board the stage, "he never kept me waiting. A lesson you should have learned, Mr. Farrell."

That goddamn Lassiter, thought the fuming Farrell as the stage rattled out of town. Lassiter returning from the grave had caused him to miss his assignation with widow Clayfield, who was going east to live out her days.

Payment for that thorn in the side, as well as earlier wounds to pride and pocketbook, would be settled with Lassiter's blood, so Farrell vowed on that bright spring morning.

THE NEXT MORNING Melody was sweeping the cramped rooms she was now using as headquarters for the freight company. The building consisted of two rooms, one the office and kitchen, the other a bedroom.

After the long hard winter, spring was most welcome. The sun through the side windows was warm and actually, for a change, lifted her spirits. She stood in the doorway, breathing in the crisp mountain air. Putting the broom aside, she slowly unwound the yard of scrap cloth she had used to keep dust off her golden hair.

Sounds of a horse caused her to look around. It was a black saddler such as that man Lassiter used to ride. Then she lifted her eyes to the rider. Her heart gave a thump and her knees turned to jelly, for the man in the saddle looked so much like Lassiter it was uncanny.

As he dismounted and strode toward her she had to grip the edge of the door in order to keep from collapsing. Her eyes were riveted to the face, the dark brows, the piercing blue eyes, the straight nose, and wide mouth, slightly upturned at the corners.

"Melody," he called to her.

My God, it *sounded* like Lassiter.

"Don't look so scared," he said, coming to stand in front of her. As she stared, a faint breeze rustled the ends of the black hair showing beneath his flat-crowned hat. "I'm not a ghost."

He looked over her slender shoulder into the freight company office. "Vance around?" Now there was hardness in his voice.

She told him that Vance had gone to Denver. "Along with his wild dreams," she added with a shaky laugh.

She stood with her head bowed, a slight tremor at the shoulders. Putting a fist under her chin, he forced her to look up at him. At first he had thought she wept, but her eyes were dry.

"Glad there's no tears," he said. "I thought you might be shedding a few for him."

"Tears for him? Never."

"Glad to hear he didn't overwhelm you. I hear he's got quite a way with the ladies."

"Oh, he has." Ragged laughter again. "I married him."

Lassiter's only reaction was a slight grimace. He asked how it had happened.

"I got panicky," she replied.

"You seemed a young woman with spunk. I'm surprised you caved in to him."

Her lips twitched, but fire touched the light gray eyes. "I was alone. Uncle Josh was dead. Uncle Herm down at Rimrock with one leg missing. And only the good Lord knows what else is wrong with him."

"They took off Herm's leg?"

"Weeks went by and the wound just didn't seem to heal. He's been drinking a lot since. The doctor wrote that he was trying to get him sober enough for travel. But Uncle Herm has never arrived. . . ."

To a point, Lassiter could understand her reaction to grim news, desertion by a husband, the health and alcoholic problems of an uncle. A woman alone, defenseless. But somehow he had thought her less fragile than most.

"I even thought *you* were gone. Dead, buried." Spoken in almost an accusatory tone, leaning close to peer up into his face, seeing his pale cheeks that had been covered by the beard for so long. There was a look in her eyes that seemed to pin the blame for her misfortune on him.

100

"Well, I didn't die on you. Thanks to a certain Roma."

"Whom you charmed, no doubt."

His laugh was like a chill wind. "Hardly."

"Well, you needn't be so nasty about it." Then, hand clamped to her eyes, she suddenly sank to a bench in the office. Tears dripped through her fingers. "Some people said such awful things about you when they thought you were dead. And others . . . Oh, I just don't know what to believe."

An old kitchen table, on which numerous papers were scattered, was used as a desk. Ink blots darkened the wood next to an inkwell and several pens. Two windows let in sunlight. A third window had a diagonal crack and a fourth was boarded up for lack of glass.

When Melody finished her spate of tears, she wiped her eyes on a lacy handkerchief, then looked at him defiantly. "Well, that's over with, thank goodness. It's been building in me for weeks, I guess."

"Good to get it out of your system."

Melody leaned back against the wall, legs outstretched from the bench. Her dress, faded green, had wilted lace at collar and cuffs. She gestured at the sorry furnishings, the walls stained with seepage from winter storms. "As you can see, your investment has gone to the dogs." A braying started up in the barn nearby. "Or to the mules, I guess is more appropriate," she added without humor.

"Herm and I put in nearly twenty thousand dollars," Lassiter reminded. "What happened to that?"

"It just went." She dragged herself over to the table that served as her desk and plopped into a chair. "There's no record of how it was spent, so far as I can tell."

She pushed a ledger across the table, but he didn't reach for it.

"In other words," he said, "I'm betting you never got to see much of it."

"I'm frankly surprised you'd pass up a chance to accuse me of stealing it. Giving me the benefit of the doubt is contrary to your reputation."

"My reputation, so-called, has been hammered together over the years by people I stepped on. People who dislike me. The other side of the coin is those that do. Talk to them sometime, Miss . . . Oh, beg your pardon, it's *Mrs*. Vanderson now."

"Your voice is so cold."

When he looked at her steadily, she gripped the arms of her chair. "It seems I'm always saying the wrong thing to you. But seeing you after all those months when I thought you were dead . . . you'll never know what a shock it was."

She asked for details of his absence and he told her about Roma nursing him. Then, while Melody was writing up a bill of lading for a customer, he hunted up Dad Hornbeck. He found him in a combination bunkhouse and cookshack adjacent to the barn. The old man was recovering from his wound. Although he couldn't be dead certain, he would bet money that it was Ed Kiley who had shot him. After that incident, most of the crew had quit. Melody was trying to do it alone.

That afternoon Lassiter wrote a long letter to Herm Falconer down at Rimrock, telling him essentially what he had related to Melody. But letting Herm know that the niece needed him desperately.

For two days Lassiter worked on the three freight wagons that were still serviceable. But all were in poor shape. He spent the time tightening bolts and replacing planks in one wagon bed that had worn through from the attrition of heavy loads. At least it was spring and they wouldn't have to cope with passes blocked with twenty-foot drifts.

Each day he talked with Hornbeck. At first the old man seemed steeped in gloom, but Lassiter finally cheered him up and he appeared to take heart. Believing that North-guard had a chance for survival, with Lassiter at the helm, slim though it might be.

On the third night they got to talking about Vanderson. "You think he'll ever come back?" Lassiter wanted to know.

"Hope not."

"Vance ran out on me," Lassiter said grimly, and told how it had happened.

"Sounds like him," the old man said angrily. "For Melody's sake, I hope he busts his goddamn neck somewheres."

"I agree."

"I know for a fact that he took almost the last dollar Melody had in the cashbox afore he lit out."

"Trouble is, Herm spoiled him rotten as a kid."

"He's a man now." The brown eyes in Hornbeck's wrinkled face were glittering. "Seems to me he's been outa short britches for quite a spell."

Lassiter wanted to get off the subject of Vanderson, because the back of his neck got hot every time he thought of what the man had done; panicked at the mine, stolen from

Melody. "Fact is," Lassiter said, "Josh let everything go to hell so there wasn't much to turn over to his brother Herm or the niece. In all his letters to Herm he never let on about the reason for his troubles. We didn't even know he'd gotten married."

"I can tell you why it all went to hell."

"Was figuring you'd get around to it," Lassiter said with a hard smile. He refilled their coffee cups from a dented pot, then sat down again. A lamp, turned low, threw their shadows on the plank wall.

"That new wife Josh had, all curls an' big eyes. Damn handsome."

"So Melody said."

"But reckon she didn't tell you the rest of it. Mebby she don't even know."

"Tell me, Dad." Lassiter sipped coffee while Hornbeck talked.

"When the lady got herself with child, she turned into a wildcat. She'd cuss the old man out somethin' fierce. Claimin' she never wanted the kid. Don't rightly know how Josh managed to put up with her. But toward the last, she told Josh to quit struttin' around like a rooster because he was gonna be a pa. She told him the kid wasn't his. It was somebody else's kid."

Lassiter's dark brows lifted. "She told Josh a thing like that?"

"I was right there an' heard it with my own ears."

"Helluva thing to tell a husband. Specially one Josh's age."

"I never felt so sorry for anybody in my life, 'cause Josh was so proud of the kid that was a-comin'. Tellin' everybody it'd be a boy. . . ."

"She ever say who the father was?"

"Not right out. But she hinted it was Kane Farrell." Lassiter paled. "I tell you, Josh like to went crazy from then on," Hornbeck continued. "One night he got in a poker game at Dixie's, it was still Dixie's then. He caught Farrell pullin' an ace outa his boot. Farrell, who'd just come into the game, denied it. Josh wasn't wearin' a gun that night, but I was. He wanted me to loan him mine. But I wouldn't."

"If Josh had tried to pull a gun on Farrell, his brains would've been on the floor."

"Just what I told Josh." Hornbeck looked grim. He drank from a tin cup, then wiped his lips on the back of a hand. "I figured that was what Farrell was aimin' for. To git Josh riled enough to make some damned fool move, then kill him."

"Not the first time Farrell's pulled that trick."

"Farrell's a real son of a bitch. An' what that female done to Josh was shameful. But she paid for it."

"How?"

"She an' the kid both died when she was tryin' to give birth."

A sad story, Lassiter had to admit, one of an older man who had let a good-looking woman scatter his wits.

The next morning he heard a creak of heavy wheels. From the cookshack window he saw a laden freight wagon pulled by a six-mule team just swinging onto the main road. What surprised him was Melody, wrapped in a heavy coat, handling the lines. A wide-brimmed hat was cinched in place by a chin strap. She seemed to be alone.

Lassiter yelled for her to wait, but she kept going. He saddled up and went after her. At first she looked annoyed, but brought the outfit to a halt.

"What do you think you're doing?" he demanded, swinging his horse close to the wagon.

"What I usually do when there's nobody else around to drive for me."

"Damn it, I'm around!"

"I didn't know whether to ask you or not."

He swore. That morning he had ridden over to Running Springs to try to hire some men. But no one wanted to work for Northguard.

Without a word, Lassiter tied his black horse to the tailgate and hoisted himself aboard. "Move over," he ordered brusquely. And before she could reply, the pressure of his hip caused her to shift positions on the seat.

"I don't like this, Lassiter," she said indignantly.

"You shouldn't be out in these mountains alone."

"I've managed so far."

"You're forgetting what happened to Dad Hornbeck," he reminded.

She toed a rifle that lay on the floorboards at her feet. "I'm quite capable of taking care of myself."

"Anybody who wanted to take over this outfit wouldn't have much trouble."

"You mean to say I'm not capable of protecting myself?"

"I mean just that."

"Because I'm a woman, I suppose." Her gray eyes sizzled.

"No, because a driver has all he can do to keep the outfit moving. You need somebody else along to spot trouble."

"Yourself, I suppose."

"No, you. I'm taking over the team."

Before she could reply, he snatched the lines out of her hands. Once he had the big wagon on the move again, he asked how far up the mountain she intended to go. He had to ask her three times before she answered in a sullen voice.

"The town of Dexter."

"What's your cargo?"

"Nails and nuts and bolts and iron braces. For new shoring at the big mine up there."

"Who'd you get to load it?"

She named two men he'd spoken to that morning about working full time for Northguard. They had refused him, but had worked a small job for her. Probably feeling reasonably safe from Farrell while in Aspen City, but vulnerable once they were on the road.

"Everything's been in the barn for two weeks. It should have been delivered long before this. Now will you please give me back the reins? . . ."

"You just set tight. And keep your eyes peeled for trouble."

"Lassiter, it's an overnight trip to Dexter."

"What's that supposed to mean?"

She looked exasperated. "Just how are we supposed to sleep is what I mean."

"How'd you manage when Dad Hornbeck was along. Or somebody else you picked up as swamper?"

"They've been perfect gentlemen. Every one."

He flashed a hard smile. "And you don't think I will be, I suppose."

"I only know what my husband said . . ."

"I'm not surprised at anything he'd say."

"He said you're quite a hand with the ladies."

"He must've been looking in a mirror when he said that."

She colored slightly, knowing he referred to the way she had been taken in by Vanderson.

They were some miles above Aspen Creek when he urged her to take his horse and go home. He'd get the cargo to Dexter. After thinking it over, he had decided there was no reason she should wear herself out on the long trip.

"We've gone this far," she said stiffly. "I'll continue."

110

They travelled another six or seven miles in silence, grinding around the narrow curves on a road that ran through a forest of pine and aspen. Towering peaks rose on either side, some still wearing what remained of winter snow. As they climbed, it grew colder. A sharp wind whistled from a high pass ahead.

They came to a mountain village where a few buildings of unpainted lumber were bunched at the foot of a granite wall. Residents came to stare at them. There was a shaking of heads as they saw the sign Northguard Freight Company painted on the side of the wagon.

"They don't think I'll ever last," Melody said under her breath. "But I'll show them." Her voice cracked.

"Spunk is half the battle," Lassiter said, after they watered the mules and then fed them.

But he knew there was more involved than spunk. There were the matters of finances and equipment. Not to mention competition from Kane Farrell's freight line with its tough crews and new wagons. At any point, Lassiter half-expected to run into one of the Farrell outfits. He'd try to stand them off as best he could if it came to a fight, and he'd see that Melody was unharmed. He didn't expect her to be much of a shot, but with both their rifles they'd have a chance.

However, they met no one on the road except some prospectors, with a string of burros carrying unbelievable loads.

Shortly before dark they rolled into Dexter. Jared Adams, superintendent of the Glory Mine, looked over the bill of lading Melody showed him. He was in the mine office, a small, cluttered building with a steeply slanted roof that discouraged a buildup of winter snows.

"You're some weeks late," Adams said with a superior smile. He was a large, red-faced man whose great mound of belly was partially concealed by a brown vest. Shirtsleeves were rolled up over soft, pale forearms. He was sprawled in a swivel chair at a rolltop desk. He handed the bill of lading back to Melody.

"We're too late?" she faltered.

"Much."

Lassiter had been standing in the doorway of the overheated office. He pretended he hadn't heard the super's remark. "I'll need a man or two to help unload the cargo," he said to Adams.

The man swung around in his swivel chair

to sweep Lassiter with a flinty eye. "The cargo is unacceptable because of the delay."

As Lassiter stepped deeper into the building, his boots thumping on the plank floor, Adams licked his lips.

"Her Uncle Josh died and she's trying to run the company herself," Lassiter said coldly. "People have been throwing wrenches into the machinery. That's why the delay. So there's no reason for you to try and back out of the agreement."

Adams regained some of the composure that Lassiter's cold gaze had partially erased. He said that Kane Farrell was bringing what was needed in a few days. "Need I say more?" he finished.

"Yeah, you can whistle up two men to help me unload."

Melody, her face flaming, cried, "Lassiter, you're only making matters worse. . . ."

Adams whitened. "*Lassiter?* But he's dead. . . ."

"Not very," Lassiter put in. "You're late getting the news up here in the mountains."

Without leaving his chair, Adams flung up a window next to to the desk and shouted, "Marsh! I need help!"

"Yessiree!" responded a deep male voice.

"Now there's bound to be trouble," Melody wailed. "And it was so . . . so unnecessary."

"Adams here has to learn that when he makes a contract he'd better keep it!"

Melody stood rigid, fingertips at her mouth as she stared out of the windows. "Oh, my God," she breathed as two big men came at a run from the mine warehouse next door.

The one in the lead had coarse hair the color of straw, was a good four inches taller than Lassiter, and outweighed him by at least sixty pounds. He jerked the door open so violently that it rattled in its hinges.

"You got trouble, Mr. Adams?" he bellowed, looking around. Yellowish eyes were riveted to the slender dark man near the desk.

"*Him!*" Adams shouted, pointing a forefinger at Lassiter.

"Let's get him, Clyde," Marsh yelled over his shoulder to the second man, making it sound no more significant than brushing aside a fly.

Marsh was reaching for a belted gun as his head turned to speak to the large black-haired man lumbering behind him.

Without waiting for the pair to get set, Lassiter lunged. A crushing blow landed on

114

Marsh's jaw. As the man's head snapped back, Lassiter rammed a hard shoulder into his chest. The force of it knocked Marsh backwards into the advancing Clyde. Both men went down. As Marsh struck the slatted boardwalk, his gun was jarred from his hand.

Without losing a step, Lassiter bent down and whipped a fist across Marsh's face. Blood spurted from a smashed nose. Then he turned on Clyde who was picking himself up from the path that led from office to warehouse.

By then Lassiter's gun was in hand, the hammer cocked back. Clyde Dover, a brawny man in his late twenties, came onto his toes as he stared into the ominous maw of the .44. His jaw dropped.

"Pull your gun," Lassiter ordered him. "With thumb and forefinger. Put it down on the walk."

When Dover hesitated, Lassiter said, "If you even look like trouble, you're dead. You hear me, Clyde?"

Dover looked down at Marsh who was out cold at his feet. Blood ran down Marsh's jaw from the broken nose. Without a word, Dover did as Lassiter had ordered. His gun thumped to the walk.

Keeping an eye on Dover, Lassiter scooped up both weapons by the trigger guards. "Get inside," he ordered the man, "and drag Marsh in with you."

Adams stood woodenly beside his desk, his face the color of fresh whitewash. A coil of rope hung by a hook near a window. "Tie Dover's wrists," Lassiter snapped at Adams. When Adams, with a trembling hand, cut off a length of rope and bound Dover's wrists, Lassiter ordered him to do likewise to the unconscious Jody Marsh.

When the trouble started, Melody had paled and looked like a frightened fawn ready to run to the safety of friendly woods. But now the shock was gradually leaving her face. It was replaced with the faintest of smiles. Her gray eyes actually glowed with excitement.

Four roustabouts had come to the warehouse door, their faces reflecting awe at the speed with which the two big men had been dispatched. None seemed anxious to challenge Lassiter's gun.

"Adams, tell them to unload the wagon," Lassiter ordered. Then he added wryly, "I don't figure to give them a hand. I've earned a rest, don't you think?"

Melody laughed. The portly Adams swallowed and said, "Yes indeed you have earned a rest."

From a window he shouted orders, saying that the four men were to unload the wagon and quickly. When the job was done, Adams paid Melody the price agreed upon weeks before. Paid in cash.

Keeping an eye on the four roustabouts, Lassiter marched Dover and a groggy Marsh to the wagon where he made them sit on the lowered tailgate. Because his wrists were bound, Marsh had no way to wipe blood from the lower half of his face. "What the hell you figure to do next?" he growled.

Lassiter ignored him and turned to Adams, who seemed to have shriveled from an arrogant overweight mine superintendent to a pale copy of his former self. Now he was just a fat man who was still in shock at the swift and brutal way Lassiter had handled his two bodyguards.

But he did attempt to save face by saying, "You've made a couple of enemies today, Lassiter."

"Enemies I've already got. From Denver to the Mex border, from the California line to El Paso. Two more don't mean a damn thing."

Lassiter gave a hard laugh. He untied his

horse from the tailgate of the empty wagon where the two men were already seated.

"You drive," he told Melody as he mounted up. "I'll be keeping an eye open."

Lassiter watched from the saddle, his Henry rifle across a thigh as a cheerful Melody started back down the mountain.

"Why in hell didn't Adams tell us it was Lassiter?" Marsh muttered. "We'd have come shootin' instead of swingin' our fists."

Lassiter rode close, which caused Marsh's bloodied face to look apprehensive. "Either one of you ever make a move against Mrs. Vanderson, I'll be on your trail. Once I start after a man I never quit till I get him."

Both of them seemed impressed.

Lassiter rode fifty yards back up the road to see if Adams might have ignored Lassiter's warning and gotten help either from his mine or the village nearby. But there was no sign of anyone.

When they were about four miles from the mine, Lassiter told Melody to halt the wagon. He ordered the pair off the tailgate. "Now you can walk."

Clouds had sailed in to darken the sun. A chill wind had come up during the last mile.

"Cut us loose, Lassiter," Marsh whined as he looked at the ominous sky. Pines rustled in the wind. A large pine cone plopped to the ground and rolled onto the road.

"Just start walking, boys," Lassiter said. "And if you get any grand ideas about coming after us, I guarantee you'll never see another sunrise."

_____ *11*

As NIGHTFALL APPROACHED, he found them a campsite, sheltered from the road by a stand of pines. After watering and feeding the mules, and putting his black horse on good grass, he went hunting. All he could bag was a large jack rabbit.

He built a fire and skinned the animal. Then broiled the meat on flat stones.

She sat so close to him that he could feel her tremble.

"You're frightened up here, just the two of us," he said. "Don't be. Nothing's going to hurt you."

"I'm not afraid as long . . ." She turned and looked at the play of firelight across his strong features. "As long as you're with me," she concluded in a low voice.

When they had finished eating, she licked grease from her fingers. "Never have I tasted anything as good as that rabbit." He shrugged. Then she whispered, "May I say something, Lassiter?"

"Sure, go ahead."

"You were marvelous today. Simply *marvelous*."

"Adams figured to give you trouble. I gave him some instead."

"That poor man was badly frightened." Laughter bubbled from her lips. Then she sobered. "I haven't been very nice to you and I'm sorry."

"It doesn't matter now."

"For one thing, it was such a shock to see you alive when I thought you were dead. And then there were the things Vance kept saying about you. . . ."

"Such as?"

"That you intended to cheat Uncle Herm."

"I would never cheat Herm Falconer. Or anybody, for that matter."

When it started to sprinkle, he got several tarps from the freighter and made a bed for them under the wagon where they'd be out of the rain.

"We better be together tonight," Lassiter said. "It'll be freezing up here before morning. We'll need the body warmth of both of us."

Light from the dying fire was reflected in her eyes as she thought about it. Then she gave a deep sigh and said, "I guess it's the only way."

By the time he pulled off his boots, the rain had turned into a downpour. He lay under the wagon, his back to hers.

"It's no feather bed," he said over his shoulder, "but it'll have to do."

She reached back under the tarp for his hand. She gave it a squeeze. "I'd be afraid out here alone. But not with you along."

"I sleep light. If I hear anything in the night, I'll be ready."

Then she made an impulsive move. Sitting up under the wagon, she leaned over him. The feel of soft lips against his cheek was surprising. He didn't say anything. But after the hectic experience of the late afternoon, the gesture was most welcome. Turning his head, he met her lips with his own.

For only an instant did it cross his mind that she was another man's wife. Man? A weak-kneed snivelling crybaby. Any guilt he might have felt slid off as easily as water from a greased sheet of iron.

In the morning she avoided his eyes. "I suppose you think I'm awful."

He kissed her, but she pushed away. "It mustn't happen again," she said hoarsely, and started to run a comb through her long pale hair. . . .

The story of how Lassiter had handled the two toughs up at the Glory Mine soon spread through the mountains. Mostly it was Melody who would go into detail about how Lassiter had made Dover and Marsh ride on the tailgate of the wagon before turning them loose. Most of the time, when Lassiter was near, she acted as though she was walking three feet off the ground. And her gray eyes would acquire a strange glow.

But Lassiter pretended indifference. He had to remind himself that there were more important things to consider, such as his determination to revive the fortunes of the Northguard Freight Company. He kept waiting for a reply to his letters written to Herm Falconer down at Rimrock.

Later that week Bert Oliver appeared at the company headquarters in Aspen Creek. The lanky former Confederate soldier said that Bluegate buzzed with news that the freight company had taken a turn for the better. Now he wanted to be a part of Lassiter's game to bring down Kane Farrell.

"You're the only man around here with guts enough to stand up to him," Oliver said gravely in his drawl. "An' I'd like to be with you."

Lassiter studied him, knowing from the leathery skin and deep eye creases that he must be close to forty or even more. Oliver seemed to sense his hesitation.

"In the war I was a dead shot. My job was to ride rifle guard on the mail wagon. A lot of blue bellies tried to jump me. None of 'em ever made it."

A grinning Lassiter welcomed him with outstretched hand.

Later in the week, Lassiter recruited three more men who had heard he was hiring. He gave it to them straight. Wages would be tops, but they wouldn't be paid until finances improved. About all Lassiter could promise for the moment were full stomachs.

The men were agreeable. At least they'd eat until the money started rolling in. Jobs in the area were hard to come by until local ranches started hiring extra hands for the spring roundup, which was over a month away.

Business picked up, but it was mostly

short hauls. What Lassiter wanted was a big one. It came when Melody was notified by mail that a shipment expected by the Bitterroot Mining Company had arrived via the railroad and was now at Montclair, a week's trip to the north.

That same day Lassiter rode into the mountains for a talk with Saul Betancourt, superintendent of the Bitterroot Mine, who had been waiting since the previous fall for equipment that would enable him to start the construction of a smelter.

Betancourt, a lean man in high-laced boots and wearing a heavy jacket, greeted Lassiter gravely. "I heard about the trouble you gave Adams over at the Glory Mine. He's a pompous ass. I guess you taught him a lesson."

Betancourt listened to what Lassiter had to say about the shipment up at Montclair. Then he sighed and ran a hand over short-cropped brown hair. "I more or less promised the business to Farrell."

But Lassiter argued the case for Northguard. And when he had finished, Betancourt said, "I agree with everything you say. Sure I realize that Farrell is undercutting your price to drive Northguard out of business."

"If that happens," Lassiter put in,

124

"freight rates will go high as the moon. He'll not only be top dog in these parts, but the only dog."

"And he'll have every mining company in a box," Betancourt added.

"In a box with the lid nailed down."

Betancourt thought about it. They were in his spacious office with its wall maps and surveying equipment. A window overlooked a new tunnel that a crew of men were digging into the side of a mountain.

"Lassiter, do you think you can handle the shipment?"

"I've got good men. We'll handle it."

For a moment Betancourt studied the rugged looking man with the penetrating blue eyes. Then a broad grin broke across his brown face. "Tell you the truth, I've been hesitant about Farrell. A gent with his rep as a cardsharp is apt to deal off the bottom of the deck in business matters as well."

"I wouldn't trust him any further than I could see a scorpion's shadow."

Betancourt laughed, then pursed his lips and fingered the brass-framed spectacles that rested on his button nose. "I thought for a time the railroad might run a spur line down here. But no chance of that now, I understand. And I do want to get that smelter built."

"You keep the stuff you need for the smelter coming to Montclair. We'll see that you get fast delivery up here at Bitterroot."

"I've a hunch you won't let Farrell push you around."

"It may not be easy," Lassiter admitted. "But here in the West, what is?"

Lassiter was just entering Aspen Creek the next morning when he saw a blooded roan at the rail in front of Northguard headquarters. Lassiter dismounted next to the splendid animal. It bore a fine saddle with KF etched in the saddle skirt.

He heard voices coming from the office. First Melody's then Kane Farrell's, through a partially opened window.

". . . and I think the offer is fair enough," Farrell was saying smoothly.

"I suppose it is from your standpoint." Melody sat at the table that was used as a desk, nervously shuffling some papers. Farrell stood before her, hands behind his back. He was half-turned so that Lassiter could see the classic profile.

"I'm sure you understand by now that running a freight line is no business for a female."

126

Through the window Lassiter saw Melody's chin come up and for a moment thought Farrell had said the wrong thing. He was surprised to see Melody's shoulders slump, as if the fight had gone out of her.

"I . . . I do dread violence," she said in a voice so low it barely carried to the window.

"I've only given you a few facts, Mrs. Vanderson. The innocent will suffer if this foolish feud is allowed to continue."

"I'm thinking of Dad Hornbeck wounded. And Lord knows how many others before it's over."

"As I explained, there are always those on the fringe who would shoot an old man like Hornbeck. Just to try and cut themselves a piece of the cake, so to speak."

"An old man like that, shot for no reason," she said in despair.

"That's the way those things happen. Who knows who may be next? As I said earlier, perhaps even Lassiter."

She bit her lips. "Oh, no. . . ,"

"He's lived a charmed life. But a lot of men want to see him dead."

"A horrible way to live, with that threat hanging over his head."

"He'd be better off to go deep into Mexico

and live out his days. He'll last longer than he will around here."

"You really think so?"

Farrell nodded and drew a sheet of paper from the inside pocket of a knee-length leather coat. His breeches were fawn colored. The only blemish to his attire were some specks of mud around the built-up heels of his dark brown boots.

"If you'll just sign this agreement, Mrs. Vanderson. Your freight line in exchange for my bank draft of four thousand dollars. Which I say is quite fair, under the circumstances."

The sound of the door opening caused Farrell to turn his head. His green eyes narrowed at the sight of Lassiter. He gave a curt nod of recognition.

"I understood from the villagers that you were to be gone at least three days," Farrell said through lips thinned from pressure.

"You are back early," Melody said. Then, "Mr. Farrell has offered to buy me out. . . ."

"So I heard." Lassiter kept his eyes on the dandified Farrell. "Business up the mountain didn't take as long as I figured." He closed the door.

"What do you think I should do, Lassiter?" Melody asked in a tight voice.

"Take his offer, if you want. Maybe consider yourself lucky. Then you can head back east where you belong."

That caused her to straighten up in the chair, shoulders squared, mouth set in a stubborn line. "You mean just . . . just quit?" Then she struck the desktop with a small fist, making the inkwell jump. "Well, for your information, I intend to fight for what is right."

Lassiter gave a fierce smile. "Glad to hear you say that."

An angry flush darkened Farrell's cheeks. "I suggest you pay my offer careful consideration, Mrs. Vanderson. Don't let Lassiter's presence sway you."

"It was my decision," Melody said firmly. "Lassiter had nothing to do with it." Her voice no longer wavered, indicating a woman unable to make up her own mind.

When Farrell started to speak angrily, Lassiter shook his head. "Leave her alone," he warned.

Farrell's height seemed to increase above the six-foot mark as he drew himself up. His sculptured chin lifted. In the deadly silence, his right hand fingers twitched only inches from the open front of his leather coat, itching to reach for a weapon. Lassiter tensed, ready for him.

Abruptly, Farrell strode to the door. "By the way, Sheriff Dancur rode up with me today. He happened to have some business at the store here." Then his green eyes swung to Melody. "I hope you don't awaken some midnight and realize the awful forces you've unleashed by your unwillingness to accept a fair offer."

"Get out of here, Farrell," Lassiter said coolly. "And don't come back."

Lassiter stepped outside in case, sheriff's presence or not, Farrell made a try for his gun. At least out here Melody would be spared the possibility of being hit by a bullet.

But Farrell rode down the street, past the Aspen Saloon. Two men came riding out from the far side of the building. Lassiter's lips formed a hard grin. Farrell hadn't risked coming up here alone. He recognized Ed Kiley's towering figure. The small and dark man he didn't know. In a few moments, Bo Dancur came swaggering out of the store, mounted up and they all started down the steep road to Bluegate.

Melody came to stand at Lassiter's side. "For a minute there I almost thought you wanted me to sell," she said, looking up at him, the sun shining on her golden hair. "I'd have given you all of the four thousand. It certainly wasn't as much as you put into the company, but . . ."

"I was hoping you'd show Farrell some backbone. And you did." He smiled at her.

Then he told about the agreement with Betancourt of the Bitterroot Mining Company.

"How wonderful, Lassiter!" she cried, clapping her hands. "We'll make it yet. The two of us."

That was when he noticed the tenderness in her eyes, the sweet smile. His face closed. In the first place, she was married, despite what had happened between them that rainy night in the mountains. Besides that, as soon as Herm was able to come to Aspen City and take over for his niece, Lassiter intended to clear out. Lately he had noticed little things Melody let slip, the way she looked at him, all since that night after he had saved her shipment at the Glory Mine. But he knew he couldn't just ride off and leave Herm and Melody to face the ambitious Kane Farrell. No, that part of it he'd have to solve before he pulled out for new horizons.

To handle the big load from rail's end at

Montclair to the Bitterroot Mine in the mountains would take an additional nine wagons, Lassiter estimated. He put out word that he wanted teamsters with wagons to work on a percentage. He was also hiring a crew, so went the story that was soon spread over the Bluegate Basin.

Teamsters with one or two wagons, who had been working the short end of the stick because of the bad winter, came in with him. Some had to be sent on their way because Lassiter knew their equipment would never stand the pounding of all those rough miles.

He wanted a crew of twenty-six men, two men to each of the twelve wagons, plus two more to take care of the extra mules. He finally got four teamsters with wagons and managed to buy five more with payment deferred until fall. On the same basis he picked up the mules needed for the long drive.

One prerequisite for being hired on by Northguard was that each man have a rifle and revolver and ammunition. Northguard lacked the funds to supply additional arms, Lassiter explained.

Melody went around humming under her breath, the gray eyes had a new sparkle.

Even Dad Hornbeck noticed the change in her. "Our gal Melody looks as happy as if she'd been out all day smellin' the wild flowers."

Most of the hired men had experience on freight lines. Those without experience were shown the rudiments of mule skinning. Lassiter couldn't be too particular, men for hire were hard to come by. Word of the trouble between Northguard and Farrell made many would-be prospects back off.

Each driver was furnished with twenty feet of rawhide attached to a two-foot hickory handle, with a buckskin popper on the end. The indispensable bull whip.

Experts practicing in the wagon yard sent their bull whips cracking with such regularity that it sounded like a miniature cannonade. Lassiter was pleased with the wrangler and nighthawk who had been hired on, both hard-jawed men with hands scarred from years of roping.

At first, Lassiter had leaned toward using oxen rather than mules. And Bert Oliver, who had had some experience in freighting, agreed that oxen were probably better for hauling heavy machinery, even though they were slower. One advantage was that they could live off grass alone and in this high country spring grass was plentiful. For mules, grain would have to be hauled, which meant a loss of valuable cargo space. But when it came right down to it, Lassiter wondered where he would be able to round up a hundred and fifty head of oxen, including replacements, on such short notice. So he decided it would be mules.

After the big crew was hired, each man took turns at cooking. Oliver wondered aloud if it wasn't a woman's place to cook full time. But Lassiter shook his head. "She's got other things to do, Bert. Same as the rest of us."

"But the good Lord put her an' her kind on earth to take care of men folks. At least that's what my Pa always said."

"Times are changing. There's a woman up in Colorado who runs a cattle ranch. And one back in Kansas I've heard of who's farming four sections of land. The only help they get is from the men they hire."

Oliver looked skeptical and rubbed one of his bushy sideburns. "If my Daddy could come back from the grave an' hear this, he'd plumb drop through the floor."

"The way I've got it figured, Bert," Lassiter said with a tight smile, "It's your night to scrape up a meal for us."

They ate together and then spread their blankets in the cramped quarters. Because there wasn't room for all of them inside, some slept in the yard under the trees.

The evening before they were to pull out, Melody asked Lassiter to have supper with her. She had made a delicious stew and a pie of dried apples. During the meal, she talked of her girlhood in the east.

"My uncles never liked my father, although I never understood why," Melody said between sips of coffee. "But after he died, they seemed to mellow and forgave their sister, my mother. They would send us money, which my mother always returned. She was the unforgiving one, it seems. Although we did come out to visit Uncle Josh one time."

Lassiter well remembered the scrawny girl and buxom mother.

As they were finishing the pie, Melody asked for more details about his life when he was recovering from the near-fatal wound. When he spoke of Roma, his voice softened and he sat staring at the plank wall that was splashed with lamplight.

"Were you in love with her?" Melody probed, watching him through thick, pale lashes.

"She was a friend. A good friend."

"From your voice, I think it was deeper

than friendship." A little catch in Melody's voice caused Lassiter to turn in his chair to stare at her. The chair creaked from his weight. The wick of the single lamp was smoking slightly. He leaned over and turned it down.

All of a sudden she seemed forlorn. He reached across the table and took her hands. "Don't be jealous of Roma." Then he added with a faint grin, "Maybe I'm the one who should be jealous, you with a husband. . . ."

It was just something that had slipped out. Suddenly her gray eyes seemed filled with hope.

"Vance will never come back," she said, the light of joy gone from her eyes. "I'll have to take the rather drastic step for a woman and file for divorce." She looked at Lassiter. "And that will be the end of Mr. Vance Vanderson, so far as I'm concerned."

He thought it best to make no comment. Already once tonight he had put his foot in it.

"I want to get rolling by dawn, so I better head for my blankets."

He got up as she removed her apron, threw it over a chair, and went across the room, her heels rapping on the bare floor. She opened the door to her sleeping quarters. There she stood, waiting, hands at her sides, head tilted.

Although she presented an appealing figure, he didn't pick up her obvious invitation.

"If I don't see you in the morning," he said lightly, "say a prayer for us."

He walked over and thanked her for the supper, then kissed the tip of her nose. But as he started to turn away, she clutched at his arms. As her fingers tightened, one part of his mind said, "Why not?" And he actually lifted his hands to her shoulders.

"I've got to go," he said suddenly.

"Can't you . . . stay?"

Pretending he hadn't heard, he hurried to the door, gave her a wave of the hand, and stepped out into the moon-swept darkness.

It was not quite daylight when Lassiter and the men ate breakfast. But they were ready to roll when the eastern lid of the horizon lifted just enough to let out a thick gray streak of light.

Melody hurried from the office, tightening a shawl across her shoulders. All the men eyed her appreciatively as she came closer to the wagons.

"Lassiter, be careful," she said, panting from her run.

"We'll be back before you know it," he said confidently.

From the saddle of his black horse he blew her a kiss, which she threw back to him. He was reflecting on how pretty she looked in a bright yellow dress, her hair pinned up. She'd make a good wife for some man. Too bad she had allowed herself to be hoodwinked by Vanderson.

He hadn't slept well. His mind had been on Melody. And on Roma with her flashing eyes, the strong white teeth that could so playfully nip his flesh, the rounded limbs that at times were so lively.

Cool off, Lassiter, he warned himself, then gave a short laugh as he rode to the lead wagon. "Vamonos! Let's go!" he shouted at the men and as the wagons began creaking into motion, he added a second command, so familiar in the freighting business. "Stretch 'em out!"

_____ *12*

ON THE MORNING Lassiter left for Montclair, Vance Vanderson was at High Pass, twenty miles west. He was on his way south and intended to bypass Bluegate and most certainly Aspen City. He wanted nothing to remind him of his brief but hectic association with Melody. She had turned out to be a nosy bitch with her litany of "Where are you going? What time will you be home, or what day, rather . . . Isn't that more money than you intended spending? . . . We're not rich, you know . . . Did you *have* to get in a poker game? You know Farrell's a cheat. You told me so yourself."

That last remark produced their worst quarrel, mainly because he feared it would get back to Farrell. He had been fairly drunk the night he told her about sitting next to Farrell in several games and surreptitiously slipping extra cards into his boot top.

To have someone spread the word that Farrell was a cheat would enrage the man. No, he'd give Bluegate a wide berth. And he certainly had no wish to see his unresponsive wife.

That was why he intended keeping to the mountains, even though it was longer, rather than chance running into her or others who might ask embarrassing questions.

He'd stop by Rimrock and see his ailing stepfather. Recently he'd heard Herm was still there. But he had become stricken with the same disease that had taken his brother

Josh. Herm couldn't stay away from a bottle when things went wrong. Losing his leg had been a mortal blow to his pride, so the doctor had written Vance in Denver. He knew Herm would be good for a few dollars if he stopped in while passing through Rimrock. And when Herm finally took off, which seemed inevitable, the way he was drinking, what he had left would go to his loyal stepson, Vance. Just thinking of it brought a hard smile to his lips. He certainly had more right to the estate, whatever remained, than Melody, who was only a niece.

One thing he regretted was Herm's investing eleven thousand dollars in the sorry freight line. Vanderson would have made much better use of the money by taking a flyer in mining stocks. In Denver he'd been caught up in the excitement of buying and selling, but lacked the necessary capital. To make a killing would take thousands, not the hundreds that seemed to be about the extent of his poke at any given time.

He was eating breakfast in the combination saloon and general store where he'd played poker the night before. Long after midnight he was the big winner. At the start it had been a low-stakes game, but as the evening progressed the ante was gradually raised. By three in the morning he had cleaned out all the other players. Most of them were drifters or miners, plus a few cowhands who worked the mountain ranches.

He had gone out back and locked himself in the privy and counted his money by the light of matches. His heart soared. He was over five hundred dollars to the good—his luck was changing. His handsome face was lighted by a wide grin. There'd been too many long dry months for comfort. His good luck here in High Pass left no doubt that he was going to have a prosperous year.

As he was finishing his breakfast at the end of the bar, some men came in. They had the look of the mountains about them, bearded and roughly dressed. He thought of suggesting a game, then decided against it. There were six of them and if he was caught padding his hand from extra cards it could be disastrous. Last night a shotgun guard had been on duty, but this morning there was only a gray-haired bartender who shuffled rather than walked.

Apparently the men had just met up with each other outside town, for they talked as if they hadn't been together for a spell. Vanderson was just sopping up the last of his egg with a cold biscuit when he heard Melody's name mentioned.

Holding his breath, he listened, head cocked. According to a large man with a full red beard, Melody had hired a new crew and was said to be prospering. Kane Farrell even seemed to accept the new status, so stated the bearded man. She had bought extra wagons and seemed on the verge of obtaining some big contracts. The man mentioned that one bit of business was to haul much needed equipment to the Bitterroot Mine, one of the largest in the mountains.

Vanderson was excited. By God, his luck *was* changing. Hearing Melody's good fortune was indeed pleasing to his ears. But then in looking back, he always did have a rather warm association with Lady Luck. His luck came unexpectedly and in strange ways.

Instead of pushing over the mountains and heading south as he intended, he went east from High Pass straight to Aspen City. He would make up for the quarrel with Melody, using his considerable experience in crushing female hearts and, if in the mood, putting them back together again. There was no reason why he shouldn't share in his wife's good fortune, he thought with a short laugh.

The following day Melody was washing the dishes used in the noon meal she had shared with Dad Hornbeck, in the headquarters building. His wound was healing and these days he always carried a rifle. She knew he thought he was protecting her, something she didn't need. She could take care of herself. But it did give the old man something to think about.

Being around Lassiter had taught her self-reliance. She had never understood the meaning of love as she did now. There had been times in her short but turbulent marriage when she had vowed she would fall in love with her husband if it killed her.

But Lassiter was a different story. Closing her eyes, she pictured him, tall and lean with the ink-black hair, his face darkened from exposure. And the startling blue eyes, his most arresting feature. She felt her heart lurch pleasantly.

"Melody, my darling! I'm *here!*"

She was so entranced that the male voice fairly sang through her mind, because for one glorious moment she thought it might be Lassiter, come back early for one reason or other.

But in the next breath she realized the voice wasn't Lassiter's. She had been standing in a bar of warm sunlight coming through a side window, holding a tin plate she had been about to wipe and put away. Standing on the other side of the table stood Vance Vanderson, wearing the boyish smile he once told her was guaranteed to set female hearts racing. The conceited fool, she recalled thinking at the time.

At first she was plainly surprised to see him again. She had considered him out of her life for good. He continued to smile at her, as if he had just been down to Bluegate for the day instead of having been gone for weeks up to Denver and the Lord only knew where else.

Her surprise was turning to anger when he skirted the table and caught her by an elbow, so that she dropped the plate. It went banging across the floor. He pulled her close and planted his lips on hers. His tongue moved inside her mouth. She was powerless to resist because he was gripping her shoulders.

Although the kiss had left her completely chilled, he seemed impressed by his accomplishment. She thought of wiping a hand across her lips, then decided not to go that far. He did have a violent temper and could change in a flash from gentleman to demon.

He had never struck her, although it had been threatened.

"Whew!" he exclaimed. "What a welcome you gave me!"

She stared. My God, he actually seemed to believe it.

She backed up so he couldn't grab her again. It was time to settle a few things, she told herself. Among them was the fact that she didn't love him and that so far as she was concerned he could get right back in the saddle and ride out of her life, as he had done before.

But before she could open her mouth, he was dumping gold coins among the papers on her desk. One of them rolled to the floor, which caused him to give a cheerful cry as he snatched it up. Something like a little kid who has found a bright shiny penny, she thought.

As she watched him with a puzzled frown, he stacked the gold coins and added some silver dollars and even a ten dollar bill. They seldom saw paper money in the mountains.

He made a dramatic gesture at the money. "There represents hours of toil, my love."

"You mean you *worked* for it?"

"Every nickel. You seem surprised."

"Frankly . . ."

"I've turned over a new leaf," he interrupted. "Marriage to you has given me a new sense of responsibility."

She smoothed the green dress that he had twisted in his violent embrace. "Oh, I find that hard to believe."

"True, so help me God." He stood, fairly tall, wide through the shoulders, with light brown hair showing under his tipped back hat. The matching mustache was thick and hooked down past the corners of his mouth. Sincerity swam in his hazel eyes. "I worked for a time in a gambling hall and then one night I met this preacher."

"Don't tell me you got religion!" she started to scoff.

"The Reverend Collins. I talked to him about you. And above all, he stressed the sanctity of marriage and he told me to come back to you just as quick as I could."

"I can't imagine you being influenced by a preacher."

"I vowed that I wouldn't return to you without money. So I got a job with a freight line. It took a lot of dangerous hauls into the Rockies to earn that money. I got so I could handle mules real good. Some are stubborn as hell, though. 'Scuse the cuss word, Melody."

"Oh, I'm used to worse than that."

She had been slowly backing away from him, but he suddenly closed the gap and slipped a long arm around her waist.

"Let's," he whispered, and started to push her toward the bedroom door.

All she could think of to say was, "Somebody might come in."

He looked thoughtful. "Well, if you think it best we wait for tonight, maybe we should. Won't be anybody to interrupt us then. Got any coffee?"

Somehow she had to get rid of him before Lassiter returned. Perhaps he would move on of his own accord.

Many times that day he mentioned the long hours he had put in to earn the money. "Just to give it to you, Melody."

She had locked the money in the safe. Perhaps fifty dollars of it was due to his benevolence. But the rest of it had come out of the company weeks ago. Loans, some of it. Or sums he had taken from the cash drawer. Many times she had caught him helping himself. But he always had a plausible explanation: one of the wagons needing a new tongue or anything he might name that would cost money.

When Dad Hornbeck came in for his supper there was a definite strain. Hornbeck didn't offer to shake hands. "So you come back," he grunted, a sour look on his seamed face.

The lamb was overdone, the parsnips from the root cellar blackened globs of vegetable.

Melody apologized to Hornbeck for the meal. He said, "Reckon I'll be takin' my meals at the cookshack till the boys git back."

After Hornbeck had gone and Vance was drying the dishes she had washed, he said, "I figure we oughta get rid of Old Hornbeck."

Melody's head came up. *We*, Vance had said. It made her stiffen with anger. Just because she had married him in a moment of despair and self-pity didn't mean she was obligated to let him share in the company. But each time she tried to make her point, he deftly danced away like an experienced swordsman in a duel. And he would invariably start talking about his great new friend, the Reverend Collins.

"I can remember the times the reverend would say that a wife's duty was to please a husband. It's God's law, Melody. Over and over he would say it."

148

"Vance, I think you and I should have a serious talk."

Vanderson slumped in a chair, fingers locked behind his head, staring at the ceiling. She supposed that many women would consider themselves fortunate to have such a boyishly handsome man for a husband.

"Go ahead, talk, Melody. But let me tell you the reverend used to say that if a wife turned her back on her husband, she'd end up in perdition, sure as hell," He laughed. "Hell being the same as perdition."

"Vance, I do appreciate your bringing me some money, but. . . ."

His right arm snaked out suddenly so that he caught her arm before she could draw back. "You look sleepy. Best we went to bed."

"I just couldn't tonight, Vance," burst from her lips. "I'm sorry, but I . . . I couldn't. . . ."

She fled to the bedroom, slammed the door and locked it.

The reaction was surprisingly mild compared to some of his tantrums when not getting his own way.

"You take all the time you want," He spoke loud enough for her to hear him through the door. "Tomorrow's soon enough, though I sure got a big ache for you."

In the morning she did something that she should have done before. But surprise at seeing him again and his windy tales about the preacher and the hard work he had done in order to earn money had thrown her off balance.

She told him about Lassiter.

He was lifting a forkful of eggs to his mouth. He dropped the fork. It took him a few moments to recover from his surprise. "You talking about *Lassiter?*"

His obvious consternation pleased her greatly. She was only sorry she had not told him when he first arrived. He might have kept on going.

"Lassiter's dead," he breathed.

"Very much alive."

At his insistence, she told him as much as she knew about Lassiter's six month disappearance, his miraculous recovery from a near-fatal bullet wound.

"But I went to his funeral," he said, sounding bewildered. What he said next surprised and disappointed her. She knew that Lassiter had no use for Vance and she assumed it worked both ways.

Vanderson said, "That's the best news

150

I've heard in ages." He sounded enthusiastic. "Ol' Lassiter alive. Will I be glad to shake his hand. Where is he?"

She told him about the new crew that Lassiter had taken up to Montclair.

"When he gets back I'll be more'n glad to do my share," Vance said heartily.

He was energetically finishing the eggs she had cooked. Melody watched him, hands in her lap, not knowing what to say. She had thought that the mere mention of Lassiter being alive would cause him to hit the trail. But this apparently was a new Vance Vanderson, one she didn't know.

Perhaps, she conceded, the Reverend Collins had had some influence on him after all.

13

ON A GRADE the air was filled with shouts from bullwhackers. The popping of their bullwhips made a sound like Chinese New Year.

Lassiter smiled at the overcast morning as the wagons creaked and rattled on the rough road. He thought back several days to when the residents of Aspen Creek had come to cheer them on their way. If the freight line proved to be a success, and it looked as if it might, then the whole area would prosper. And he intended that it would.

Drivers had different ideas about handling a team. Three of them preferred a jerkline. They would ride astride the near wheel mule, one hand on the jerkline, a long single rein threaded through loops and finally anchored at the bit of the lead mule. This animal would respond to jerks on the line which would signal it to turn right or left or come to a halt. The others mules followed its lead.

Lassiter rode up to the lead wagon where Bert Oliver was handling the reins. "Three more days and we'll be in Montclair," Lassiter said to the lanky southerner.

Lassiter rode down the line, checking to make sure that each man had a rifle in a sling or scabbard within reach, as well as a revolver at the belt. It was so important in view of the contract between Northguard and the Bitterroot Mining Company. It called for one hundred sixty-five dollars a ton per day from Montclair to the foot of the mountains, and up the steep hill up to the Bitterroot. A fair enough price, he and Betancourt had agreed. And Melody certainly had seemed pleased when he spelled it out for her.

For now the mules were easy to handle because they were pulling empty wagons. But when they were loaded it would probably take some doing before they got over balking at the heavy loads.

At times Lassiter scouted ahead. Then he would travel a half a mile or so along their backtrail to make sure there was no potential trouble. He began to fret. It was unlike Farrell to let them move so easily across the country.

The last time their paths had crossed was in New Mexico, where Lassiter had been instrumental in breaking up a gang of rustlers that was threatening to bankrupt the county. Farrell was behind it. They had always been enemies, but from then on the enmity was like a raw sore that would heal only when one of them was dead at the hands of the other. They were bound to tangle in a fight to the death. Farrell hated Lassiter with all the venom of a stepped-on rattler. It was a worry, knowing that despite the depths of Farrell's feelings, the man had made no move.

During the trip to Montclair, Lassiter began to think about Melody, with only Dad Hornbeck to protect her. If Farrell kept out of it, for one reason or another, and they were able to be paid for this initial contract, then all would be well. If Farrell didn't stay out of it. . . . Lassiter refused to dwell on the possibility of failure.

But if Farrell did catch them by surprise, then all Lassiter prayed for was enough breath left in his body to finish the bastard off, to keep him from ruining Melody.

Each morning after ten or so Lassiter began to hunt for a clearing that could easily be reached from the road. On the fourth morning he found one quickly. Sam Birkener had been designated as cook. He was a fat, slow-moving man who usually wore a puzzled frown, as if he couldn't quite make out what was happening around him. That day he whipped up antelope stew for the noon meal, from the animal Lassiter had shot from the saddle an hour earlier.

As was customary on the early stop, the mules were watered by the teamsters. Swampers broke out the sacks of grain that were carried in each wagon. The mules were then fed in long canvas troughs to minimize waste. After the mules were turned loose onto the grass, the men had their noon meal. Shortly past noon they were ready to roll again.

So far, they had made nearly twenty miles

a day. But of course the wagons were empty and there was a gentle downgrade all the way. It would be different coming back with a load.

Just before sundown, Lassiter ordered the train to corral by alternate wagons, the first wagon turning right, the second left, the others following suit until making a complete circle.

While this was being done, Lassiter rode on the perimeter of their camp far enough out to spot potential danger. But he turned up nothing. A cookfire sent sparks shooting into the darkening sky. When a breeze came up, the wagons parked close to a stand of pines had their sides brushed by tree limbs.

Lassiter returned from his scouting expedition in time to fill his plate with the last of the stew. The men had already eaten and were busily sanding their tin plates so as to have them ready for breakfast.

Shortly past midnight, Lassiter crawled out of his blankets. He reached out for his boots, fumbled in the darkness, then pulled them tight on his feet. He picked up his rifle and walked silently away from the sleeping men. Ahead were the mules, held in a rope corral under the watchful eye of Willie Barr.

Barr was alert and hissed a challenge when he saw Lassiter's moving shadow.

Lassiter whispered his name and Barr relaxed.

"See anything?" Lassiter asked the lean shadow.

"Nary a thing, boss. You edgy?"

"A little. I don't know why. Something in the air, maybe. Indians say they listen to the leaves. A good idea."

"Come to think of it, I feel kinda tight through the gut myself," said Barr, looking over his shoulder into the darkness.

A blur of shadow caught Lassiter's eye at the periphery of his vision. Whatever it was moved swiftly between the two aspens.

"Who's out there!" Lassiter bellowed, cocking his Henry rifle.

A spot of orange-red blinked at him and a bullet screamed off the iron brace of a wagon tongue. He fired at the flash. A man moaned.

"Fred!" the same man cried. "The sunnuvabitch got me!"

More shouting and more shots. One of the panicked mules screamed and toppled over. Other animals surged against the rope corral, threatening to bring it down.

"Don't let 'em stampede!" Lassiter

yelled. Doubled over, he darted into the trees, heading toward the man he had shot.

Behind him the camp was in an uproar. Men in ghostly longjohns grabbing rifles, shouting questions.

At a hard run, Lassiter stumbled over something yielding. And the next thing he knew he was falling forward to his knees as a gun went off almost in his face. Close enough to feel a faint scorching of powder burn across the right cheek. A man was crouched just ahead of him, coming now to his feet. Lassiter pumped a bullet into his middle. As the man collapsed, Lassiter sprinted toward a knot of mounted men. Their horses were milling about.

"Look out, there he is!" one of the men screeched, gesturing at Lassiter.

The sound died in him; a shot from Lassiter's rifle knocked him backward off the rump of his horse.

More shots were now cutting loose from the camp. Bullets slammed into trees. Deep in the shadowed pines, a horse let out a high-pitched scream. Almost greater than the cry of pain from its rider. Lassiter at a panting run fired again. Another man went down, either from the Henry rifle or from a weapon in camp.

"Let's clear out!" came a man's strident cry from deeper in the trees.

As if in reply there was a sudden thunder of hoof beats as four horses, three with riders, the fourth riderless, burst across a clearing and into the aspens on the far side.

"Hold it!" Lassiter shouted back to the camp. "Hold your fire, boys. This is Lassiter."

When no more shots came winging into the stand of timber, Lassiter cocked his head and listened to the diminishing sounds of horses on the run.

Sam Birkener, Oliver and several others came running up, stepping gingerly in their bare feet. It took cajolery and threats to finally get the mules quieted down. When this was done, Lassiter struck matches. Two men and a horse were down. The horse was thrashing about, uttering pitiful cries. Lassiter put his rifle muzzle to its head and pulled the trigger.

One of the attackers was still alive, but barely. The other was shot through the heart.

By flickering matchlight, Lassiter studied the wounded man. The man, lying on his back, was clenching and unclenching his hands. His midsection was soggy with blood.

Lassiter hunkered down, his face hard. Had it not been for him being awakened by some sixth sense, most of them could by now be dead in their blankets.

"How much did Farrell pay you for this?" Lassiter demanded softly.

"Lew, he's the one done the dickerin'. Lew, he said we . . . we had you dead to rights. . . ."

"You admit Farrell put you up to this."

"Yeah," the man gasped. "He's the one Lew dickered with. You better watch out for Lew. He'll be back an' your brains'll be on the ground."

"Lew Tremont you talkin' about?" came Bert Oliver's southern drawl out of the shadows.

"If you know him," the wounded man said defiantly, "you know there ain't nobody tougher."

"This is Lew layin' here dead," Oliver called over.

With great effort, the wounded man came to his elbows and looked at the dead face Oliver was lifting into the matchlight.

"Holy Kee-ryst," the man said with a shudder.

The sight of the dead leader of the surprise attack, a bullet in the heart, seemed to stun him. Nerve as well as blood seemed to drain from his ravaged body. All that had kept him going was the hope of retribution by Lew Tremont. Now even that hope was dashed. One of his supporting elbows collapsed and he fell over on his side. When Lassiter tried to rouse him, he found that the man had expired.

"Anybody know him?" Lassiter asked as he held a lighted match alongside the dead face. But none of them had ever seen him before. His brutal features had not even relaxed in death.

Lassiter was reloading his rifle. Now that the fight appeared over, at least for the present, he felt a letdown. His nerves quivered. "From here on out, we better have night guards," Lassiter said, "Tonight was too damned close."

"You seen somebody move in them trees yonder," said Willie Barr, the nighthawk. "Wasn't for you, ain't no tellin' where we'd be now."

Lassiter volunteered for the first trick of guard duty and the lanky Oliver would side him until relieved by another pair who would remain awake until dawn.

After a hurried breakfast, they buried the two dead men. In one of Lew Tremont's pockets Lassiter had found an agreement between the man and Kane Farrell. Tremont was to become foreman of Farrell's Twin Horn Ranch.

Lassiter swore softly. Farrell would have to be hunting himself a new foreman. But the agreement definitely tied Farrell in with the dead Tremont. Something that might open Sheriff Bo Dancur's sleepy eyes. Perhaps not. It was no secret that the sheriff and Farrell seemed to hit it off. A mighty important development in the months Lassiter had been away recovering from his wound.

It was a sober outfit that pulled onto the road that morning to continue the trek to Montclair. They couldn't help but consider themselves fortunate. Two of the enemy in their graves but not a one of the Northguard outfit even scratched.

"Don't brag about it," Lassiter cautioned. "Might change our luck."

But he knew they spoke the truth. If the night riders had been able to stampede the mules, they could have shot down the Lassiter men at their leisure as they leaped from their blankets.

Finally, when they were being worn thin with boredom on the long rough road, Lassiter went ahead to scout. He was soon back, after seeing a blur of smoke on the horizon.

"We're almost there!" he shouted and the men cheered.

That noon they made camp in a clearing next to a huge warehouse of unpainted lumber, so new the air reeked with the smell of green lumber. Lassiter glanced at the town, a collection of shacks for railroad and warehouse workers. There was less than a block of rutted street that comprised the business district of Montclair, a saloon, brothel, and general store.

A tall, blond girl in a spangled dress lounging in a doorway spotted Lassiter. She beckoned.

Lassiter saw the eagerness in the eyes of his crew and called a meeting.

"First we load, then we split the crew in half. Every man in the first bunch gets two hours for saloon or whatever. But I want 'em back in two hours. And I do mean two hours. Understand?"

There was an eager nodding of heads.

"Then the second bunch can go. Same thing applies to them."

Lassiter had been trying to see the railroad rep, but the man was in conference, one of the bookkeepers told him. A switch engine on a siding blew smoke and wheezed. There was a clatter of couplings as a string of empty cars was hooked up. Activity was everywhere. Montclair couldn't help but one day become a city. Business for the southern part of the territory would be routed through Montclair. Every pound of merchandise discharged by the railroad would be carried south by freighter. A great potential for the business. A fact that Kane Farrell no doubt had foreseen, hence his eagerness to get into the business.

When Lassiter again tried to see the railroad rep and was put off, his jaw hardened. He ordered the first two wagons to pull up at a loading platform. The others would come up in turn.

Then he went into the warehouse. Even large as it was it couldn't handle all the freight brought in by the railroad. Large boxes and many crates were piled outside under the extended eaves.

The man Lassiter wanted to see was Leland Ordway.

"I want to see him. *Now!*" thundered an exasperated Lassiter at a bookkeeper. The man scampered off his high stool and rushed toward a door at the rear of the big building.

Presently the bookkeeper returned, but

keeping well out of Lassiter's way. "Ord-way, he's a comin'. I told him you were powerful mad."

Presently Ordway came strolling up through the piles of merchandise. He was eating an apple, no doubt from a local resident's root cellar.

Ordway halted in front of Lassiter, one brow lifted. "I understand you're slightly put out. Which seems to indicate that we're getting off to a rather bad start, wouldn't you say?"

Lassiter fought an urge to hit him.

14

ORDWAY CARRIED HIS coat over an arm. He tossed the apple core over his shoulder onto the warehouse floor. Then, stepping around Lassiter, he entered a rather spacious office and plopped down in a swivel chair before an elaborately carved rolltop desk. He did not suggest Lassiter take a chair.

Lassiter stepped to the man's desk, fuming at the discourtesy. He showed him the contract with the mining company. As Ordway reached for the document, possibly to tear it up, Lassiter returned it to his pocket.

"As you can see, I'm here to pick up freight for Bitterroot," Lassiter said coldly.

Ordway leaned back in his chair and stared up at him out of a round face, each cheek a mound of flesh. His nose a miniature map of broken capillaries. His round gut was cinched in by a too tight belt. His shirt was spotless and he wore sleeve holders and cuff guards. He tossed his black coat onto the seat of a chair. Ordway's brief laughter was like the rumble of distant thunder. Smiling, he picked up a cigar from a humidor, bit off an end which he spat on the floor, then put the cigar in his mouth.

"Well, I'll tell you how it is, mister . . . what was the name again?"

"Lassiter."

"Well, Mr. Lassiter. . . ."

"Just Lassiter. Plain Lassiter."

"You have a nasty note in your voice, sir, which amuses me not." Ordway stirred his bulk in the chair and glared, while Lassiter held himself in. The man had not offered to shake hands or even a place to sit.

"I want to pick up the Bitterroot cargo and be on my way."

"I'm afraid you don't have the job."

It didn't surprise Lassiter too much. All along he had been braced for such an eventuality. He allowed a faint hard smile to slide across his lips. "Maybe you'd better explain just why I don't have the job."

Ordway sat up straighter, fleshy hands resting on his knees. The iris of the eye he cocked was shot with yellow. "A simple statement of facts, sir. The freight contract you showed me has been cancelled. It has been awarded to Farrell Freight Lines by the Bitterroot Mining Company."

Lassiter again waved his contract under Ordway's nose. "Take a look at it. That's the signature of the superintendent of the company."

"I was told you'd probably be a hard man to deal with."

"When I'm double-crossed, I'm hell on spiked wheels, Mr. Ordway." He drew the paper out of the man's reach and put it back in his pocket.

A sheen of sweat began to glisten on Ordway's upper lip. "Threatening me will avail you nothing," he blustered. "You had better consider your position."

Lassiter's laugh was chilling.

"I am a representative of the Western and South Fork Railroad," Ordway said huffily. "I have at my disposal some thirty very tough men."

"I have twenty-six men," Lassiter said. "We'll match you any day of the week, Ordway."

"Twenty-six men?" Ordway gulped. "How many wagons do you have, for God's sake?"

"If you'd take the trouble to look out the window, you'd see I have twelve."

"But I . . . I was told you'd have three at the most." He got up and looked out the west window, then sat down again.

"We've gone far enough in this stupid little game," Lassiter said angrily. "I want the wagons loaded. . . ."

"Mr. Farrell graciously offered to buy your wagons so you could be on your way to new territory, as he put it." Ordway nervously rubbed his jowls. "But I don't know about *twelve* wagons. He authorized me to offer you a hundred dollars a wagon."

"Just a gesture on his part. He knows damn well I'd never take him up on it."

"I don't care for your attitude," Ordway muttered, sounding unhappy that he hadn't come up with something better to say.

"Quit straining your brain trying to figure it out." Lassiter slapped his coat pocket. "In here is my authorization to pick up the Bitterroot freight. Now get word to Farrell, if

167

he's here. Tell him I'm taking over the cargo. And if he wants to try and stop me, to get to it."

"Unfortunately, Farrell is not here to argue his own case. He returned to Bluegate two days ago."

"How much did he pay you, Ordway?"

"*I beg your pardon!*" Ordway screamed. "Are you insinuating I'd take a bribe?"

He bounded to his feet, every square inch of corpulence trembling with indignation. Beads of perspiration danced on his rather low forehead beneath a Prussian haircut, as he strode to the office door.

"Tell Blackshear I need him!" he roared to his white-shirted clerk, who shot his employer a frightened look, then scampered from the building.

The shouting had brought Bert Oliver slouching up to one of the tall sliding warehouse doors that was partially open. "Trouble, boss?" he called through the doorway.

Without turning his head, Lassiter said, "Tell the boys to stand by . . . just in case."

As Oliver ducked out of the warehouse and began shouting orders, Ordway's round face lost even more color.

"I . . . I didn't expect you to be in such force. Farrell gave no indication. . . ."

"Hoping you'd be fool enough to pull a gun on me and I'd be unlucky enough to kill you. Then he'd have my neck in a noose. Something's he's wanted for a few years."

A heavy step caused Ordway to regain some of his composure as an immense black-bearded man came stomping into the office.

"Your spindly-legged clerk said you needed me, Mr. Ordway," Blackshear said with a wide grin that revealed a missing front tooth. He jerked a thumb at Lassiter. "This the trouble he was talkin' about?"

He turned lazily, all two hundred and fifty-odd pounds of a hard muscle, to give Lassiter a taunting smile. His eyes, a washed out hazel, glowed under bushy brows and the low-pulled brim of a brown hat. He wore a brown shirt and fringed calf-skin vest. A Colt .45, on a belt decorated with conchas, had ivory grips. Pinned to the vest was a badge: TOWN MARSHAL.

"I've got a contract to pick up some freight," Lassiter said in a level voice. "I'm here to do it."

"What you say about it, Mr. Ordway?"

"Blackshear is the marshal of Montclair," Ordway started to say, but Lassiter interrupted him.

"The railroad's marshal, you mean."

169

Still in a lazy tone as if he had all the time in the world, Blackshear said, "This is the fella Mr. Farrell was talkin' about, I reckon."

"Farrell again, eh?" Lassiter said with twisted lips.

"A fine gentleman." Blackshear took a hitch at his gunbelt. "Now I figure it just might do you a heap of good to cool off in our jail for a few days. Till we can git Mr. Farrell up here to straighten things out."

Suddenly Lassiter had enough of the sparring. His next move was so explosive that Blackshear had barely time to blink as he tried to reach his gun. Lassiter was on him with all the fury of an enraged grizzly. The gun with the fancy ivory grips thudded to the floor and skated under the rolltop desk. In the same movement, Lassiter got one hand at the back of Blackshear's shirt and vest. He spun the big man toward the door. In order to try and retain balance, Blackshear was forced to dance on his toes. At the same time he lashed out with wild swings of his tremendous arms.

Lassiter ducked one blow, but a fist to his temple landed with such force that lights burst in his head. By then Lassiter had both hands at the back of Blackshear's belt. He swung him as he would heave a bale of hay. As Blackshear spun around he stumbled over Lassiter's outstretched leg. It sent him crashing into the rolltop desk, his weight crumpling pigeon holes as if they were made of mud. One whole end of the desk was knocked loose. When Blackshear fell headlong, the floor shook.

The man lay face down, gasping, stunned from his impact with the floor. In that moment Lassiter tore free a pair of manacles from Blackshear's hip pocket. Before the man could recover, he had both wrists manacled behind his back.

Only then did Lassiter straighten up, barely breathing hard. A pale Ordway stood trembling as he stared numbly at the wreckage of his desk. Then at the hulking semiconscious Blackshear, made immobile by his own manacles.

Startled faces of warehouse workers crowded the doorways. Behind them were Lassiter's men, each with a rifle. Every one of them looked grim. Lassiter eyed a stunned Ordway.

"Blackshear's likely got keys to the handcuffs in his pocket," Lassiter said. "But don't turn him loose till I'm an hour out of town."

"I . . . I understand," Ordway mumbled.

"On second thought, make it two hours. Now, do I get help to load the freight?"

Ordway was mopping his face on a soggy handkerchief. "My God, you moved like a tornado. Farrell gave no indication that you were so dangerous." He gave Blackshear on the floor a look of mingled disgust and disappointment, then issued the order that the Northguard wagons were to be loaded.

Three hours later Lassiter and his men were finished with the job, every one of them bone weary and dripping with sweat.

"You boys still deserve some fun," Lassiter said tentatively. "But how about making it one hour instead of two?"

"Hell with the fun," Bert Oliver put in gravely, as Lassiter thought he might. "Fun'll come later. Main thing now is to git this load to Bitterroot."

The men agreed, some reluctantly. Lassiter was glad the decision had been made for him. He wanted to get south of Montclair before dark.

He found Blackshear sitting on the floor of Ordway's office, his back to the wall. He glowered. The timid clerk was picking up the last of the shattered desk. Ordway slumped in a chair, looking ill.

One of Blackshear's eyes was purplish and closing. He had a cut above the right ear and a gashed cheekbone. One of the heavy arms was specked with dried blood from a long cut.

"Consider yourself lucky today, Blackshear," Lassiter said. "A few bumps and bruises. You could be dead."

"Unlock these goddamn handcuffs. . . ."

Lassiter shook his head. "When you do get free, don't come after me. I'm warning you."

"I'll fix you, Lassiter," Blackshear threatened.

"I can tell you this. You get within fifty yards of my outfit and I'll blow you right out of your boots."

Then Lassiter reminded Ordway not to unlock the manacles for two hours.

Outside the warehouse a bearded man fell in step with Lassiter. "A lot of us folks hereabouts have been hopin' to see Blackshear taken down a peg. Reckon that bully won't be quite so tough from here on out." The man chuckled.

At their camp, twelve miles out of Montclair, Lassiter assigned guards for the night. He was in the first trick.

Bert Oliver, sanding his tin plate for

173

morning, gave a dry chuckle. "Hope you don't git in no bind with Sheriff Dancur for roughin' up Montclair's town marshal." Flames from the dying cookfire lighted his long, solemn face. "Mebby you didn't know it, but Blackshear an' Dancur are cousins."

"Like usual, seems I've got a habit of stepping into a snake pit," Lassiter said lightly.

"Dancur got his cousin that job at Montclair to git rid of him. Was causin' Bo some trouble, was the way I heard it."

Each night on the return trip, Lassiter was doubly cautious, awakening several times so as to prowl the area. Farrell had tried for him twice, once in the night raid on the mules. And again, no doubt by bribing Ordway to deny him the cargo designated for the Bitterroot Mining Company.

After the long grinding haul upgrade to the mountain village of High Point where the mine was located, the men were ready for relaxation. They found it late that afternoon in the High Point Saloon.

Meanwhile, Lassiter was in the mine office, telling Betancourt, the superintendent, about the two attempts to keep him from honoring the mining company contract, the night attack and then Blackshear.

"Farrell tried, but didn't make it," Lassiter finished.

Betancourt clapped him on the back later. "My foreman reports that everything arrived in good shape."

Lassiter slipped a hand over the pocket containing the bank draft Betancourt had given him. Along with a promise of new business as soon as it arrived by railroad at Montclair. He couldn't wait to show the bank draft to Melody. Proof that the long haul had been a success. And they had not lost a single man.

15

KANE FARRELL BARELY heard Blackshear rambling on about the trouble up at Montclair. Blackshear had come south on a fast horse, following the encounter with Lassiter. He arrived at the big house at the edge of Bluegate just as Farrell was getting ready to go downtown for a night of poker at Shanagan's.

"I was about to lock Lassiter up when his crew jumped me," Blackshear said as he sipped the fine whiskey Farrell had poured. The bottle, on a small table, had a label that showed two colonels, one in blue, the other in Rebel gray, sabers lifted in one hand, glasses in the other. Colonel's Choice.

Blackshear drank more of the whiskey while waiting for Farrell to make some comment. But he stood, with back turned, in front of the oversize fireplace that was unlighted because of the mild evening. He was staring up at a broad leather belt displayed diagonally across the stones of the fireplace chimney. Time and the elements had dulled the silver so that it was in need of a good polishing. But intricate etching around the border of the buckle and the large classic "L" reflected the work of a craftsman.

"So you were jumped by Lassiter's crew," Farrell said at last. His eyes reminded Blackshear of green ice. A shiver danced across Blackshear's shoulders. "Why didn't you have twice as many men to side you?" Farrell went on.

"Wa'al, to tell the truth, I figured it'd just be me an' Lassiter. . . ."

"You *figured!*" Farrell's lips twitched. "Did it ever occur to you that conjecture never won a war? It takes direct action."

Blackshear ran a tongue tip over blunt teeth as he puzzled over "conjecture." One eye was slightly swollen and the various bruises and abrasions were still raw on his bearded face.

"I'll finish the bastard next time." Blackshear reddened at memory of his humiliation at Montclair, before the warehouse crew and passersby.

"There's another man about your size who also has a grudge against Lassiter," Farrell mused as he stared at the giant slouched in a leather chair, glass of whiskey gripped in powerful fingers. "It would be quite a show if the two of you confronted Lassiter."

Blackshear bristled at the suggestion that he might need help. "I can handle Lassiter alone." The bearded jaw was outthrust, the small eyes bright with hatred. "Long as somebody keeps his men off my back," he added.

"I guess you weren't listening to me. I said the two of you. And that is exactly what I meant to say."

"But I want him myself. . . ."

Farrell's elegant hand made a gesture of annoyance. "So far, Lassiter has been able to squirm out of every trap I've set. This time I want to make sure of him and have a little sport out of it at the same time."

"The two of us, huh? Me an' . . . this other fella."

"Exactly." Farrell smiled as if commending a small child who has just mastered simple addition. "In fact, I think the rest of the county should have an opportunity to witness the spectacle."

"Spectacle?" Blackshear frowned in puzzlement. "What you mean?"

"Roman gladiators . . . Oh, never mind." Farrell gave a short laugh as he was carried away by the excitement of the idea. "I'll see that tickets are sold."

"You mean like for a show."

"Now you're beginning to understand. You see, most men are thrilled by the sight of blood on a fellow human, although they seldom admit it. They enjoy watching someone suffer."

Blackshear chuckled and helped himself to more whiskey.

"I'll see that your cousin Bo is conveniently out of town during the event," Farrell continued. "In case some nervous ladies start screaming for him to arrest you gladiators. The crowd at the warehouse will be Roman citizens from Nero's time. . . ."

Blackshear looked blank.

"Yes, it'll be held at the big warehouse here in town. Only those that pay can witness the spectacle of the century. To see an arrogant Lassiter beaten to his knees and then stomped to death. How does that sound to you?"

"The stompin' part of it I like. With Lassiter's face under my boot heels." Then a frown ridged a pockmarked stretch of flesh between his eyes. "But what'll Bo say about Lassiter gittin' kilt?"

"I told you. Bo will be out of town. And after the deed's done, it's too late to worry. Wouldn't you say?"

"All I know is I like the part about Lassiter bein' dead."

"Of course you and Marsh may have to clear out for a spell. It'll soon blow over and you'll have plenty of money."

"Yeah. . . ."

"In six months hardly anyone will even remember that Lassiter was smashed to a pulp on the floor of the Farrell Freight Lines warehouse. How does two thousand dollars sound to you, Art?"

"Jeezus! Two thousand *dollars?*"

"All yours. And two thousand for Marsh."

"Who's this Marsh?"

"Works up at the Glory Mine. Lassiter's crew jumped him like they did you. You'll meet him. Now I want you to stay away from whiskey and eat lots of beefsteak and potatoes and run a few miles every day. Do you understand?"

"Well . . . yeah." Blackshear drained his glass and held it up for Farrell to see. "Guess this'll be my last till it gits over with. How soon we do it?"

"Soon." Farrell was excited. "I'll get Lassiter to town, one way or another." He started to laugh as he pictured Melody Vanderson as the perfect bait for his trap. Then he turned and stared up at the elaborately carved silver buckle of Lassiter's belt. He had bribed Miegs, the undertaker, to remove it from the body everyone assumed to be Lassiter's; Farrell had wanted it as a reminder of his triumph over an old enemy.

Of course even now he could call Lassiter out and play the game of "may the best man win." But after downing the Texas Kid recently, he had come to the conclusion that he was too valuable a commodity to risk in foolish ventures. Not when there were others to do the job for him. The Texas Kid had been incredibly fast. Almost too much so.

On the day Lassiter left the Bitterroot Mine for the long trip downgrade to Aspen City, Kane Farrell was in the town's saloon a block from the rather squalid headquarters of the Northguard Freight Company. He called one of the local drifters over to his table, gave the man a silver dollar and an envelope he was to deliver. Then he sat back to wait, feeling excitement as his plan got under way.

At the freight office, Vanderson was yawning. He was alone. His eyes were reddened from lack of sleep, the brown hair rumpled. He was at the desk, trying to figure out how much the company would make out of the Bitterroot business. A shabbily dressed man shuffled in. The man handed him an envelope and departed.

Vanderson tore open the envelope and read the few hurried lines written in a fine hand. Then he glanced at the closed door of the sleeping quarters. Melody was sleeping late because they had sat up long past midnight, drinking coffee and arguing. He sensed he was gradually wearing her down. And this was necessary, he believed. For she had to be definitely on his side by the time Lassiter got back. All along, Vanderson had tried to convince her that his going away some weeks ago had been for the benefit of their marriage. No, he hadn't run out on her; he wanted that understood. And he just wasn't a letter writer, not until he had good

181

news. And when he finally had it, he thought seeing her in person would be better than a letter. After all, he had brought her money, hadn't he? Money earned by sweat and aching muscle.

Last night, at least, had been a milestone. While still pleading his cause, and Melody so sleepy she could hardly keep her eyes open, he managed to slip into her bed before she realized it. She tried to order him out and when that failed, began to plead with him.

But he kept talking and maneuvering. Finally she seemed convinced when he stressed her wifely duties. Really forced instead of convinced, if he wanted to be honest about it, she had suffered in silence through the rest of it.

But she would come around completely before long. Last night had been a chink in the dam of her resistance. Each night would be that much easier until finally she looked forward to it. As he was sure she had when they were first married. Or at least she had seemed to.

All this had been streaming pleasantly through his head as he toyed with a column of figures that would reveal the approximate profit from the Bitterroot haul. He was even considering a return to her blankets that morning, to wake her up in proper married fashion. That was when the drifter came shuffling in with the note from Kane Farrell.

Vanderson swore. He didn't want to see Farrell, damn it, not when he needed to concentrate on things here at home. But he didn't dare refuse. Farrell knew too much about him. For instance, the night Bert Oliver had been trimmed out of five thousand dollars. After convincing Farrell that he had worked big games before, Farrell gave him his chance. Of course, if Farrell tried to implicate him, he would be exposing his own hand in the cheating. But Vanderson had been around long enough to know that the big thieves usually squirmed out of trouble. It was the small fry who spent miserable years on a prison rock pile.

The small saloon smelled of unwashed flesh and stale beer. Farrell sat at a table, looking as if he resented the odors. The bottle at his elbow was not the usual Colonel's Choice. Farrell was immaculately dressed in a knee-length leather coat and navy pants. He waved him to a chair, then leaned across the stained table and quietly told him what he wanted done.

Vanderson tugged at his mustache

thoughtfully when Farrell was finished. "How can I be sure to get her to town on any certain date?"

"You're her husband, need I point out. Don't ask her, *order* her. Don't let that fluff of pale hair and pink cheeks put a ring in your nose."

Vanderson reddened. "I'm head of my own household. . . ."

"Then I'll expect her in town on the twentieth. At my place. Get her there in midafternoon."

"I tell you, Farrell, I'd rather not be a party to this. . . ."

Farrell gave him a look of disgust. "My friend, may I remind you of certain . . . forgeries?"

It took Vanderson a moment to realize what Farrell meant. Then it hit him like a blow to the stomach. He had forgotten about being talked into forging a sheepman's name on a bill of sale a few months back. It was for a thousand head. Farrell had taken most of the profit from the scheme, Vanderson recalled bitterly.

He was about to bristle and say that Farrell was equally guilty. But something in the man's superior smile, the knowing eyes, was a reminder that the forgeries had been committed by the hand of Vance Vanderson. Farrell had remained in the background and had no apparent connection with the dirty business.

"I'll have Melody at your place on the twentieth," he said lamely.

"Good. It's the first step in getting Lassiter into our little trap."

"*Lassiter!*" Vanderson's face drained. "What is this all about?"

"I assume Lassiter doesn't know you're back yet."

"Haven't seen him."

"But you'd like to be rid of him."

"God yes. I've dreaded facing up to him."

"If you listen carefully, you'll never be troubled by him again. Either you *or* your wife."

Something in Farrell's green eyes caused the back of Vanderson's neck to chill. Was Farrell trying to tell him that during his absence Lassiter had moved in? Moved in all the way? Was that what Farrell's knowing smile meant, the wise look in the green eyes? Vanderson swallowed and, thinking of Lassiter, slid a hand onto the comforting grips of the revolver worn under his coat.

Roma whirled, her skirts sailing out. Then she began a series of high kicks to the beat of Rex's tom-tom. Holding her skirts in such a way that the males in the audience had their view restricted to the lacy edge of pantaloons.

The town was Dry Bar, high in the mountains, with the usual circle of gawkers come to see the medicine show. Doc, slender and ornately costumed as he assumed a mandarin in far off Cathay would be, gave his speech from the small platform on the highly decorated wagon.

After sales were made, they started on their way. Roma was anxious to reach Bluegate as soon as possible. Doc thought a town of that size should give them several days of work. Also, Doc hoped she wouldn't be disappointed should she meet up with that fellow Lassiter again. From the first, even as badly wounded as he was, Doc had decided that Lassiter was a hardcase with a life of his own. A life not likely to be shared with a woman. At least not for any length of time. He knew that was what Roma was counting on. She would like marriage, but if not, she was smart enough to accept companionship instead.

Rex was curled up in the second wagon, driven by Roma, reading from a well-thumbed copy of the *Iliad*. How many times had Rex read it? Uncounted times. And the books by other Greeks and the plays of Shakespeare. Doc had found Rex at a precarious point in his life. As a tragedian in a travelling Shakespeare company, he became mixed up with a woman in Santa Fe. She happened to be married. Her fiery-tempered husband used a knife. The scars on Rex didn't show when he had on his clothes.

"My wounded pigeons," Doc referred to the two members of his company, Rex and Roma.

He had found Roma stumbling along a prairie road. She was swollen in various places from a beating with a horse whip. Angrily she showed them her wounds. Her gypsy family had betrothed her to a man she didn't like. When she refused him, her brother beat her and she ran away.

"Only a few more days and we'll be in Bluegate," Roma called happily to Rex. But he was asleep, the book he had been reading in his lap.

She calculated the days in her mind. They would arrive on the twenty-first of the month. At times when she first joined the company, as Doc liked to refer to it, and things had gone badly, she would comfort Doc or Rex in her tent. She failed to see anything wicked about bringing pleasure to another human being. But after meeting Lassiter, everything changed. For the first time in her young life she knew love. Doc and Rex understood and left her alone.

Her black eyes glowed as she contemplated her reunion with Lassiter. By now he had probably settled the business he had come back to finish. He had never told her very much, but a lot of it she had learned from his ravings when he was so ill from his wound.

Doc and Rex would have to go on without her. She and Lassiter would probably live out their lives in Bluegate. She liked the sound of it. She was a very contented young woman. She hummed a Romany song as she drove the team.

16

THE MOMENT LASSITER and the wagons rolled into Aspen City after the long haul down the mountain from the Bitterroot Mine, he saw a familiar figure waving a hand and smiling broadly. Lassiter gave Vance Vanderson a spare nod.

"The best news I ever heard in my life

was that you're alive, not dead," Vanderson enthused.

Lassiter looked down at the proffered hand, then into the hazel eyes that seemed bright with sincerity. "The last time I remember seeing of you, you were running for your life to the back of a mine tunnel."

"And I was yelling every step of the way for you to follow and we'd make a stand."

"You did that?" Lassiter asked mildly.

"Sure I did. I thought you were behind me all the time."

Lassiter gave him a hard smile, then saw Melody hurrying from the office to join them. For her sake, he shook Vanderson's hand.

"I was off trying to earn money enough to help keep Melody going," Vanderson said. "Melody, tell Lassiter how much I brought home to you."

Melody smoothed her dress as to give herself time to think, then said, "It was around five hundred dollars."

Lassiter was unimpressed. He wondered where the man had gotten his hands on that much money. Not by the sweat of his brow, he would bet.

Later he got Melody aside and gave her

the bank draft. She was surprised at the amount.

Dad Hornbeck prepared roast venison for the evening meal. Melody and her husband were invited to eat with the crew. They crowded into the room adjoining the barn and sat on benches at two long tables.

Melody sat at the head of the table where Lassiter was eating. She wanted to know all about the long trip. However, Lassiter minimized the night attack by the Farrell men and his later encounter with Art Blackshear at Montclair. But Bert Oliver wasn't satisfied to leave it at that. The garrulous southerner told it all. Lassiter wanted to kick him under the table, but was sitting too far away. He didn't want Melody to start worrying.

While Oliver was talking, Lassiter noticed that Vanderson squirmed in his seat. Probably out of boredom.

When the meal was finished, Vanderson spoke solemnly to Lassiter, saying how he intended to cooperate. "You just name what you want done and I'll do it."

"I'll remember." Lassiter's smile was for Melody's benefit. Despite their success with the Bitterroot business, he sensed she was unhappy. She seemed ill-at-ease and dark shadows were noticeable under her gray eyes. All because her goddamn wayward husband had decided to come home.

Finally Vanderson walked around the table to stand next to Melody's chair. "If you boys'll excuse us, I think my wife and I will retire now." He reached down to take Melody by an elbow. He drew her up from the chair. "Come, my dear," he urged.

She complimented Hornbeck on the supper he had cooked for them, but the old man only shrugged. He seemed embarrassed by her obvious distress.

Lassiter felt sorry for her, too. Vanderson was making such a show of taking her to bed. Wearing a confident smile, his eyes bright with triumph, as if to say, "You boys don't have what I've got."

Melody was white-faced.

In the bedroom she turned on him. "Did you have to make such a spectacle out of us retiring for the night?"

"What in the world is wrong with that. I'm sure they all know what husband and wife do behind closed doors."

"Why couldn't you have waited until they left the room?"

"Maybe I just wanted to let them know that you belong to me. They should keep their hands off."

"I belong to *nobody*."

Her vehemence surprised him. So he decided to back off. "I didn't mean you actually belong to me. . . ."

"Vance, I feel that you're up to something. I don't know what it is, but I assume I'll find out soon."

"How can you even think such a thing?"

"Probably trying to figure some way to steal Northguard out from under me."

"My God, I'm only trying to be nice, to make up for those horrible weeks I was away from you."

As she stared at him she wondered at her unstable mind, the day she had impulsively agreed to marry him. That day he had slipped into the big house in Bluegate, before Farrell had taken it over, apparently concerned solely with her welfare. He had just learned, so he claimed, that her late Uncle Josh borrowed heavily from Kane Farrell and that the note was suddenly due.

"Yes, I know," she had replied sadly.

"I understand you're going to move your freight line to Aspen City." That was when he came close and took her hands. On that morning it seemed that his was the only comforting presence, and this following the horror of a meeting with Farrell. There had been shouting and tears.

"Where else can I go but Aspen City?" she asked Vance.

"I'll help you move. Together we'll make a success out of the company and Mr. Kane Farrell be damned."

"Together?"

"It's a rather backhanded way of asking you to marry me."

It startled rather than filled her with joy. He seemed a decent young man. And who else did she have? Lassiter dead and Uncle Herm apparently rooted permanently down in Rimrock.

Who else could she turn to but Vance Vanderson? She felt strongly that Farrell wouldn't back off after taking the grand house, the stable, and the warehouse her Uncle Josh had built. No, he would harass her every step of the way. Although she had made brave talk, following Lassiter's death, that she could run the company herself, others told her differently so often that she had begun to believe it.

She had written Uncle Herm time and again at the hospital in Rimrock and had received only a few garbled sentences in return. Finally, she wrote to the doctor who replied that Herman Falconer, having lost a leg, was drinking himself into an early grave because of it. And no, there was nothing anyone could do about it.

Impulsively and desperately, she had whispered, "I'll marry you, Vance."

When he hooked a forefinger under her chin to force her to meet his lips, she almost backed away. The pressure of his lips sent no rockets roaring through her, did not make her tremble and her heart soar. It was just . . . nothing.

Now, standing with the backs of her knees against the bed, she knew that marrying him had been a terrible mistake. In the first place, she instinctively knew he didn't love her. And she certainly didn't love him.

As he removed his jacket and hung it over the back of a chair, she could see that he planned a repetition of recent nights.

"You're not sleeping here tonight." She saw him stiffen and squint at her.

"My dear, I thought we removed the last obstacle to our happiness here in this room. I enjoyed myself and assumed you did also."

"Sleep in the lean-to with the men."

"I'd be the laughingstock of the town. My own wife throwing me out of our bedroom."

Under his steady gaze and that small smile

194

under the mustache, she felt her defenses start to crumble. But she straightened her shoulders, determined not to give in to him.

"I might as well tell you now as later. I want a . . ."

"Divorce," he finished for her. Which she confirmed with a vigorous nod of her head, no longer able to trust her voice.

"It's Lassiter who put that idea into your head."

"Not at all," she responded quickly. Too quickly, she wondered, for his eyes had taken on a strange glow?

Slinging his coat under an arm, he stalked to the door. He looked back at her there beside the bed, face pale and hands clenched at her sides.

"I don't want to hear you ever mention divorce again," he said in a flat voice. "In the first place, no judge would give you one. Besides, I'd never let you drag me into court. We'll forget about tonight so you can collect yourself and realize your obligations. But tomorrow night I'll expect you to be a wife to me. And we'll have no more of this nonsense."

But she was stubborn and refused to bend. Move slowly, he cautioned himself, for there was the possibility that if he pushed it she might run to Lassiter for protection. That prospect chilled him. Eventually, he knew, if he handled it right, he could wear her down.

A few days later he felt the need to get away and rode into Bluegate. At Shanagan's he found Farrell talking to the saloon owner. Shanagan moved away when Vanderson came to stand next to Farrell. There were only a few other customers at the opposite end of the bar. Vanderson felt uncomfortable because Farrell hadn't spoken or offered him a drink, but just kept staring sideways out of those green eyes.

"You must enjoy horseback riding," Farrell finally said in a nasty voice.

Vanderson gave him a blank look.

"You must enjoy it to make the long ride in today when you're coming in at the end of the week."

Farrell pointed at the large calendar on the backbar with a big circle around the twenty-first of the month. Suddenly Vanderson remembered. He was supposed to bring Melody in on the twentieth.

"I'll be here, so don't worry about it," Vanderson said with a tense smile. Actually, he had forgotten all about Farrell's grand plan to use Melody as bait for Lassiter.

With a shot of the splendid Colonel's Choice warming his stomach, reality began to loom coldly in Vanderson's mind. Would Melody in her present mood come to town with him?

"Trouble with the wife?" Farrell asked after studying him.

"Hell, no. What made you ask that?"

"You've got that look that all married men seem to get periodically."

Vanderson voiced the possibility that Melody might ignore all entreaties to get her to town. He was laying the groundwork, just in case. Then he saw that the face under the dark red hair had twisted in a fury.

"She's to be at my place on the twentieth."

"Yes, I understand, but . . ."

"Just what seems to be your problem with the lady?" Farrell asked in icy tones.

Vanderson was so keyed up that the invitation to unload his grief was too tempting to resist. Among his many complaints against Melody was that she was about as responsive as a lump of coal.

"Vance, you're a bigger damn fool that I thought," Farrell cut in.

Vanderson felt himself redden. "I'm doing my best, damn it!"

"I guess I didn't make myself clear the other day about those forgeries . . ."

Vanderson was alarmed. He looked past Farrell's big shoulder to the other drinkers down the bar. "Not so loud," Vanderson hissed.

"Loud? I'll shout it. If you don't start acting like a man." Farrell leaned an elbow on the varnished barlip. "I'm surprised you'd let a puff of blond hair get the upper hand."

"She's not easy to handle . . ."

"Double your belt and use it on her backside. You'd be surprised how little touches like that can get a woman thinking your way in a big hurry."

"I suppose."

"And when you bring her to town, make sure she's in a good mood. With everything else on my mind, I have no time for a surly female."

Farrell got a pen, ink, and sheet of paper from Shanagan and then wrote a note, neatly printing each letter. Vanderson looked over his shoulder. What he read, caused his heartbeat to quicken.

"But Lassiter will be gone on the twentieth."

"This will bring him back." Farrell folded

the note and slipped it into Vanderson's shirt pocket.

When Vanderson had left the saloon, Farrell called Shanagan over. "How're the tickets going?"

"Great."

"I want the place jammed."

"There'll be well over a thousand on hand, Farrell."

"As long as the two of us are going to hang around and grow rich in this lump of mud known as Bluegate, how about calling me Kane?"

"You call me Tex."

"You don't talk like a Texican."

"So many sheriffs down there was lookin' for me," Shanagan said with a straight face, "I figured to borrow the name."

Farrell laughed. Before it was over, they would do a lot of business together, he was sure. Such as selling tickets at five dollars each, a small fortune for some, for the privilege of witnessing a spectacle. And in the exchange of money for a ticket, a promise was elicited not to discuss what was planned in the Farrell Freight Lines warehouse on the twenty-first of the month.

17

UPON HIS RETURN from Bitterroot, Lassiter's main problem was keeping the crew intact until the next shipment for the mining company arrived by rail at Montclair. But he was finally forced to lay off some of the men. However, he managed to keep five wagons busy with short hauls of supplies to mines and isolated villages.

At first he was happy to note that Vanderson slept with the men instead of his wife. Serves him right, he thought. But even so, Melody seemed thinned down and the circles under the gray eyes more pronounced. If she would only complain, he'd throw Vanderson out. But she never discussed her marital problems.

Many short hauls kept Lassiter busy. At least that part of the operation was smoothing out. It did nothing to cheer up Melody. Her temper grew short.

One morning she said in a voice a little too shrill, "Well, I've made my peace with Vance. I suppose it's better this way."

Lassiter didn't get a chance to ask her to elaborate because she kept to her bedroom for the rest of the day. But that night Vanderson failed to join the crew at the big lean-to.

Uncertainty as to Farrell's next move was putting a strain on them all, Lassiter well knew.

One day he took a wagon to Bluegate for supplies. While there, it came to him strongly to seek out Farrell, challenge him and get the dirty business ended. But unfortunately the man happened to be out of town that day.

On the twentieth of the month Lassiter returned from a haul into the mountains. At least Vanderson was doing the job Melody had given him, scheduling the hauls. It kept him out of mischief. Even so, Lassiter knew Melody was not getting along with her husband, although she pretended to be cheerful.

On the day of Lassiter's return, Bert Oliver and three men had gone to town for supplies needed to feed the men and to keep things going. The long Reb face was grave as Oliver squatted beside Lassiter who had removed a freighter wheel and was applying axle grease with a rag.

"Strange feelin' in town I had," Olvier said, giving Lassiter a steady look.

"Bert, we're s'posed to be friends. You can tell it plainer than that."

"The whole town is buzzin' like ten thousand bees."

"How do you mean?"

"There's somethin' gonna happen, but damned if I could find out what. Every time I asked somebody, they claimed I was just imaginin' things an' they'd walk away."

"And you figure all this concerns us in some way?"

"A bad feelin' I got."

"I get hunches myself," Lassiter said, wiping his hands on a grease rag. "Sometimes they're right. Other times they don't mean a damned thing."

"Last year I drifted through Mexico. A coupla days before a big bullfight, when a real famous torero was comin' to town, I'd git that same feelin' deep in my gut."

Lassiter gave a tight smile. "A bullfight in Bluegate, you mean?"

"It's the same as one, damn if it ain't."

"Hmmmmm," Lassiter was thoughtful.

"Tried to git Shanagan to talk but he jist looked me in the eye an' claimed he didn't know what I was talkin' about. But in his saloon I seen fellas starin' at me, then when

I'd look back they'd pretend they was lookin' somewhere else."

"You sure about all this, Bert?"

"An' along the bar, I'd see fellas nudgin' each other an' grinnin', like they was about to bust. They'd look slantwise where I was standin'. Give me a funny feelin'. Like they knowed somethin' was gonna happen that was secret."

Lassiter reached for the wheel he had leaned against the wagon. A stack of bricks supported the front axle he had been greasing. Hunched down, he was staring at the headquarters building across the wagon yard. He'd gotten back nearly an hour ago. And after pulling the front wheel that had screeched all the way up the mountain and back, he'd pushed everything else from his mind but getting to the root of the screech. What bothered him was that he had had time to do all that and yet Melody hadn't appeared. Usually when one of the wagons pulled in she'd be down asking how the trip had gone. She seemed interested in everything that pertained to the freight business.

Very strange that Melody hadn't come down from the office to welcome him home.

"I'm going to see the boss," Lassiter announced. "Will you put that wheel back on?"

Oliver nodded.

There was a strange silence in the office with its desk and safe and benches. He called her name, but there was no reply. He rapped on the bedroom door and called her name again. Still no answer. He rattled the knob. It turned. The door was unlocked.

He stepped inside. The air smelled faintly of her perfume. A light green coverlet was on the bed. Two pillows reminded him of heads side by side. Hers and her husband's. A shiver ran down his spine. If ever she told him she could no longer stand Vanderson then he'd take steps to keep the man away from her. But she suffered in silence and whenever he tried to get her to talk about it, she'd just shake her head and walk away.

For the first time he noticed an envelope on the floor. Evidently it had once been propped up by a pillow on the bed, but a breeze through an open window had blown it down.

His mouth went dry when he picked it up and saw that it was addressed to him. Personal. He tore the envelope.

Lassiter: Melody Vanderson is my guest at the big house in town. I want you to join us for a business discussion. I can't stress enough the importance of our meeting. She tells me there have been attempts on her life. That is why she sought sanctuary with me.

To lessen any chance of harm coming to her from these enemies, I must insist that you come alone. Any show of force on your part could mean disaster for her.

As an intelligent man, I know you can read between the lines and realize that discretion is vital.

The note was unsigned. Not that a signature was necessary. Who else but Kane Farrell? With no signature and the text in block letters, Farrell was protecting himself. In case something went wrong, he would disclaim all knowledge of the kidnapping. And what else was it but that? Lassiter felt such a rush of anger that had Farrell walked in the door he would have tried to kill him with his bare hands.

As first Lassiter was so enraged that he crumpled the note and threw it into a corner of the room and stormed to the door. Did

Farrell for one minute think he could bluff him into not coming to Bluegate with every available man?

Before reaching the door, however, he stopped and turned everything over in his mind. He picked up the crumpled note and reread it. The threat to Melody's safety was spelled out. No, he couldn't risk it. He calmed down sufficiently to maintain a straight face as he hunted up Dad Hornbeck. He found the old man in a small barn where he was mending a mule harness.

Lassiter asked if he had seen Melody. Hornbeck nodded. He had seen her ride out with her husband earlier that day. "On the Bluegate road," finished the old man.

"How did Melody seem?" Lassiter asked coolly.

Hornbeck rubbed his wrinkled chin, looking puzzled. "Same as usual, near as I could tell. 'Course she was on the road by the time I seen her an' it was a far piece. Somethin' wrong?"

Lassiter almost showed the old man the note, but remembered the veiled threats. Melody would be in danger if he made a wrong move.

"No, nothing's wrong." Lassiter shook

his head. "I'm going to town. See you when I get back." Would he ever get back?

He almost let go with a blast of bitter laughter. What would he find in town? Melody in a trap, no doubt. Well, he'd get her out of it, one way or another. But at what cost? That was something for the fates to decide. It was out of his hands. All he could do was follow Farrell's directions for the present. And play the rest of the game by the cards he drew. The gall of Farrell, he thought angrily, to make a captive of an innocent young woman such as Melody Vanderson. Even acknowledging her married name put a bitter taste in his mouth. For he felt strongly that somewhere in the woodpile was Vance Vanderson.

The trip to Bluegate seemed endless. Today he had no eye for the sweep of color from wildflowers, the intense green of cottonwoods and aspen in their spring finery, nor even a second glance at a beige-colored bobcat that bounded across the road ahead of him.

The only humans he met were in a large blue wagon with Farrell Freight Lines painted on the side. It was a double outfit, wagon and trailer, pulled by twelve mules, coming from the direction of town.

As the outfit approached, Lassiter pulled off the road and sat in his saddle, one hand clamped to the butt of his holstered .44. Both teamster and swamper were strangers, but apparently knew him by sight.

"You seem mad as hell, Lassiter," called the bearded and heavyset teamster. "But ain't our fault. We only work for Farrell!"

Lassiter didn't take time to dwell on what the man might have meant by "fault." It was later that he learned.

_____ *18*

NEVER HAD MELODY been so upset as she was that day when her husband told her that Lassiter had been injured and was in Bluegate, asking for her. They left in a spring wagon by the rear door of the office.

Only when they were a mile or so down the mountain did she wonder aloud.

"You acted almost as if you didn't want anyone to see us leave. You did tell Dad Hornbeck, didn't you?"

"Sure I did." He flashed his boyish grin which he thought would wipe the puzzled look from her face. "Now don't fret. Lassiter will be all right once he sees you."

She felt it a strange thing for him to say, knowing his intense jealousy of Lassiter.

But she didn't dwell on it. All that mattered now was to reach Lassiter's side to see how badly he had been injured. Vance had said that a wagon tipped over and he had been caught by a wheel.

It seemed hours before she saw the haze of smoke from cook fires and the blacksmith shop. The town seemed busier than usual, she noted as they wound away from the business district. She found herself in front of the house her Uncle Josh had built for that harridan of a wife.

Her jaw dropped. "Lassiter is *here?*"

"Doc Overmeyer thought he should have comfort. And he's got it here."

He drove around to a side door, hopped out and tied the team to a post. Then he helped her out of the wagon. They went up a short flight of steps to a wide veranda that ran to the front of the house. He opened a door and she hurried inside. He closed the door. She heard a key turn in a lock.

But before she could speak, Kane Farrell appeared, elegantly dressed in a fine black wool suit, his dark red hair neatly combed. He was smiling.

"Well, Vance, I see you didn't let me down." He sounded pleased.

"Where is Lassiter!" Melody cried, looking down a long hallway to a parlor she knew so well.

"Oh, I have a feeling Lassiter will be along," Farrell said with a smile. "Come, my dear." He beckoned.

"Which means Lassiter wasn't injured at all!" she cried. "Vance, you tricked me!"

She tried to run, but they each grabbed her by an arm. Though she kicked and tried to bite, she was helpless. She was literally dragged to a large bedroom that used to be Josh Falconer's. Familiar tall dark chests of drawers, the big bureau, and a canopied bed dominated the room.

There were three women in the room. One of them was buxom with hennaed hair and large brown eyes, in a flowing green dress with lace trim that failed to cover her rather extravagant curves. She was probably in her late thirties. The other two were pretty, younger, with rouged faces and tight-fitting dresses.

"I'm Blanche," the older woman announced. "And these are two of my girls. We've been hired to keep watch over you for the night. I'm sure we can do it." She gave a soft laugh.

When Vance and Farrell released her wrists, she tried to run. But Blanche was surprisingly swift. She was dragged back to the bedroom.

Farrell produced a chain. While the three women held a squirming Melody, a hand clapped to her mouth, the chain was padlocked around Melody's waist. The other end was fastened to a leg of the bed.

"I'll scream!" Melody threatened when the hand was removed from her mouth.

Vance leaned close. "You do that and you won't have any teeth."

"Damn you, Vance," she said angrily, but he only shrugged and left the room. She was alone with the three women.

"Just calm down, honey," Blanche said quietly. "It's a job with us, nothing more."

Melody took a closer look at the woman. Her voice cued her in. One day when she first came to live with Uncle Josh, she had gotten lost downtown. And as she passed a two-story building at a dead-end street, this woman came to a doorway. "I think you're lost, honey. You better get back on Center Street."

Melody saw the girls in the windows and

211

turned red, realizing that she was in front of a parlor house at the end of a deserted side street.

Farrell and Vance returned to the bedroom. "Lassiter's coming," Farrell told her coldly. "Keep your mouth shut, hear?"

"Goddamn you both!" she stormed at her husband and Farrell. "When Lassiter gets here he'll . . ."

"Do nothing." Farrell gave her an angry look. In his earlier struggle with her, his hair had become mussed and his face so slick with sweat that he was now mopping it with a white handkerchief. Subduing her hadn't been easy.

"Lassiter will do *something*," she said defiantly.

"Lassiter won't be alive to see the sun go down tomorrow," Farrell said in such a vicious tone that she was stunned. She stared at the green-eyed tense face that held all the fury of an aroused mountain lion.

"What are you going to do to Lassiter?" she asked breathlessly.

"When you hear sustained shouting tomorrow, you'll know he's down for the final count. When this is followed by silence, you'll know he's finished."

"Finished?" she heard herself say numbly.

"Dead," Farrell supplied her with a hard smile.

Lassiter came bounding up the veranda steps to face Farrell in the doorway. "Where is she?" he demanded.

"Come in, come in." Farrell stood aside and Lassiter strode into the parlor. Something hard rammed his backbone.

"Stand hitched," Vanderson said from behind him, "or I'll blow a hole in your spine I can ram a fist through."

A door at the end of a hallway opened to a bedroom. Through the doorway he could see Melody sitting tensely on the edge of a bed.

"Lassiter," she said hoarsely, her voice tormented.

She was with three women. The tall strapping woman he recognized as the local madam. He didn't know the girls, but could guess their occupation.

"Close the door, Blanche," Farrell ordered. The door closed. He turned to Lassiter. "She's safe enough, for now."

"What the hell is this all about?" The gun muzzle was still grinding against his back.

"You'll find out tomorrow."

"Turn her loose," Lassiter demanded. "Then you and I can settle our differences."

Farrell laughed harshly. "We'll settle our differences, but in a way you're not expecting."

Lassiter narrowed his eyes, wondering what Farrell meant. But before he had time to reflect the front door opened. Ed Kiley and another man he didn't know entered the parlor. Both of them held rifles at the ready.

"We buried Holzer, thinkin' it was you," Kiley said roughly. "Next time we won't make no such mistake."

Farrell said, "If you make any fool move, Melody Vanderson is a goner. Remember that, my friend."

Lassiter turned his head as far as it would go and glared back at Vanderson. "You'd let him threaten your wife?"

"Shut up, Lassiter," Farrell warned. "Kiley, not too hard now." And a rifle barrel crashed against the side of Lassiter's head. He sank down into a sea of blinding white lights and then a rush of darkness.

When he regained consciousness he was lying on a large bed, wearing leg irons. His hands were menacled in front. A rope looped through the manacles was tied to a bedpost.

214

Kiley and the other man occupied chairs, rifles across their laps.

"Tell me, Kiley, just what is this all about?" Lassiter said. His head throbbed and his stomach was all knotted up in worry over Melody.

"You just set. You'll be fed in an hour or so. An' you can take care of yourself. But you make any fool moves an' Lew here has got orders to shoot the gal. I'll take care of you."

Farrell had opened the door to hear the last. "Believe him, Lassiter. Every word he said is true."

"And I even get fed. The condemned has the final meal, eh?"

"Don't act so glib. I want you hale and hearty for tomorrow." Farrel's smile was icy as he closed the door.

Somehow Lassiter sweated out the long night. He catnapped only to awaken with a start to realize his surroundings. Kiley's companion at one time was snoring softly in his chair, but Kiley was wide awake, his eyes glittering in the glow of a turned-down lamp.

Finally a faint streak of gray lighted the eastern sky. Lassiter's mouth tasted as if it had been a camp for beavers. His arms were

215

asleep because of their awkward position tied to the bedpost.

After breakfast, the rope attached to the manacles was removed and he was able to sit up in bed and eat three eggs and a mound of potatoes. He learned that Blanche was the cook, which proved she had talents other than dispensing pleasure to lonely males. At one time her establishment had been on Joy Street, but indignant housewives, who were flocking into the town by then, had managed to get it changed from a suggestion of pleasure to plain E Street.

As the morning hours crept by, Lassiter was suddenly aware of a distant humming sound. He'd been hearing it for some time, but it hadn't registered until then. It reminded him of a great swarm of bees. He knew what it really was. Voices. Hundreds of them.

Then he was remembering his arrival in town yesterday, the unusual activity, men swarming in the streets. Others were crowding into town by horseback and wagon. Probably payday, had crossed his mind. It was one thing that would lure not only cowhands and miners to Bluegate but also ranchers and their families from the scrub outfits out on the flats.

There were few fine ranches such as Farrell's Twin Horn that he'd won from Silas Borodenker in a midnight poker game. Two days after signing over his ranch, the old man had gone out to the privy behind Shanagan's, put the muzzle of a carbine into his mouth and worked the trigger with a big toe. They found him slumped on the four-holer, his brains on the plank wall.

One more mark against Farrell, Lassiter was thinking as his ankles were untied from the bedposts. He was ushered into the parlor. Farrell stood in front of the cold fireplace, looking amused. He gave Lassiter a slight bow in the manner of a grand duke. Today he wore a corduroy jacket and brown pants. His boots bore a high polish.

Vanderson entered the room, losing color when he saw Lassiter's glare.

"Is Melody all right?" Lassiter demanded.

"Perfectly," Farrell said. He jerked a thumb at Vanderson who walked down a long hallway and flung open a bedroom door. Melody could be seen sitting on the edge of the bed. Her wrists and ankles were roped so that she was bent over.

"Untie her, for Crissakes," Lassiter shouted.

"That's for her husband to determine.

She's in his hands now." Farrell seemed to be enjoying himself. "Blanche and her girls have done their job. And very well, I might add."

Then he stepped to the mantel where Lassiter's .44 and Henry rifle had been placed. Farrell said, "I like the heft of your revolver, Lassiter. I'll keep it for my personal weapon. Each time it is fired, I'll think of you."

Lassiter glanced along the hallway, feeling helpless. Melody still sat on the bed, chin up, eyes steady, although she probably had had little sleep. Not that her goddamned husband could care. Had it not been for her being so close, he would have tried some desperate move. To make any rash attempt to escape would only endanger her life. He looked at Vanderson who had come back to the parlor, trying on his boyish smile under the mustache. But it wavered.

Farrell was gesturing at the wide belt with the silver buckle and initial "L" that was displayed above the fireplace. "I'll have it polished and put in a glass case," Farrell said. "A reminder of how I won the game after all." He gave Lassiter a hard smile.

"You haven't won it yet," Lassiter reminded, which caused Farrell to laugh.

218

Farrell turned on Vanderson. "Keep an eye on your wife."

"But I'd like to see it. Can't you fix it so I can?"

"See *what?*" Lassiter cut in narrowly.

Farrell ignored him. "If somehow she should get loose," Farrell was saying, "are you man enough to kill her?" Farrell used the same tone of voice as if saying, "Are you you man enough to finish your whiskey?" That was the worth of a human life to Farrell, Lassiter thought grimly.

Vanderson licked his lips. "You and me all the way, Kane. You know that for sure now."

It was hard for Lassiter to realize that the boyish face was twisted in eagerness to have Farrell believe him. Lassiter tried to inject a measure of doubt as he said, "Whatever Farrell's promised, Vanderson, you'll find out it's only dead ash."

"Farrell will keep his word with me," Vanderson said firmly.

"By the time you find out, it'll be too late for you," Lassiter pointed out.

"Keep your mouth shut, Lassiter," Farrell ordered calmly. "I'm sick of your voice. Thank God, after today I won't have to hear it ever again." He gave Lassiter such a look of triumph that Lassiter felt a knifing chill spread across his shoulders.

Farrell glanced at the face of a thick gold watch. "Almost time. Are you ready, Lassiter?" He drew a gun from under his coat.

"Ready for what?"

Two men entered the parlor. Lassiter recognized them as hands from Farrell's Twin Horn outfit. Farrell jerked his head at Vanderson, who strode down the hall to the bedroom. There he removed a gun from under his coat and held the muzzle deep in Melody's thick golden hair. Her face blanched.

Under Farrell's cocked gun, Lassiter's manacles were removed. His wrists and upper arms were then roped, hands behind his back. Then he was pushed out to the veranda. His black horse stood saddled at the foot of the steps.

For two solid weeks the sale of tickets at Shanagan's had been brisk. Each ticket represented hard-earned money. Five silver dollars each was a high price to pay for entertainment in a lonely outpost such as Bluegate. But the promise of witnessing sheer drama instead of being faced with the usual dull days made it seem worthwhile.

Although the purchaser of each ticket had been warned to keep his mouth shut, some couldn't help but let it slip to their wives. Most of the male population was womanless, but in this instance the few wives banded together. Today's so-called "entertainment" was too much. It amounted to cold-blooded murder. A delegation of indignant women marched to the sheriff's office the day of the event only to find a hand-lettered sign in the office window stating that Bo Dancur had gone north on County business, along with his deputy, and wouldn't return for several days.

Even so, the ladies had been able to dissuade a few of the ticket buyers from attending what they termed a pagan carnival.

Roma was astounded by the activity in Bluegate. It wasn't a Western village, but verging on a metropolis. "Rex, this is where I will live and raise my children!" she cried.

Rex Ambrose gave her a tolerant smile.

Doc's experienced eye was roving the crowded streets, seeking a good spot to set up their operation. He found one in vacant land adjoining the Mercantile. With the tom-tom, Roma's flashing teeth, agile body and swaying midnight hair, plus Doc's mellifluous tones, they soon had an audience. While Doc was making his lofty presentation concerning the elixir from ancient Cathay, Roma tugged at the sleeve of a passing middle-aged woman.

"Do you happen to know a man named Lassiter?" Roma asked, her black eyes shining with excitement.

The woman turned on her as if she might have been a leper. "Do I know him? He cost my man five dollars we sorely needed for other things. That's what he's done. I wish him no good luck on this black Saturday."

The woman, herding two small wide-eyed children along the walk, left Roma in a momentary state of confusion. But it soon passed as the slender aristocratic looking Rex played a drum roll on his tom-tom. Her cue for another wild session of gypsy dancing, much to the enjoyment of the crowd.

She wondered about the murmur of voices coming from a large building on an adjoining street. More of a subdued roar than a murmur, come to think of it, she decided. Men were streaming toward the building entrance, kicking up dust, laughing, pounding one another on the back, acting like excited schoolboys about to sneak into some forbidden circus sideshow.

19

AT THE NORTH end of town, Lassiter was marched to his saddle horse at the foot of the veranda steps by the two Twin Horn men. Each held a rifle which they used as prods. They were replacements for Ed Kiley and companion who were dozing after the long night as guards for Lassiter.

Farrell, a look of excitement on his rather handsome face, was already mounted on a bay. He began to play out a catch rope to make a loop.

One of the Twin Horn men, Parky Brimmer, lank and with a frozen grin, was forcing Lassiter into the saddle. He was mounting awkwardly because of the hands bound behind his back. The other man, burly and with a sandy beard, was Si Ukase. He gave Lassiter a final jab with his rifle.

As Lassiter settled in the saddle, Farrell aimed a loop of his catch rope at Lassiter. "I'll just drop this over your head to make sure you behave."

Once Farrell got him to wherever he intended, a sixth sense told Lassiter, it would all be over. As the noose sailed expertly,

Lassiter suddenly ducked. He yelled at the top of his voice and at the same time slammed bootheels into the black flanks of his horse. The sound of Lassiter's explosive voice and the sudden jab of bootheels sent the black horse into an instant hard run.

Lassiter, bent low in the saddle, saw the noose sail harmlessly past his head as the horse bolted. Strength of knees hugging the horse's barrel compensated for the absence of hands to help hold him in the saddle. He was bent over so far that at each lunge of the speeding horse, he was punched in the stomach by the saddlehorn. His horse went pounding between a cottage and a fair-sized barn.

"Won't do you a damn bit of good!" Farrell was shouting. This followed by a gunshot deliberately wide of the mark. A bullet slammed into the barn wall. "Get him!" Farrell yelled at Ukase and Brimmer.

And they appeared suddenly out of the dust on two fast horses, coming in from an angle. Ukase was the nearer and with his sandy beard blowing in the wind, reached out for Lassiter. But Lassiter rammed him in the side with the crown of his head. A surprised yell broke from Ukase. He sailed from the saddle and into a large clump of weeds. He seemed to bounce.

The second man, taller and thinned down, with a flop-brimmed hat, snatched at Lassiter's reins that were loosely tied at the saddlehorn. The shoulder of his big roan crashed into Lassiter's mount, causing it to stumble. But Brimmer, a hard grin frozen on his lips, failed to relinquish his hold on Lassiter's reins. Despite the two horses bumping into each other and swerving along a narrow alley, Lassiter managed to keep his seat.

But in the flash of an eye wink, Lassiter quit his saddle. Bootheels slammed into the alley hardpan with such an impact he felt it up his spine. Momentum sent him stumbling to one knee. Pain flashed up his thigh. He reached his feet as Farrell yelled an order at Brimmer.

But Lassiter was dancing around the rump of Farrell's plunging horse. He took off at full speed, skirted a shed, and started across a vacant lot, running awkwardly because of his bound wrists.

Momentarily alone, he looked desperately for something he could use to cut the ropes at wrists and arms. All he saw was the shiny upper half of a shattered bottle lying in a weed patch. But that would take too long and time he didn't have. As he ran, something prickly slapped one cheek. The familiar scratch of hemp. He heard a horse behind him as a noose settled over his shoulders. It slid down his arms and then was yanked tight. It jerked him backwards, so that he slammed into the ground on his shoulder blades.

"I got him, Farrell!" the burly Ukase yelled.

"Good work!" Farrell came riding up, Brimmer behind him.

Ukase and Brimmer boosted Lassiter into the saddle of the black horse Farrell had led up. They slammed him down so hard on the saddle that Lassiter gave a grunt of pain. It brought an ugly smile to Farrell's lips.

"You bastard," he cried. "You don't even know what pain is . . . yet!"

A swelling rumble of voices was pouring from the big warehouse. At the end of the street, straight as a string, the road up the mountain to the Black Arrow Mine was a scar in the bright sunlight. A thread of smoke at the mine vanished into cloud cover.

All around the warehouse were stacks of lumber and crates and barrels of merchandise to be freighted by Farrell's wagons.

They were moved out to clear the vast interior for the crowd of spectators, come to witness the "fight of the century," as one man was yelling exuberantly.

At the entrance Lassiter was hauled from the saddle. Ukase had him by one arm, Brimmer the other. Farrell was behind, giving Lassiter an occasional shove toward the building.

A man stepped from the crowded warehouse, saw the quartette approaching on foot and ducked back inside. "Lassiter's almost here, boys!" he shouted, which brought a cheer from the crowd.

Another man gave Lassiter a broad wink. "I bet that you can do it. I seen you fight before an' I know you can whip 'em both!"

"*Two* men?" Lassiter yelled above the excited voices.

The speaker, Ben Haley, looked surprised. "Hell, you put up a thousand dollars that you could beat them two hombres Shanagan dug up!"

"That's enough, Haley!" Farrell barked. Haley's jaw dropped at the reprimand.

"Never meant nothin', Mr. Farrell, I only . . ."

Over big double doors, now wide open, the sign FARRELL FREIGHT LINES

227

seemed the final mockery to a battered Lassiter.

A sea of excited faces greeted Lassiter as he was shoved into the oversize building. In the center was a cleared space but around it men were packed solidly as minnows in a bottle.

Those nearest the door gaped at Lassiter with wrists and arms roped, held by two of Farrell's men. And Farrell, elegantly attired, with polished nails and a fresh white shirt, now being sweated into, which no doubt displeased the man.

"Why's he tied?" several men chorused.

"Lassiter tried to back out of his bet!" Farrell said loudly so as to reach every ear in the vast audience.

"Liar!" Lassiter shouted, his face an angry red.

"We hauled him off his horse just as he was about to leave town!" Farrell went on.

This brought an instant roar of disapproval from the crowd. Bottles were tilted. A sharp odor of alcohol in the air that was stained from dust and sweat and tobacco smoke.

Lassiter raised his voice to be heard, but couldn't compete against the tumult. It seemed as if the high ceiling with its heavy rafter, walls of raw lumber fairly bulged from the raucous sounds. Men were jammed back against the walls, the shorter ones kneeling or sitting on the floor.

"It was your idea, Lassiter!" a bearded men shouted angrily and shook a fist in his face. "I never believed it possible, but now I figure this Lassiter's got a yellow streak down his back as wide as a mule's ass!"

This followed by a roar of approval.

"Watch the doors, boys, so he doesn't try and get away!" Farrell was yelling. "Shanagan's going to cut him loose!"

Shanagan produced a knife, stepped behind Lassiter and began sawing at ropes that bound arms and wrists. "Wish to hell I'd never gone along with this, Lassiter," could barely be heard above the surge of voices. The ropes fell away. Returning circulation sent icy needles along the arms and shoulders.

"Blackshear's got the first round!" Farrell shouted, caught up now in the fever of the place, the raw smell of sweat and whiskey. "Jody Marsh takes the second, and so on. Still not too late to put your money on Lassiter."

There were no takers. Farrell laughed. Those who had had the bad judgement to bet on Lassiter in the first place merely glared, having no doubt now that they were losers.

Lassiter stared along an aisle through the bodies where Blackshear appeared. This followed by a mighty roar that seemed to threaten the roof. Jody Marsh was pounding an encouraging hand on Blackshear's back.

The size of the two men grinning together was awesome. Rage ripped through Lassiter as his eyes met with Farrell's. He started to lunge forward, but a phalanx of bodies blocked him. As the swelling roar increased, Lassiter looked wildly for an exit he might use. Damned if he was going to stand here and let not one man but two beat him into the floor. As all attention was focused now on the advancing Blackshear who was flexing the muscles of his enormous shoulders, Lassiter spun. He made a grab for the revolver at Brimmer's belt, but Ukase thrust out a leg. Lassiter sprawled over it. Before he could right himself, he was seized by many hands. Some men had him by the arms, others around the middle and the legs. Angrily he fought, shouting above the waves of sound that it was all a mistake, that he had never bragged that he could whip both men. It was a goddamned lie!

Only those in close were able to hear him above the bedlam.

"Turn him my way, boys!" Blackshear yelled, all six-feet three-inches and two hundred and fifty pounds of bone and muscle.

And as the combined weight of many men swung Lassiter toward the giant challenger, Blackshear shot a fist at the jaw. Lassiter saw it coming, jerked his head so that knuckles only grazed a cheekbone.

"Turn him loose," Farrell ordered. "It's him and Blackshear . . . for now!"

There were to be four minute rounds, it was agreed. Shrunken little Miegs in his black undertaker's suit, was the time keeper. In one hand he held a large gold watch.

"All right, you sons of bitches!" Lassiter started to peel off his shirt. But Blackshear leaped in and with a triumphant roar ripped the shirt from Lassiter's back.

Blackshear, already shirtless, showed off bulging muscles as he threw Lassiter's wadded up shirt into the crowd. Then he slammed a solid right to the breastbone. The force of the blow rattled Lassiter's teeth and another one knocked him back several steps. Hands reached out and shoved him back. A volcano of noise erupted from the crowd as

231

Blackshear came roaring in, both fists swinging.

It seemed to the vociferous crowd that Blackshear was about to finish the fight before it had even gotten started. But Lassiter, amazingly light on his feet, spun away at the last possible moment. He landed two jolting lefts to the big man's exposed left side. Blackshear grunted and hunched over. Then they began hammering each other from one end of the clear space to the other. Dust from their shuffling feet rose from the floor in layers and drifted toward the rafters.

Finally in all the yelling, Lassiter heard the thin voice of the undertaker, "End of Round One!"

Lassiter made the mistake of turning his head when a three-legged stool was shoved under him. Blackshear took that moment to elbow him on the jaw. So much power was behind the blow that Lassiter felt it to his ankles. The blow produced another mighty uproar from the onlookers.

"Watch yourself there, Blackshear," Farrell warned loudly; but with a trace of a smile. "We want this to be a fair fight!"

Lassiter wanted to laugh. Fair fight. The biggest joke of the century.

He sank to the stool and rinsed his mouth

from a water bottle someone shoved on him. His nerves were raw. Farrell's treachery not only to him but to Melody was like a myriad of red hot splinters driven into the flesh. He had suffered a battering in the first round, he'd be the first to admit. His breathing was ragged and he tasted blood where the inside of his mouth had been cut on a tooth. Was it possible that the bullet fired into his back over six months before and the long convalescence that followed had drained him?

He caught sight of Kane Farrell through the crowd. The man was shoving thumbs into a wide belt. It left his coat open so that Lassiter glimpsed heel plates of a holstered revolver.

If he could lunge through the crowd, get his hand on the gun, ram it into Farrell's back. And force the man to do his bidding. Then the day might end well after all.

He got to his feet, eyes on Farrell not ten feet away.

At that moment the reedy voice of the town undertaker was barely audible above the noise. "Round Two!" he shouted.

But before Lassiter could make his move toward Farrell, he caught a blur of movement from a corner of his eye. The crowd was going wild. Cheers for Jody Marsh, the big man Lassiter had tangled with up at the Glory Mine. No hard breathing for Marsh. He was fresh, wearing a spotless white shirt. A broad grin knifed across the heavy face. A man with more finesse than Blackshear's raw power, Lassiter had to admit.

They came together, Lassiter clinging to the front of the white shirt while he got his breath. Marsh kept trying to beat him off, but Lassiter had his chin tucked against the broad chest and refused to have his hold broken.

"I'm gonna beat you to your knees, then Blackshear'll finish it!" Marsh snarled and tried an underhand to the groin. Lassiter, however, had sensed his intentions and twisted aside. He hit the bigger man in the mouth, splitting both lips. Dazed and angered, Marsh rushed in. Lassiter took a blow high on the forehead, but one to the jaw rocked him.

He started backing. Vision in one eye blurred. Marsh seemed distant and almost ghostly, with incredibly long arms that punched him out of the blurry vagueness. His head felt as if it had been stepped on by a mule team. Another blow jarred his skull again. Another exploded his breath. Paralyzing pain enveloped him like a shroud.

Somehow he fought his way back from the edge of blackness. A fist almost crumpled his nose, but not quite, for he was able somehow to jerk back his head in time. A fist landed viciously against his stomach. It seemed to him that the building tilted first one way, then the other and with it the banks of yelling sweated faces.

As Marsh paused to hitch up his pants, Lassiter swung hard at the slight paunch overhanging the belt. Air gushed from the man's lungs. He staggered. Lassiter caught him on the jaw with lefts and rights. The crowd was going mad as Marsh staggered.

"End of Round Two!" could hardly be heard above the roaring in the big warehouse.

Lassiter sank to his stool. He was getting the range of Marsh's jaw. A few more solid blows like the last pair Lassiter had landed and Marsh would be down. But Lassiter forgot about the change in combatants at each round.

A rested Blackshear loomed up, not even waiting till Lassiter got off the stool. He crashed into him with all the force of a runaway team. Lassiter grabbed Blackshear's forearms, slick with sweat and went over backwards, pulling Blackshear with him. Blackshear landed on top of him.

For just a moment his breath was gone. And then he recovered and began to hammer away at both kidneys. When Blackshear got him by the throat, Lassiter drove both arms upward between the hands, forcing them apart.

And in the same movement, Lassiter squirmed out from under the heavyweight, somersaulted on the floor and reached his feet. In the piercing din that followed, he felt heartened, despite himself. For some of the shouting was for him.

Blackshear bounded to his feet, rushed Lassiter again. From one end of the cleared space to the other they fought. A deep cut on Lassiter's right cheek made him aware of the warmth of his own blood. It trickled downward, soaking into the gout of black chest hair.

Lassiter danced back and as he got set for another rush by the larger man, he heard the squeaky voice of Miegs, the undertaker-timekeeper.

"Hell with it," Lassiter heard him say above the noisy crowd. "Nobody pays no attention to me. Don't need rounds. I say let 'em fight it out. The winner is the one still on his feet!"

He grinned at Farrell, who gave him a nod of appreciation.

The words of the timekeeper had caused a fresh outburst from the spectators. The eyes of most of them glassy with excitement and whiskey. They seemed to sense that this day they were witnessing history in the making. Never before had one man the guts to challenge two bigger men as opponents. A sight to behold. The events of this day to be passed on down to great-grandchildren.

And as Miegs stepped back into the howling mob, Marsh swaggered up to hover at Lassiter's back while Blackshear began to hammer his midsection and jaw. But Lassiter cleverly managed to avoid the heat of most punches by twisting his body at just the right angle so that the power was lessened, and at times lost altogether.

"Hey, Shanagan!" one of the onlookers roared through cupped hands. "Ain't fair. Two men on one . . . and at the same time!"

"Shut up an' set down!" others cried.

Whatever reply Shanagan made was lost in the thunder of voices. Lassiter danced out of range of both men, pulling great draughts of air into his lungs. In the past, he had been hard-pressed at times to survive the brawny fists of tricksters. Now he was faced with not one, but two. He would have to make a bold move and quickly, because common sense told him he couldn't survive for long the onslaught of four fists beating on his body. What would happen if he lost consciousness? What then, a knife blade sneaked between the ribs? Boot heels crashing down on an exposed face? As this skipped across his mind, his ears were continually assaulted by wave after wave of the raucous voices of the aroused crowd.

Blackshear's knuckles against his jaw suddenly sent him reeling backward. He spat blood and kept backing, his mouth filled with blood and mucus. Marsh struck him on the back of the head. Each blow now sounded like the slap of wet canvas against a wall.

From beneath tangled black brows, Marsh stared at him in disbelief. "You ain't human!" Marsh yelled just before Lassiter broke his nose.

Despite himself, Lassiter tasted a raw edge of fear. Blackshear hit him a solid blow to the temple that set up a clanging, as if great bells rolled around inside his skull. As Lassiter reeled, Marsh clubbed him on the kidney. It was almost a paralyzing blow, but somehow Lassiter managed to twist aside, using elbows to fend off Blackshear while he got his bearings and some of his breath.

Pandemonium rocked the building. Mules in a nearby corral brayed in unison.

"Now," Lassiter told himself. Now he had to gamble.

Lassiter spun suddenly, his back to Blackshear as he sensed rather than heard Jody Marsh closing in behind him. The swell of raw voices in the warehouse seemed to rattle the walls. Marsh had his right fist drawn far back, ready to slam it into Lassiter's rib cage with all the force of a hurled stone.

But Lassiter moved so quickly, it caught the man off balance. Before Marsh could make a correction, Lassiter had spun out of the range of Blackshear's deadly fist. And it occurred to Lassiter suddenly it was he dealing out the punishment now, the two dancing bears giving ground.

At that moment Marsh's jaw was fully exposed. The startled look on his face turned blank as Lassiter found the range of that shelf of bone and solid flesh. Lassiter's heels came up from the floor as he swung with every ounce of strength remaining in his body. Marsh's eyes crossed. His head bobbled like a ball on a string as he crashed face down to the floor. Before Lassiter could twist around to confront the remaining menace, Blackshear grabbed him from behind.

"I'll finish you off, you son of a bitch!" Blackshear cried.

With another great surge of strength, Lassiter rammed backward with his right elbow into the pit of Blackshear's stomach. It produced a noise like escaping steam.

As Blackshear bent over from the blow, Lassiter broke the man's hold. Blackshear was staggering, hunched over as he gasped for breath. Lassiter didn't wait, but stepped in and threw a solid right to the cheekbone. Skin split as if cleaved with an ax blade. Then he smashed the lips for a second time, punishing the nose until it bled like a fountain.

"Ain't no fair," Blackshear blurted and went down while searching for Farrell's face in the wildly cheering crowd. "He's gotta wait till Marsh gits on his feet. . . ."

Somehow the big man staggered to his feet and met Lassiter's onslaught to jaw and midsection. Lassiter's howl of laughter added to Blackshear's inane protest, mingled with the fresh outburst from the crowd that roared through the building like a tornado. This time when Blackshear dropped, he lay a few feet from the unconscious Marsh. Men were pounding one another on the back, yelling, grinning.

The little man who had told Lassiter earlier that he had bet on him, was holding aloft a sack of money. No one could hear the jingle of coins because of the noise.

In the press of bodies the water bottle that once had been passed to Lassiter was tipped over. Water belched from the mouth. Lassiter snatched it, tipped back his head and took a long drink. Never had anything tasted as good. He shook his head to try and drive away the fuzziness. Sweat spun into the sunlight from his damp hair.

Shanagan thrust his beefy face close to Lassiter's.

Lassiter stared at him.

In the embarrassing moment, Shanagan said, "Free whiskey at my place for you, Lassiter. For as long as you want it."

Without replying, Lassiter thrust his way through the screaming men. Some touched his arms, his shoulders. "Great fight, Lassiter . . . greatest I ever seen . . ." sang at him from all quarters.

He saw Farrell standing with a look of disbelief on his face. Lassiter said, "I'll never

241

forget your hand in this." Farrell slid away into the crowd.

Lassiter still breathed hard and every muscle in his body seemed as if it had been put to the supreme test. It hurt to stand up straight and he knew he had a face that would frighten small children.

Lassiter was delayed by men wanting to congratulate him. At last he was able to push his way outside. The pandemonium followed him. Somehow he found his horse where it had been tied to a rack outside the warehouse.

Numbly he got into the saddle. The crowd milled around the horse, shouting Lassiter's name.

He saw Farrell's big bay horse where it had been left at the rack, nervously twitching its tail because of the press of bodies.

Just because the horse was nearby didn't necessarily mean that Farrell had stayed at the warehouse. He might have walked to his house in anger and frustration, Lassiter told himself, probably kicking savagely at every stone in his path.

A hard smile touched Lassiter's swollen lips as he pictured the possibility of finishing it all on this eventful day. To hell with the fact that his mind was blurred, that his right hand was in no shape for gunspeed. "Get it over with!" kept hammering through his head.

Some of the men started to follow him, but he twisted in the saddle, shouting, "I don't want company!"

Most of the crowd turned back, but some didn't. The former knew he was edgy and they wanted to avoid trouble. Besides, there was drinking to do at Shanagan's, along with discussion of Bluegate's historic day.

<hr>

20

As LASSITER TURNED his horse away from the mob, he heard a woman frantically calling his name. It sounded vaguely like Roma, but looking around in his benumbed state he saw only a wall of exuberant male faces.

An older man with a downsweep of gray moustache drew his attention. The man expressed the majority opinion. "A fella your size whippin' two big men . . . ain't never been done before. You won me a little money, Lassiter. Won't never forget it."

Lassiter nodded his head. Other voices said, "I'm for you, Lassiter . . . Me, too . . . And me . . ."

He was a block away when he saw something coming across a vacant lot, green with spring weeds. Because his vision was slightly distorted, he had to squint with his good eye, his head back. It was female, he could tell, because of the long hair and the swaying hips when she walked. And she had pale hair and was holding a long rip in her shirt with one hand. Every few feet she would look back over her shoulder.

And then she saw Lassiter. A hand flew to her mouth and the eyes widened either in surprise or revulsion, he couldn't tell which. One thing he did know, it was Melody and her shirt was torn and she seemed frightened.

"Lassiter!" she cried and started to run toward him.

He closed the distance between them. The move of dismounting in a hurry brought a flurry of pain. "Melody, what happened?"

She put her forehead against his chest and began to cry.

His shirt was gone and his chest, smeared with blood, was now dampened by her tears.

"How'd you free your hands?" he asked, remembering she had been tied.

"I . . . I tricked Vance. I . . . I promised him . . ." Her face reddened with embarrassment, but she plunged on. "He was so anxious, he cut me loose . . ." She drew a deep breath. "When his back was turned, I hit him with a bookend."

"I hope you killed the son of a bitch!"

"Oh, don't say that. Even about Vance . . ."

"Why the hell didn't he stay away, instead of coming back to foul up your life . . . ?"

"I'm through with him, Lassiter." Her jaw was set in a firm line, the wet eyes bright with anger. "When he told me what Farrell had planned for you, I just couldn't believe it."

"Let's go see him." He gave her a hand up behind him on the black horse. "I've got some personal business to settle with him. I'll start the hunt for him at Farrell's."

"But you're in no shape, Lassiter. You have no idea how awful you look. Your hands are swollen and your poor face . . ." She shuddered. "Please don't go to Farrell's."

"Need my guns."

"Dad Hornbeck will loan you his."

"No."

"Farrell might be there."

He jerked a thumb at the crowd that had disobeyed his request not to follow him and were exuberantly trailing along. "Those boys won't let Farrell pull any fancy stunts. I'll meet him face up . . ."

"Oh, *Lassiter* . . ."

He could feel her tears against his bare back.

Farrell's front door was ajar. Lassiter dismounted, teeth clenched with the pain. He managed to climb the veranda steps.

"Vance!" he called from the veranda. "Farrell?"

There was no sound from the big house.

Melody, at the foot of the veranda steps, had both fists at her mouth. Then as Lassiter started for the door, she ran up the steps to be at his side.

"Get away," he warned. "There may be trouble."

"I intend to share that trouble . . . with you." She was defiant. "And don't try to stop me."

A small smile flickered across his misshapen mouth. "Stay out here."

Already the sun had changed so that the parlor was mostly in shadow. Ropes that had bound Melody lay over the arm of the sofa. The only sound was a scrape of bootheels when he shifted his feet. It took him a moment to realize, in his foggy state, that he had produced the sound himself.

As he looked numbly around the ornate furnishings, the heavy Spanish furniture, several oil paintings, for the first time in his life he had to restrain a savage impulse to smash everything in sight.

He got his weapons from the mantel where Farrell had placed them. Somehow he buckled on his gunbelt, even though his knuckles were so swollen he could barely move them.

He reached up and pulled down his belt with the silver buckle. He handed it to Melody, who had followed him inside. "Take care of it," he said thickly.

As time passed it had come to him that despite the urge to settle everything here and now, he was in no condition even to face up to Vanderson. Let alone Kane Farrell. At long last his mind was clearing so that he could accept reality.

By the time they were five miles out of Bluegate, riding double, they changed positions. Melody rode in the saddle and Lassiter straddled the horse's rump. He clung to her, a bruised cheek resting on her shoulder. At times he dozed.

They were in that position when entering Aspen Creek. Word quickly spread when

Lassiter's swollen features were seen. A crowd gathered.

Oliver and Hornbeck helped Lassiter from the back of the horse and led him limping into the office. Melody insisted he take the bed, but he refused. He'd sleep on the floor because she insisted on being within call should he need her during the night.

It took a combination of arnica plus laudanum to smooth out the world for Lassiter. Pain was minimized by the opium derivative and his cleansed wounds no longer throbbed as strongly as before.

Bert Oliver got a zinc tub from the back porch and Melody heated pan after pan of water on the stove. So as not to be embarrassed by his nudity, she retired to the bedroom.

The warm water and suds was so relaxing he almost fell asleep in the tub. Melody had loaned him a bar of her French soap.

"I'll smell like a Paris whore," Lassiter told Oliver with a wink.

Oliver and Hornbeck straddled chairs. "Farrell's got to be trimmed down to size," Hornbeck said with a wag of his graying head. "This time he's gone too damned far."

Oliver agreed. "That stunt he pulled on you today is worse'n anything he's done so far. An' that's been plenty. Usin' his cooked cards to trim old man Borodenker outa the Twin Horn ranch. Not to mention the five thousand he euchered me out of." Oliver swore.

"You don't know the half of what he's done," Lassiter said. It hurt him to speak because of the lacerated lips.

When he was dressed and Oliver and Hornbeck had dragged the tub outside and emptied it in the yard, Melody came to stand in the doorway with Lassiter. "I want you to do something for me," she said, including them all.

"Name it," Hornbeck said, and Oliver nodded.

"If my husband even tries to get near this building, run him off."

"You're through with him, I hope," Hornbeck said.

"Definitely. I'm divorcing him. And then . . ." Turning, she looked up into Lassiter's battered features with a smile.

He was instantly on his guard. Was she considering a switch of affections from her no-account husband to him? Not that he thought he was much of a catch for one so young. But maybe she thought so. There was no denying a special look in her gray eyes since he had survived Farrell's double trap at the warehouse. And he remembered snatches of whispered words on the long ride out from town.

But it was time he moved along, he well knew. Already he had spent over six months in the interests of Northguard, including his long convalescence. It was time that Herm Falconer put away the bottle and got his bootheels anchored on Mother Earth. Herm wasn't the first man in history to have lost a leg.

He considered sending Bert Oliver down to Rimrock in a wagon to bring Herm back. Providing the man would come. There was always a chance Herm would get his back bowed and refuse to stir. Both he and his late brother Josh were noted for their mule blood. Despite their stubbornness, both men were likeable and Lassiter had been drawn to them for some years. Now all he wanted was to end the threat of Kane Farrell so that Melody could operate her freight line without fear. There was no denying that there were hazards enough, the natural kind, in trying to make such a venture pay off. Heavy snows and avalanches and wrecked wagons and mule teams stricken with one ailment or another. Having someone like Farrell adding to her troubles made it that much more difficult to achieve success.

No, he'd get things settled up, one way or another, then head out. Herm could take over and send him the money he had invested in the company, whenever he got his hands on some. And if he never got paid back, what of it? To Lassiter, all he cared about was to put a hand in his pocket and feel enough gold coins to get him through a few more days. He had no desire for riches, to be the biggest cowman on the range or the most prosperous merchant in a frontier town. He remembered his own father, always striving, scheming. And when he died his estate consisted of a horse and a new pair of boots. And even the boots were a size too small for Lassiter's feet.

Wherever he moved about the West he made friends. Most friendships lasting, as with the Falconer brothers. He'd known them well over ten years and there was never any hesitation to offer assistance if one of them was in trouble. And they would do likewise. Now Josh was gone, all because he had gone soft in the head and traded his life for a softly scented body and a dazzling smile, so everyone said. And even behind Josh's demise was the shadow of Farrell. It was Farrell's child Josh's wife had been carrying. And that flung in his face by the vindictive woman was what had beaten Josh to his knees, as if by a leaden whip.

That evening, the day after the fight, Melody insisted on a special supper for Lassiter. Dad Hornbeck rode out of town with a rifle and a pack mule and returned with a fine buck deer.

Lassiter sat in the sun, on a bench, a bottle of whiskey in his lap as he watched Hornbeck expertly butcher the deer. By then the old man's wound was completely healed. His wounding only another mark against Farrell, Lassiter thought grimly as the bloodied knife peeled back the deer skin.

Dad Hornbeck could look after Melody, Lassiter was musing, after the old man had left the yard. But first there was the matter of Farrell. He took another generous gulp of the whiskey Bert Oliver had provided. It slid easily down his throat and acted as balm for his numerous hurts. But he wouldn't allow the whiskey to fog his brain. If ever he needed a clear head, it was now.

Farrell wouldn't back off from another defeat at the hands of his old enemy, Lassiter. Not only had he lost money but prestige as well, when the Roman carnival turned out so badly for him. Not to mention the other times over the years they had tangled. Each time Lassiter had been fortunate enough to thwart Farrell's grand plans for sudden wealth.

But Lassiter was realist enough to know that one day the coin was going to come down tails instead of heads. That would be the day of reckoning, but he would be ready for it. He prayed only that the day could be postponed until his knuckles returned to normal size and the left side of his rib cage didn't cause him pain every time he twisted suddenly.

He took another drink. Hearing a step, he turned and saw Melody come out of the office. She joined him on the bench and leaned back against the office wall. Taking one of his swollen hands in both of hers, she drew it to her mouth and kissed it. The warmth and softness of her lips was like a jolt of lightning through his healing body. But he decided not to let it show. Now was not the time for a deeper involvement.

So intent was he on ways to try and get Melody to look on him less romantically, that he didn't realize he was being observed from a stand of pines some fifty feet across the yard.

21

A PAIR OF fierce black eyes in the shadowed trees took in the scene on the bench in front of the Northguard Freight Company office. *Her* Lassiter, sharing a bench with that honey-headed girl. Oh, the girl was pretty enough, Roma supposed. But she hated her with all the passion of her Romany heritage.

At her elbow, Rex said softly, "Well, now you know. So let's get back to town and be on our way to new fields."

Roma mounted her horse and spurred it in the direction of Bluegate, her hair streaming out behind like black silk. Only when she finally slowed the sweated mount was Rex able to catch up to her.

"I warned you long ago not to let your affections for that Lassiter get to the boiling point," Rex said, mopping his aristocratic features with a handkerchief.

"It is why he came back here. Because of that female. It is why he refused to let me come with him. Because of her. I see it all now."

"Doc says we might work our way East. Possibly clear to the big river. It will do you good to get away from memories of Lassiter. Perhaps at long last you might look on me with favor." He gave a wry smile and she laughed outright. He looked hurt.

When they finally arrived back in town, she told Doc that she was staying behind. He and Rex would have to go ahead without her. Both men were surprised and disappointed. But she was adamant.

She was remembering the handsome man with dark red hair who had told her in so many words that he was Lassiter's sworn enemy.

"Two sworn enemies are better than one."

Rex looked at her in surprise and Doc, who was smoking a cheroot beside the wagon, said, "What did you say about sworn enemies?"

"It's from an old gypsy poem," Roma snapped, not wishing to discuss the matter. Her emotions were too obvious; she had spoken of enemies without even realizing it.

Well, Lassiter would one day soon learn that he couldn't put his bootheel in Roma's face and not expect her to show her claws. She smiled into the darkness. The town was quieting down after the big day. Many wagons were still rumbling out of town.

Farrell also often thought of the girl he

had seen in the crowd at the warehouse on the day of the fight.

He remembered standing by one of the warehouse walls, his mouth dry as he saw Lassiter riding out of town, sharing a horse with Melody Vanderson. How he longed to put a bullet into that insufferable black-haired bastard and knock him out of the saddle. Do the job that Blackshear and Marsh had bungled. But there were too many witnesses, men shouting Lassiter's name as the black horse stepped along the road to Aspen City. A look of awe on many faces as if Lassiter might have been a Greek god. The damn fools.

No, he couldn't risk a bullet in the face of such idolatry. In his present mood, every nerve raw, he might by mistake hit the girl.

When he let a long-held breath slowly out of his lungs, he realized a girl standing nearby was also shouting Lassiter's name. But in a different way than the others, who were cheering him. She seemed almost anguished in an attempt to get him to notice her.

When Lassiter failed to respond, he recalled the anger in her black eyes, the way the attractive mouth tightened and her back arched. Even then he had thought her pretty and seeing her later, his assessment deepened. She was truly beautiful, with a proud carriage that revealed every swell and dip of her splendid figure. She wore a pair of boy's Levis and a shirt, the ends knotted about her slim waist, the material so tight across her breasts he could see the nipples. Sight of her stirred a volcanic heat that soon encompassed every centimeter of his body.

He decided to be blunt, so he caught up with her and said, "You dislike him."

Her head snapped around and she peered up with those incredible black eyes. "What did you say?"

Her voice rang cool and clear. Somehow it stirred him even more. "Lassiter, I mean. You hate him."

"How do you know that?"

"There's enough fire in your eyes to singe a mountain."

"Hah! Real fire you have not seen."

"Burn him! Maybe the two of us . . ."

But she turned on her heel and lost herself on the crowded walk. He saw her later, her walk stately, the long black hair hanging below her waist and swaying at each step. The march of her hips in the blue canvas skin of the Levis prodded his heartbeat.

In her he sensed a spark that could lead to a conflagration.

Sight of the brawny Shanagan on the walk stirred up other emotions in him. He stalked over to where the saloonman was talking with Loland of the Mercantile and Bishop of the saddle shop.

The two merchants, facing Farrell, saw the fury on his face and backed away. Shanagan turned to see who was coming and the merchants lost themselves in the crowd.

Farrell said, "I thought you claimed Blackshear and Marsh were top men."

"It was you picked 'em, Farrell," Shanagan said levelly.

The response caught Farrell by surprise. He had expected the saloonman to fawn and make excuses. Don't go off half-cocked, he warned himself, just because of today's disaster.

Somehow he forced a smile. "Well, I guess it was a time of mistakes all around."

"Lassiter's been jumped by more'n one man before today. He knows how to take on a pair of roughnecks."

"So it would seem," Farrell said.

"I didn't like you tryin' to lay the blame on me."

Careful, Farrell warned himself again

258

when he wiped the moist palm of his right hand across a vest and let his fingers slide toward the gun worn under his coat. He stilled the hand, withdrew it. Shanagan wore a tight smile, as if guessing.

And right there Farrell vowed that one day soon there would be a new sign above the saloon door, his name instead of Shanagan's.

Shanagan watched him lift both hands to his hat as if it seemed suddenly important to have it set straight on his head. He made the adjustment, then lowered his arms. The danger point was past. Farrell had himself under control once again.

Later, Farrell saw the mystery girl again. She was talking to an English-looking dude and an older man. The two men walked toward the center of town, leaving her alone at a small camp.

Farrell walked over. Removing his hat, he introduced himself. "May I buy a bottle of that elixir?" He pointed at a box of bottles.

"Doc isn't here," she said, turning to study him.

"You can sell me one," he said with an easy smile.

"It's mostly whiskey. It'll make you feel good and forget whatever is troubling you."

"Nothing troubles me . . . except the burr

in my blanket in the person of a man known as Lassiter."

He saw with satisfaction that mention of the name caused her to jump as if he had jabbed her with a pin. He thought that perhaps she was over her anger. But not so.

"What about Lassiter?" she demanded. Her voice was softly accented, but for the life of him he couldn't decide what her primary language might be.

"He's my enemy. As he seems to be yours."

"You a mind reader? How do you know so much?"

He reminded her of the crowd at the warehouse the day before. "I saw you call to him. I saw the way he ignored you."

A faint flush began to spread across her high cheek bones, while the ends of her generous mouth curled, and lightning seemed to flicker in her black eyes. "You see too damn much," she snapped.

Farrell laughed, then grew serious. "Between the two of us we might bring him down."

She suddenly seemed indifferent, but he sensed it was just a pose. "I don't want to bring him down," she said. "I just don't want to hear his name."

"Not jealous of that fetching blonde?"

Roma's lip curled. "Pale women have no fire. He'll find that out soon enough." She was staring across the flats where a team and wagon were rumbling out of town. "No doubt he has already found out."

"May I buy you some supper?"

Her head swiveled around, the eyes narrowed. "I am not hungry."

"But you must eat. In order to keep your health. And not lose that splendid figure."

"You notice that I look splendid, eh? Apparently he does not."

"He's got the blonde on his mind," Farrell said, playing his cards carefully. Don't move too fast, he cautioned himself. "She's Melody Vanderson."

"He's known her for . . . for how long you think?"

"Since she was a kid. That's what they say around here."

"So he's had her all the time." Roma thought about Farrell's proposition. "So you want to buy me supper, eh? Well, perhaps."

"It might be upsetting if he saw us together."

"So you *do* read minds." A faint smile touched her lips, then was gone.

"It would be more than upsetting if he

saw two of his sworn enemies enjoying themselves together. The collaboration might worry him."

"The collab . . . ?" She broke off, staring up into his face.

"It means he'll think we've joined forces."

"But we haven't," she said bluntly.

And she went into a tent and lowered the flaps.

There was something about her that fired the blood and he'd be damned if he'd give up so easily. He talked with her through the wall of the tent. At first she refused to answer him, then finally she stepped outside again.

"Where has he gone with the female with the honey hair?" Roma demanded thinly.

Farrell told her about the Northguard headquarters at the foot of the mountains. "It's quite a ride."

"How do I find this place, mister?"

"Farrell's the name. Kane Farrell." On the cool midmorning he told her to follow the west road out of town to a junction where a sign would point to Aspen City. "When you get back, we'll have that supper after all?"

She didn't reply.

But half an hour later, he saw her ride out of town with the English-looking dude she'd been with before, heading in the general direction of Aspen City.

22

ALTHOUGH HE KNEW he should take more time to recuperate from the savage brawl earlier in the week, Lassiter was determined to pick up another load of freight for the Bitterroot Mining Company. Word had come through that another sizeable cargo had arrived at Montclair.

Lassiter got word to his crew. Some had taken on other jobs, so he had three men to replace. This was quickly done.

"I'm going with you," Melody said firmly. But Lassiter shook his head.

"It's no place for a woman." And the moment he opened his mouth, he realized it was the worst thing he could have said. He blamed it on the various pains still scattered throughout his body. "I'm not thinking straight," he said quickly. "What I really meant was that you should stay here. Uncle Herm might show up at any time."

They had both written him, urging extrication from the morass that seemed to be trapping him down in Rimrock. To come north and take his rightful place as head of Northguard Freight Company.

Lassiter forced a smile. "After all Herm's been through, he certainly deserves to be met."

Melody's gray eyes were thoughtful as she studied his face. Then she shrugged and said, "I . . . I suppose you're right."

Lassiter breathed easier. At least he had sidestepped that small crisis.

As before, half the inhabitants of Aspen Creek came out in the cold spring dawn to see them off.

"Good luck, Lassiter," Dad Hornbeck called, and Lassiter lifted a hand to the old man who was staying behind to watch out for Melody.

Although she seemed sincere when saying her marriage was over, there was no telling what Vanderson might try in order to get back in her good graces. Not that he would make it, but he might resort to mischief in order to achieve his own ends. From what Lassiter had heard, no one had seen Vanderson since the day of the fight. Hornbeck suggested he might have returned to Denver. But Lassiter was dubious.

"Keep your eye open for him, Dad," Lassiter had told the old man. "If he gives you trouble, shoot him."

He knew how persuasive Vanderson could be with women. Melody might weaken under pressure. He really didn't know her all that well.

While Lassiter was leading his wagons north to Montclair, Vance Vanderson finally summoned nerve enough to try to see Melody. Watching for his chance, he saw her leave the office and start in the direction of the Aspen City store. She did make a fetching picture in the bright morning, wearing a brown dress, her hair done up to make her look regal. Just seeing her at a distance put an ache in him.

He hurried ahead through some pines and when she neared the store, he stepped into plain sight.

She came to an abrupt halt, her face losing color. "Vance," she said, anger tightening her voice.

"Honey, let me explain about the other day . . ."

"Keep away from me, Vance. I mean it!"

"It was all a damned mistake and if you'll just give me five minutes, I can explain everything . . ."

Something jabbed him in the spine. With-

265

out turning his head, he knew it was a gun barrel. He looked over his shoulder. Dad Hornbeck stood at his back, the wrinkled face taut with anger. He jabbed again with the rifle so hard this time that Vanderson took a few stumbling steps forward.

"Get outa here, Vanderson," the old man ordered. "You come around here again an' it's where you'll end up in a grave."

"Listen, Melody, tell him to back away, that I'm your husband and have the law on my side . . ." Vanderson was pleading because the old man seemed nervous enough to actually pull the trigger.

"You heard him, Vance, get out!" she demanded. "You know Lassiter's not here. Otherwise you wouldn't have tried this."

Although Vanderson argued and threatened, there was Melody with her blazing eyes and the old man with the rifle. It came to him like a bucket of cold water that his charm was going to fail him this time.

He tried once more, however, removing his hat so she could see the bandage on his head. "Where you hit me," he accused. "Seems to me you owe me some consideration . . ."

Melody's laughter cut like a knife. She

stepped around him and continued her walk to the store.

Some men had come out of the saloon to stand at Hornbeck's side. They glared at Vanderson. At last he knew it was too risky to remain in Aspen City, so he mounted his horse and rode out.

It was only shortly past noon when he reached Farrell's house in Bluegate. Farrell answered his knock, the green eyes boring into Vanderson's face.

"What the hell do you want?" Farrell demanded.

"First time I've felt like myself. I . . . I've been in agony. She tried to kill me and bashed my head . . ."

Farrell snorted in disgust. "Blanche said you probably got tricked by the oldest promise in history. Your wife's promise to let you go to bed with her."

The truth of it colored Vanderson's face. He removed his hat and bent over so Farrell could see the bandage. "Doc said it's a wonder she didn't beat my brains out."

"If you have any to beat out, which I doubt."

It was then that Vanderson became aware of the stunning dark-haired female who had come gliding into the parlor and now stood some distance away, watching them. Her black hair was slicked back to give the silver hoops at her earlobes more prominence. She wore a ruffled white blouse and a dark skirt with a wide yellow belt.

A real beauty, Vanderson saw at a glance.

Farrell noticed the direction of his glance. "As you can see, I'm busy."

"How I envy you being busy with that," Vanderson said under his breath, hoping to please Farrell.

"Be back in a minute, Roma," Farrell called, then he pushed Vanderson down the veranda steps and halted beside the man's buckskin horse. "Next time I give you a job to do, can you follow orders?"

Vanderson gave a tremulous smile, so great was his relief not to be completely shunned by Farrell. "Of course I can . . ."

"The new job I'm offering you is simple enough. Kill Lassiter."

Farrell had spoken so softly that Vanderson hadn't heard it at first. But then it sank in quickly like a knife blade slipped into the gut. "K . . . k . . . kill Lassiter?" he said in a shocked voice.

"You're the man for the job. I'll pay five thousand dollars."

Vanderson had to catch his breath. "Five thousand *dollars?*"

"I knew you'd be impressed." Farrell smiled benevolently, then outlined his proposition in more detail. Vanderson had no stomach for trying to face Lassiter in a gunfight, a fact he sensed Farrell shared.

"Lie in wait with a rifle," Farrell said softly, after a glance at the big house behind him. "Catch him when his back is turned. When I know he's dead, you'll get the money."

Farrell offered his hand to seal the deal. Vanderson seemed satisfied. Five thousand dollars would give him a fresh start. To hell with Melody and her freight line. Farrell would soon grind her under anyway.

When Vanderson had ridden off, Farrell knew he had set a ball rolling today. Either way he would be a winner. If Vanderson did the job, then well and good. Farrell would be rid of his old enemy once and for all.

On the other hand, should Lassiter kill Vanderson in the exchange, which was certainly a possibility, then Farrell intended to use every bit of influence at his command to see that Lassiter ended up on the gallows for murder.

23

BECAUSE HIS FREIGHT outfit moved at a much slower pace than a rider, Lassiter missed Vanderson both times that morning. Once when he was heading for Aspen City and again on the return to Bluegate. But mainly it was because the wagons had to keep to the road, while a horseman could cut across open country and save several miles.

Those who saw Lassiter enter town at the head of his string of wagons that midmorning, were surprised. They had expected he would be in bed from the effects of the savage beating he had suffered at the warehouse.

Those who saw the brutalized body, the ravaged face right after the fight would have bet that he was stumbling along his final trail. Bets were laid in Shanagan's as to whether or not he would survive. Money appeared on the bartop, most of it negative, that Lassiter wouldn't be around at the end of the month. But he was, now stepping into the saloon on his way north with twelve freight wagons and loose mules as replacements for the teams.

A silence spread over the big barroom as

Lassiter stood near the swinging doors, looking the customers over. Wounds on his face were healing and there was no longer a swelling at one eye, only a faint purple tinge to the skin. And he stood upright, not hunched as if in pain.

A few men ventured nods.

Shanagan, who had been writing figures in a ledger at the bar, looked up when there was a sudden cessation of talk. For a moment worry was stamped on the meaty face, then a tight smile slid across the mouth. He set out a bottle and glass.

"Drink all you want, Lassiter," Shanagan said after clearing his throat. "It's on the house."

Lassiter poured himself a drink and laid down a coin. He flicked his gaze over the dozen or so customers as the silence continued. He drank his whiskey, then spoke to Shanagan.

"Farrell in town?"

"Out at the ranch," Shanagan answered nervously. "Said he's gonna stay till the end of the week."

"Maybe," Lassiter grunted. He looked Shanagan in the eye and nodded at the coin he had laid on the bar. "I've got some change coming."

"But I told you, it's on the house . . ." Something sparked in Lassiter's cold blue eyes. Shanagan hurriedly gave him his change. Lassiter left by the front door.

Lassiter left his men and wagons on the main street near the mercantile and rode up to the stable that Farrell had stolen from Melody. There he received the same answer concerning Farrell as Shanagan had given. It was the same at the warehouse. At both places he was regarded with awe. It was almost as if this time he had really stepped from his grave and it was a ghost they were seeing.

If they had ever seen a man beaten half to death, it was Lassiter. Yet here he was a few days later, acting as if he'd suffered no more than a few bee stings.

He rode on up to Farrell's house where the only one around seemed to be Sam Dunsten, formerly a swamper at the saloon when it was known as Dixie's. Hunched and spindly legged, with the ends of gray hair shooting out from beneath an old hat, he was sweeping off the veranda. He stood frozen as Lassiter came riding up.

As with others encountered that day, the look on Lassiter's face caused him to lose color. Lassiter asked his question and received the same answer. Farrell was out at his Twin Horn ranch.

"Who's in the house?" Lassiter asked.

Dunsten seemed embarrassed. "Only a lady."

"Nobody else? No Farrell?"

"He left for the ranch early on this mawnin', like I said."

"I've got a message for Farrell. You get word to him that I said to stop playing games behind a woman's skirts, as he tried to do with Mrs. Vanderson. If he's got the guts, let him face up to me. He can name the time and place."

"Jeez, I dunno if'n I can remember all that."

Lassiter was about to turn away when Dunsten uttered a sob of terror and flung himself face down on the veranda flooring. Dust rose as the thin old body struck the planks.

But already Lassiter was ramming in the spurs. A gun crashed as the black horse spun away from the veranda at a driving run and pounded toward a corner of the house. A man crouched there, gripping a rifle, a wisp of smoke trailed from the muzzle. He seemed frozen with fear as Lassiter bore down. His face was ashen.

"Lassiter!" The name was a strangled sob from the throat of Vance Vanderson. "I . . . I figured you were a robber about to harm the old man . . ." He let the rifle fall. His mouth jerked in terror as Lassiter struck the ground in a running dismount, .44 in hand, the hammer eared back.

Seeing the younger man paralyzed with fear, Lassiter holstered the weapon. With a look of disgust, he snatched up the fallen rifle, looked around until spotting a slab of granite projecting from the ground some two feet or so. He stalked over, beat the rifle on the rock until the stock was shattered, then he threw it into some pines adjoining the house.

"You miserable bastard," Lassiter said through his teeth as he turned back to the trembling Vanderson.

Twice he backhanded Vanderson across the face and each time his head snapped back from force of the blows. "That's for what you did to your wife." Lassiter's lips twisted as he saw tears start to spread over the cheeks reddened from the backhands.

"Get out of Bluegate," Lassiter said savagely. "Don't let me see you again."

Something moved at a window curtain. Lassiter stiffened, dropped a hand to his gun. He had an impression of dark eyes at the lace curtain, but couldn't match a face to the eyes because of reflected sunlight on the window glass. Then the image vanished.

Turning back to Vanderson, he jerked the .45 from his holster, unloaded it, hurled the shells into the trees. Then he beat the gun sharply on the slab of stone, knocking off the hammer.

"Remember what I said, Vanderson." Lassiter rode away.

From a narrow window, Roma watched Lassiter leave. She had been tempted to call out to him, but the old flame of jealousy burned too brightly for that. He had turned from her after all she had done for him. All because of that hank of golden hair, as Kane Farrell contemptuously referred to Melody Vanderson.

She was still in bed when the gunshot had awakened her. She rushed to a side window in time to see Lassiter savagely backhanding a slender younger man.

Through the window she had seen Lassiter's face and almost melted at sight of the cuts and abrasions that were not yet fully healed. An almost maternal instinct welled up in her to nurse him again, as she had during the long weeks he was recovering from the bullet wound in the back.

But when she took a second look and saw the way his mouth was twisted and the savagery in his eyes, she backed away from the window. At first, she couldn't quite believe the things Kane Farrell said about him. But now she wondered if at heart Lassiter wasn't a killer, with no regard for fellow humans, men or women.

Farrell had left the house early that morning to go out to his ranch. He wanted to get everything set before he took her there, he explained. She guessed his intention was to get rid of traces of any previous female visitors.

If he only knew his previous love life was of no interest to her. The only thing that had drawn them together was a mutual desire to bring Lassiter to his knees.

She longed for the day she'd see him groveling in the dirt. When that happened, she would hunt up her family, make her peace with her father, then marry the member of the gypsy band he had selected to be her husband.

She was tired of running, tired of being disillusioned as she had been with Lassiter. She appreciated what Doc and Rex had done for her, taken her in when she had run away, risking the wrath of her family for giving her shelter.

Now it was time to go back and resume her rightful role in life. But first there was Lassiter. As she had told Farrell sternly, she didn't want Lassiter killed, only humiliated. Forced to beg for mercy.

Farrell had smiled, stroked her cheek and said he agreed.

24

THIS TIME THE Northguard freighters made the long trip to Montclair and the return with a full load without incident. Even Ordway, the railroad rep, did not cause trouble. But he insisted on the transfer of Bitterroot cargo to the wagons be handled through a clerk. He refused to speak to Lassiter. That suited Lassiter just fine.

When he finally arrived back in Aspen City, Melody came flying out from the office to hurl herself into his arms and stand on tiptoe to plant a welcome home kiss on his lips—right in front of everybody.

"Thank God you're safe," she breathed. Then she told him her news. Her Uncle

Herm had finally responded affirmatively to the letters she and Lassiter had written. He was leaving Rimrock and would be in Bluegate toward the end of the month.

When Lassiter read the letter Melody handed him, he said, "It's about time."

Lassiter had good news of his own. In Montclair he had learned that the Black Arrow Mine, above Bluegate, was going to reopen. For Bluegate it would mean jobs and money flowing into the town coffers.

The mine owner, Brad Dingell, had been working around the mine for two years with only a helper or two, hoping to find an extension of the original silver vein that had petered out on the previous owners. He stumbled onto a fresh vein. The deeper it went into the mountain, the broader the vein. There was quite a bit of freight piled up in the Montclair warehouse consigned to Black Arrow. Lassiter wondered why Farrell hadn't gotten wind of it and tried to grab the business.

When Dingell had returned from a fast round trip to Montclair, he waved his assay report under the noses of customers in Shanagan's. Shanagan provided a round of drinks for the house on the strength of the report. Dingell, who seldom came to town, made up for it that evening. He was thirty, with wiry red hair, a much lighter shade of red than Farrell's. Freckles peppered his fair skin.

After two quick drinks he got Shanagan's ear. "Now that I know the mine will prosper, one of the first things I'll be doin' is to be askin' for the hand of Miss Melody."

"*Miss* Melody?" Shanagan said with a lift of brows. "She's a married woman."

Dingell's freckles stood out like coffee grounds flung onto a white tablecloth. "I didn't know," he mumbled. He remembered her fondly when she first came out to visit her Uncle Josh. But since Josh had died he had been so tied up with his mine he hadn't seen her. Shanagan leaned over his bar and spoke quietly.

"Her husband's not much, though. He hangs around here."

"That's sad news you're a tellin' me, mister."

"But they haven't lived together for a spell. Don't reckon they ever will again. At least that's the story."

Dingell brightened. "Well, now, that's different." He had never even introduced himself to the girl, only admired her from afar. He had intended to keep it that way until news of his mine would eventually be positive. "I know that divorce ain't a word people like to hear, but it sure comes in handy at times."

The Bluegate school was holding a dance to raise money for a new room. Tickets were two dollars, three dollars less than for the Roman carnival at the warehouse, which no one mentioned. Men with a bent for carpentry were asked to volunteer. Lumber would be donated by affluent citizens. Money from the sale of tickets would be used for desks and books and odds and ends.

When Melody heard about it, she said they should go. Lassiter was dubious until he got to thinking about the Black Arrow Mine. It was a good bet that Dingell would be there. A chance to talk business with him.

On the evening of the dance, the schoolyard was crowded with rigs of all descriptions. The schoolhouse windows danced with lamplight and the strains of music could be heard.

Lassiter, wearing his black suit, and Melody, in pale green, arrived with some of the Northguard crew. They had the first dance. Melody was light on her feet and seemed to enjoy herself. Lassiter kept his eyes open for

Dingell and finally saw him after a dance was concluded. He came threading his way through the crowd to where Lassiter stood with Melody. Flushing, so that his freckles seemed more prominent than usual, Dingell introduced himself, then boldly asked Melody for a dance. She turned to Lassiter, who said, "By all means. Glad to meet you at last, Dingell," he added enthusiastically. "I've seen you on the street but we've never had a drink. You've been keeping pretty close to your mine, I understand. And speaking of the mine, I'd like to have a talk . . ."

But Dingell was paying no attention. He had eyes only for Melody, who danced away in his arms. They made an attractive couple, Lassiter decided. Dingell was probably five foot ten, with stocky build, but no fat. His checkered suit fit him well. He seemed to be a good dancer. Melody's head was back and she was laughing at something Dingell had said. A good sign, Lassiter thought.

Lassiter stood looking at the crowd of dancers who were enjoying a waltz played by piano, fiddle, and cornet. He saw Edgerton, the banker, dancing with his plump wife. And Loland of the Mercantile with a bony woman. Bishop of the saddle shop danced with Miss Ames, one of the school teachers.

He was aware of a ripple of excitement at the far corner of the room where Kane Farrell had just entered. With him was a stunning brunette—Roma. Hardly a man in the big room could keep his eyes off her ripe figure in green, the dress a darker shade than the one Melody wore. He saw her eyes dart about as if searching for someone. Finally they settled on him. He gave her a nod, which she ignored, turned her back on him and hugged Farrell's arm as if to show where her affections lay. The little fool, Lassiter thought. Sight of the arrogant Farrell started all the old hatreds churning.

Although guns were supposed to be checked at the cloakroom door, Lassiter would bet a double eagle against a centavo that Farrell wore a gun under the coat of his splendidly tailored light-tan suit. Lassiter wore his as well, having vowed not to be unarmed when within stinging distance of that human scorpion.

During the evening, Lassiter danced with many of the ladies, twice more with Melody, but mostly she was appropriated by Brad Dingell.

There were occasional outbursts as men

lost their tempers over such subjects as the outcome of the war, how to handle the threat of rustlers or the crooked politicians in Washington.

If fist fights erupted, they were broken up by Bo Dancur and his deputy. Two men were marched off to jail by the deputy; Dancur seemed to be having too good a time with the ladies to bother with the technical side of county business. He silenced one obstreperous male with a pistol barrel across the temple.

Whenever Farrell, with Roma in his arms, danced past Lassiter, his green eyes glowed wickedly and the familiar superior smile was on his lips. If Roma condescended to look at him at all, it was to glare. Lassiter was sorry about that. Her enmity, he assumed, stemmed from the fact he had refused to bring her with him to Bluegate.

When Melody was claimed by Brad Dingell for another dance, Lassiter found Bo Dancur at his elbow. "You know why Farrell hasn't squashed you under his heel?" the sheriff asked slyly.

"Haven't given it one damned thought," Lassiter lied. He saw ladies of marriageable age sizing up the two of them; both eligible bachelors, Dancur, the sheriff, Lassiter of

Northguard Freight Company, an exciting man of mystery. Those who considered Lassiter's reputation to be unsavory, fully expected him to one day finish off Mrs. Vanderson's husband so he could have the lady and the freight line all to himself.

Those who knew Lassiter better would say that one day he'd be gone and Bluegate would never hear of him again unless he just happened to drift through sometime in the future.

"Farrell's let you alone 'cause some folks around here look on you as kind of a hero, for the way you stood up for yourself against Blackshear an' Marsh."

"That so?"

"Otherwise, Farrell would've had you in a box long before this." Dancur gave a faint laugh and walked away.

A full moon showed its yellow disk behind the trees at the far edge of the schoolyard.

Lassiter was determined to have a talk with Dingell about giving Northguard a contract for hauling Black Arrow silver ore to the stamp mill being built at Montclair. So far, the miner had been so engrossed with Melody, he hadn't had a chance.

As this was going through his mind he saw Farrell, at a far corner of the room in earnest conversation with Vanderson. He saw Farrell place a hand on Vanderson's shoulder and whisper something. Vanderson licked his lips. It seemed to Lassiter that Farrell was asking Vanderson to do something distasteful. Or dangerous.

Suddenly he felt reckless. If there's anything planned, let's get it over with, he thought.

Lassiter made a great show of going outside to smoke a cigar, standing longer than necessary at the side door, then leisurely going down a short flight of steps to the schoolyard. On the rear of the dancehall there were few windows and only faint lamplight spilled out. Many tall bushes grew next to the building. He heard a soft sound at his back, as he began to stroll. Suddenly he ducked into a shadowy blob of shrubbery.

Vanderson came into view, peering ahead into the darkness. He gave a grunt of surprise as Lassiter stepped out into full view. Faint lamplight shone on the barrel of the gun he held in his right hand.

"Stalking your prey?" Lassiter said softly, and tore the weapon from Vanderson's fingers. But in so doing, the weapon was discharged. The gunshot sent echoes booming

285

across the schoolyard. Inside the music died with a discordant squeal.

Vanderson tried to run, but Lassiter grabbed him.

"You're breaking my arm," Vanderson yelled, as Lassiter twisted his arm up behind his back.

People came pouring from the schoolhouse even before echoes of the gunshot were dying. Melody seemed in a state of shock as she saw Lassiter in the light of a lantern Dancur had snatched up.

"What the hell's goin' on, Lassiter?" the sheriff demanded.

The lantern glow fell over Vanderson's stricken face, as Lassiter held out the revolver for Dancur to see. "A new one," Lassiter pointed out. "Even got his initials on the grips. The other one I took away from him when he tried to shoot me in the back the other day."

In the stunned silence, Vanderson sobbed, "Every time I turn around, you're at my throat. You stole my wife. Now you're trying to kill me . . ."

"Hold it," Lassiter warned. Men were streaming up, faces excited; nothing like a good fight to liven up a school dance. "It's Vanderson's gun out. Not mine."

"You tried to kill me with my own gun."

Lassiter's hard laugh cut through the buzz of voices. Women, throwing on shawls because of the crisp evening air, were crowding out.

"If you got a dollar for every lie you tell," Lassiter said roughly, "you'd be sitting on a hill of gold." What he said next, brought a gasp from the onlookers. Lassiter tightened his grip. "How much is Farrell paying you to bring me down?"

Vanderson's lips fluttered, but Dancur rescued him from having to reply. "There's no cause for you to go accusin' Farrell just because . . ."

"Did I hear my name mentioned?" Farrell sang out jauntily. The crowd parted so he could get through, Roma clinging to his arm. "What's the trouble, Sheriff?"

Dancur looked ill-at-ease, a big man squirming in his black suit, the kind of attire known locally either for "marryin', dancin', or buryin'." "Lassiter claims Vanderson was after him . . ."

"Lies!" Vanderson cried, tears streaming down his face.

Dancur leaned down to smell Vanderson's breath. "You're drunk, that's the main trouble. Go inside an' have one of the ladies pour you a bucket of black coffee." He gave him a shove and Vanderson staggered toward the steps.

What sent a cold rage through Lassiter was Farrell's laughter; the mockery in his green eyes shining in the lantern light. Lassiter handed Vanderson's gun to Dancur.

Lassiter stood tall, thumbs hooked in the wide leather belt with the silver buckle. "Maybe we should settle everything, Farrell!" His voice rang into the star-filled sky. "Get it over with!"

Farrell, a few feet away, stood perfectly still. It seemed no one drew a breath.

A pale Melody put a hand to her mouth and cried, "Lassiter, no! Don't do it!"

But the two men continued to glare at each other.

Roma suddenly leaned into the cone of lanternlight to point at Lassiter's right hand. She had to make two tries to get her voice straightened out. "It's too soon after the fight, Lassiter. You wouldn't stand a chance with Farrell." Managing a trace of scorn in the last of it. "Your poor right hand is swollen."

Farrell looked at her, then back at Lassiter. "A habit of yours, ducking behind a skirt." Turning on his heel, he took Roma's arm and walked her toward the steps.

When Lassiter started to follow, Dancur grabbed him. "I want you to leave this dance. I order you to leave!"

"Wait a minute . . ."

"Folks has come here tonight to have a good time. Not to see somebody get bloodied up . . ."

"Let's go, Lassiter," Melody said urgently. She stood alone, Dingell no longer at her side. He had gone back inside at her urging.

Melody hurried into the schoolhouse to get her coat.

Dancur drew a deep breath. "Had you faced up to Farrell tonight, you'd be layin' there dead."

Lassiter swallowed at the possibility, but he said, "Maybe not."

"Don't like to see you hang around an' pester Mrs. Vanderson. She belongs with her husband, no matter what kind of fella he might be. Ain't no woman in Bluegate ever got a dee-vorce an' we don't want to start. Her an' her husband'll git back together, long as there ain't no temptations. It's you I'm talkin' about, Lassiter."

"One thing she doesn't deserve is to have to live out her days with Vance Vanderson."

"I tell you this, Lassiter. Any twelve men in this county would vote a hangrope for anybody that would kill a man just to git to his wife."

"Who's been filling your head with this kind of mule shidd? Farrell?"

Dancur reddened in the lantern light. "Not Farrell or anybody else. Just statin' facts. Now if you'll oblige by leavin' the dance so that there won't be no more trouble . . ."

But Lassiter had walked away. Tension was beginning to drain as he went to get the wagon. Tonight he had tempted fate by boldly walking outside when he sensed Vanderson might be gunning for him. A stupid move on his part. He'd let anger and frustration sway his better judgement.

Those of the Northguard crew who had come with them, rode behind the buckboard Lassiter was driving so Melody wouldn't have to eat dust. A perfect night for an ambush, Lassiter was thinking. He drove with rifle within reach, but nothing happened.

When they got home, Melody said she was too wound up to sleep. She wanted to talk. Lassiter sat with her at the big table in the office and sipped the fresh coffee she had quickly made.

"That trouble between you and Vance tonight," she said, putting down her cup. "I wish he'd go away. And stay away."

"Seems he won't."

"He's such a fool. I've told him I want nothing more to do with him."

"Farrell's got him under his heel."

"For what reason?" Then her gray eyes widened. "Or is it true, the ugly rumor I overheard tonight."

"Don't listen to rumors, ugly or otherwise . . ."

"A rumor that he has been promised a large sum of money to . . . to eliminate someone. Could that someone possibly be you?" She ended in a gasp.

"I told you, don't listen to things like that. It's just talk. Nothing else." She had enough on her mind already without adding worry for him to the burden.

"You take it all so lightly. You're even smiling." She leaned across the table to study him in the lamplight. A piece of kindling popped in the stove where she had heated the coffee.

"I just don't want you to get yourself upset. I can take care of myself. I've been doing it for a spell, you know."

To change the subject, he asked about her girlhood. Her eyes suddenly had a distant look. "My mother denied me few things after my father died. She spoiled me terribly. But since she's been gone, I've adjusted. More or less."

"Tell me about yourself. You speak well, so you've had some education."

"Not much. But I had access to many books when I was growing up. What I read soaked into me, I guess."

They talked on. It was long past midnight. A faint breeze whistled through a crack in the wall. He finally got the subject swung back to Northguard. Mainly to the Black Arrow Mine above Bluegate.

"I planned to have a talk with Dingell tonight about us getting a freight contract. But that damned sheriff . . ." Lassiter's lips tightened. "Oh, never mind."

"I suppose it had something to do with your trouble with Vance."

"A little," Lassiter admitted, but didn't go into detail. He stood up. "I've got to get to bed. I've got to get up early to take a load up to High Pass.

"But tomorrow is Sunday. You can stay

in bed." She reached over and clasped his hands in hers. "Don't leave me tonight," she whispered hoarsely.

"I'll be within shouting distance if you need me."

"I want you closer than that. I want you . . . with me."

He debated. Her Uncle Herm was probably on his way. And that meant that Lassiter, drifter, seeker of new horizons, would be out of her life. So why not? he asked himself.

"I won't leave you tonight," he whispered.

"I swear my legs are made of India Rubber," she said with a shaky laugh. "You'll have to carry me into the bedroom."

He did, kicking the door shut behind him, lowering her gently to the bed.

"So much more comfort than that night under the wagon up on the mountain," she said with a catch in her voice. "But I loved every minute of it."

"So did I." He went out and got the lamp and brought it into the bedroom. This time he locked the door, sat down and pulled off his boots.

"Take off my shoes for me, will you, Las-

293

siter?" She lay spraddle-legged on the bed, her golden head turned on the pillow.

He did as she asked, then she whispered, "Now my stockings, my petticoat . . ."

His fingers flew to do her bidding, warm against her flesh. But he needed no further directions and in a space of seconds she lay gleaming upon the bed.

25

AT BREAKFAST MONDAY morning he told her they should leave for Dingell's Black Arrow Mine. "If we move fast, we might grab a contract to haul his ore to Montclair. . . ."

"But isn't it closer to Bitterroot? They're building a smelter and stamp mill and I've heard they're going to accept outside business."

"Closer, but steeper. I've been figuring the costs. We can freight Dingell's ore for nearly half of what it would cost him to make the haul into the mountains."

He offered more details that he had worked out over the weekend. Then he suggested she don her prettiest dress for the visit to Dingell's mine.

"You just want to show me off," she said with a dimpled smile.

"A lot to show off, believe me." he kissed her lightly, which caused her to blush.

"But only you will ever see what I've really got to show off." A new wickedness flashed into her gray eyes and she laughed and hugged his arm. "Oh, Lassiter, you've been so good for me."

"You sew up that Dingell contract and it'll please your Uncle Herm when he gets here. . . ."

"If he ever does." Her face fell. She looked up into Lassiter's dark face, at the abrasions that were nearly gone, the lips that had been so horribly mashed but were now almost back to normal. He'd have scars from the historic brawl to carry to his grave, but those that showed were minor. "I could never make it without you, Lassiter," she said fervently.

Her words made him feel uncomfortable, for they alluded to a long-time commitment.

Lassiter went to get the buckboard. The light wagon that Vanderson had used the day he took Melody to Bluegate had never been returned. By now he had probably sold it.

They started out on a warm morning, Melody wearing a light coat over a yellow dress to keep off the dust. Set squarely on her pinned-up golden hair was a bonnet with a small feather that was only a slightly darker shade than her dress.

In the war, Bert Oliver had ridden shotgun for a mail wagon in the Confederate Army, but today he was doing it for the couple in the Northguard buckboard.

Mostly that morning on the long drive, Melody talked of plans for the future, her voice warm. She hoped they could take some of the money from the Dingell business, if they were lucky enough to get it, and build a house at Aspen Creek.

"Better yet," Lassiter cut in coldly, "take back the house your Uncle Josh built in Bluegate."

"But Farrell owns it now," she exclaimed, turning in the wagon seat to squint at him against the sun.

"Farrell stole it, you mean."

She gave a little sigh and threw the coat off her shoulders, for the day was warming. She pushed up the sleeves of the dress. Her forearms were smooth and round. When he thought of them crossed at his back, he grew tense. The road here cut through a heavy stand of pines like a twisting snake, to avoid outcroppings and the shoulders of the many hills. Off the road there was plenty of seclusion. The back of his neck grew warm when thinking of them together in the shade of those tall pines. If only Bert Oliver wasn't plodding along behind the wagon on his gray horse. Well, it was his own fault for insisting the southerner accompany them. He had wanted someone at his back in case they ran into trouble. And it was just as well, he reminded himself as he began to calm. One less memory for them both to digest before the inevitable parting.

Soon they were approaching the road that led to Dingell's mine that dead ended at the big warehouse Josh Falconer had built and which was now owned by Farrell. Melody must have been thinking of it because she spoke of the hectic period when Lassiter was presumed to be in his grave.

"Farrell kept putting papers in front of me and I foolishly signed my name," she said, a note of despondency in her voice. "But I trusted him," Her voice tightened. "I hadn't realized what a snake he is."

"And with Vance Vanderson buzzing in your ear it only made the world even more confusing."

"Don't you worry about him, my darling." She gripped his right wrist with her two hands. She had surprisingly strong fingers for one so young. "I intend to divorce him. And I don't care if every woman in the county snubs me because of it. I can hold my head up with you at my side."

He made a left turn where the Black Arrow Mine road ended only forty feet or so from the north wall of the warehouse. Glancing at the sprawling structure, Lassiter found it hard to imagine it jammed with a blood-thirsty crowd, most of whom had come to see a battle to the death. Even he had to admit that with two men against one, it was a miracle he had survived.

The mine road began to climb abruptly. It was narrow and straight as a string up the mountain, to where the mine was a mere dot in the distance.

A hundred yards from the warehouse, a creek that paralleled the road all the way from the mine, made a sweeping right angle to drop over a low granite cliff and spill into a narrow valley.

From what he had heard, Lassiter could believe that cloudbursts in the mountains above the mine could turn the creek as well as the road itself into a raging river. He was beginning to see evidence of the last storm that had washed around large rocks to expose them for as much as ten inches in places above the normal roadbed. It made the uphill climb even harder. Shod hooves and wheel rims clattered over the stretches of bare rock.

"You coming all right, Bert?" Lassiter called back.

"The road to hell couldn't be much worse'n this one."

"This road'll be rough on the wagons," Lassiter mused as the buckboard wheels dipped into the wide depression dug by the creek where it made its sweeping turn. Wheels rattled over rocks and dripped water as he urged the team up a steep bank and onto the road once again. At times the buckboard tilted sickeningly when encountering a higher ledge of exposed stone. Melody hung on gamely to a seat brace and did not cry out.

At last they reached the mine entrance. Lassiter hopped down and helped Melody out of the wagon. She kept her face close to his, her feet swinging in the air as he spun her around and set her down.

"On the way back," she whispered. "Oh, if Bert Oliver wasn't along." She gave him a wicked smile.

Lassiter tied the team to a stump near the

edge of a great pile of tailings. Oliver dismounted and stretched his long bony arms. "You go ahead," he said. "I'll water the hosses."

Taking Melody's hand, Lassiter climbed with her up a path through the tailings and to a long platform, the length of two freight wagons. Just down from the mine tunnel was a rather large lean-to built against the side of the mountain. Lassiter walked down, but there was no one inside.

It took five minutes or so, calling into the maw of the mine tunnel before Brad Dingell finally shouted, "Coming," his voice faint in the distance.

While waiting for Dingell to appear, they looked around. From this elevation, Bluegate, spread out below, looked like a child's miniature city. The people scurrying about were mere dots. Smoke from many chimneys spread a faint haze over the diminutive buildings.

"Looks like an ant hill from here," Melody said.

"Remember your speech now," Lassiter reminded. "I'll let you handle everything." They had gone over what she was supposed to say to Dingell.

"But I want you to help me. . . ."

300

"Show Dingell how smart you are. I think it's important."

"But why?. . ."

"There's enough sour talk about a woman running a freight line. Show 'em you can do it, Melody."

By then they could hear Dingell's footsteps echoing from the tunnel.

When Dingell appeared and saw Melody, he flushed with embarrassment at his appearance. He wore work clothes and he needed a shave. A smudge of dirt was on one cheek.

"If I'd known a pretty lady was calling on me I'd have spruced up." He and Lassiter shook hands. "Where'd you two disappear to at the dance?"

"We had a long ride ahead of us," was all Lassiter said on the subject.

"Reckon you're here about the freight contract," he said slyly.

"Melody Vanderson has all the details," Lassiter said.

"If I may be so bold as to compliment you, ma'am, that's a purty dress. Mighty purty."

Melody thanked him, flushing slightly at the compliment.

"I'd ask you inside," Dingell waved a

301

square hand toward the lean-to. "But it's a boar's nest."

"Bachelor quarters usually are," Melody said with a warm smile.

Dingell laughed. He was shorter than Lassiter by an inch, with broad shoulders and sturdy legs. He wore high-laced miner's boots.

Under an overhang was a table and benches where Dingell took his meals when the weather was decent, as he put it. They sat in the shade. For a few moments Melody seemed ill-at-ease until Lassiter gave her a nudge. Then she handed Dingell a sheet of paper with their estimate of costs to haul the Black Arrow ore up to the stamp mill at Montclair. In a clear voice she explained how it would be cheaper than using the closer but steeper route to the Bitterroot Mine.

He scanned the paper, but seemed more interested in Melody than the figures she had presented. Lassiter was faintly amused because Dingell was so obviously taken with Melody. Well, why not? he asked himself. And Melody apparently found him pleasant. In talking, they found they had something in common, for Dingell had lived in Westport, where Melody had and her mother had lived for a time.

"You've got a good head on your shoulders for a female," Dingell said, "Not meanin' any disrespect," he added quickly. "But most of 'em kinda light in the head. Ain't that so, Lassiter?"

But Lassiter only spread his hands; they could take from that any answer they wanted.

Dingell insisted on fixing them a noon meal. Melody was agreeable. She seemed to be enjoying herself in the clear air, with the splendid view of Bluegate at the foot of the mountain. Lassiter called Bert Oliver to join them. He and Dingell shook hands.

Dingell got a chunk of roast beef from a root cellar, sharpened a knife and sliced enough meat for sandwiches, then sliced what was left of a loaf of bread. Melody pitched in to help. She seemed relaxed around Dingell, which Lassiter took as a good sign.

As they ate, Lassiter spoke of the mine road. "When the weather's bad, there'll be no chance to get wagons up here."

"Tell you how I figure to fix that. I got ore cars and tracks in the warehouse up at Montclair. You fetch the load for me. Then I'll figure the right grade for a narrow guage like they use in all mines. I'll put tracks on that hill yonder." He gestured to the left of the mine tunnel where the mountain made a gradual descent to the valley floor. "I'll figure the grade just right so I can use switchbacks all the way down. The cars can drop their load of ore at the bottom where you can pick it up."

Lassiter said it sounded like a good idea.

"I've had some experience surveying," Dingell went on, "so I'll lay out the tracks. They've got to be at just the right grade so they don't get loose an' make the cars derail."

"How will you get the empty cars back to the mine?" Melody asked.

"A good question," Dingell said approvingly. Each empty car would be brought back to the top by sheer manpower at the end of a long cable. "That is until I can get steam to turn a pulley. Main thing I'll need is a boiler. You can haul that for me, too, Lassiter. There's one for sale at Montclair and I'll arrange to buy it by mail. Had a look at it last time I was up. If it isn't sold, it's a deal."

"We'll make it up the mountain with the wagons," Lassiter said, "until you can get tracks laid."

"Shouldn't take more'n a few weeks."

They agreed that Northguard would pick up ore cars, tracks, and the boiler at Montclair, plus pulleys and cable. Lassiter estimated he could do the job with two wagons.

A contract, which they all signed, was drawn up at the table.

As they started back down the mountain, Melody was elated. "We did it, Lassiter."

"You mean you did," he said with a grin.

"Don't be silly. You did most of it."

He wanted to change the subject. "I hope he's enough of an engineer to figure out how to get those empty cars back up the mountain by cable. The switchbacks and all . . ."

"Seems to me he's quite a remarkable man. . . ."

26

LASSITER WAS A little surprised to find a new railroad rep at Montclair. Ordway, the one who had tried to get Blackshear to arrest him, was gone. The new man was Regis Boshar, a husky mustached man of middle age.

"We hope to do a lot of business with you, Lassiter."

"Business with Northguard you mean," Lassiter said with a smile as they shook hands. "I'm only a small cog in the gears of the freight line."

Roustabouts from the warehouse helped load the cargo of steel rails, ore cars, and an ungainly mass of metal that was the steam boiler. In addition there was what seemed like miles of cable, and boxes and boxes of pulleys of all sizes. Plus the hardware needed to attach them to the many posts that would be needed for the long haul from the lower level up to the mine.

On the return trip to Bluegate, Lassiter was constantly on his guard, riding his black horse ahead for a mile or so, then scouting their back trail. But nothing happened. He was as edgy as he had been on the last haul to Bitterroot. But nothing had happened on that trip, despite his worry and vigilance. And when they were within five miles or so of Bluegate, he decided this trek would be equally uneventful.

It was a clear day, the sun warm. Birds chattered in a thick grove of aspen that bordered each side of the road. Lassiter was riding twenty yards ahead of the lead wagon that Bert Oliver was driving. Sharing the seat with him was a swamper named Sid Hooper. The following wagon contained Alex Holmes and Steve Baronski. All good men that Lassiter felt he could depend on.

Without warning there were rebel yells from the east side of the road and the sudden thunder of hoofbeats. A bunch of horses suddenly spurred into violent movement from a standstill.

He barely had time to yank free his Henry rifle when riders swooped out of the woods. No Indian charge in history was more deadly than this. There were eight of them, firing from the backs of hard-running horses. Bullets peppered the sides of the lead wagon; the second wagon was being used as a flat bed to accommodate the bulky steam boiler. Bullets whanged into its metal sides and ricocheted. Rifle bullets threw gouts of dust into the air only an arm's length from the forefeet of Lassiter's plunging black horse as he swung the animal, at full gallop, into a widening curve.

Lassiter was firing back as were his men from the halted wagons. He felt a twinge of agony as Ed Kiley, in the lead of the attackers, knocked Sid Hooper tumbling from the lead wagon. Rolling to the center of the road where he lay still. Oliver was firing a rifle as fast as he could work the loading lever.

But it was Lassiter, closing fast on the

hard-riding Kiley, who had the best chance of avenging the crumpled Hooper, now bleeding in the dust.

Kiley, mounted on a big gray, tried to ram Lassiter's smaller horse. But Lassiter's superior horsemanship enabled his mount to evade the hard-driving gray. Turned as he was in the saddle, Lassiter felt something twitch the short hairs at the nape of his neck. A bullet from Kiley's rifle had come that close to causing disaster for Lassiter. A split-second later came the roar of the big .50 caliber Sharps he was carrying.

"Damn near gotcha!" Kiley yelled with a grin.

Lassiter twisted in the saddle, swung back as Kiley was checking the speed of his gray horse. Around them was the sound of battle, the incessant rattle of rifle fire, yells, screams.

Holding his rifle in one hand, Lassiter fired it like a pistol. Kiley, turning back, lost his grin. It was replaced by a spurt of blood as the bullet took out his front teeth and a portion of his skull, just above the back of the neck. He plunged from the horse in a loose-limbed roll, still holding onto the rifle as he struck the roadway, the barrel somehow tripping up the galloping gray horse, bringing it down. Above the roar of weapons came a clear, snapping sound as of a stick breaking. The gray's neck snapped as it plunged to earth, the head twisted at an unusual angle. The left front wheel of Oliver's wagon was less than inches from Kiley's ruined skull. Everything had happened in the space of time no longer than it takes for a man to draw three good breaths.

Out of the trees came the bearded Art Blackshear. Not on a horse but on solid ground, for better marksmanship than from the saddle of a plunging mount. His horse was running back into the trees.

A bullet blew a faint breath against Lassiter's right cheek as he jerked his head around. He saw the stock of a Winchester tucked against Blackshear's hairy cheek. Knowing he was too vulnerable against a marksman with bootheels anchored firmly on Mother Earth, he quit the saddle. He slid a few feet on his knees in deep grass as momentum carried him into a patch of wild flowers. Bullets flung bits of petals and stems into the air.

"Stay still, so's I can bust one into your gut!" Blackshear yelled. He was a little over ten feet away, teeth bared through the heavy beard. Before he could shift his position to cover up the fast-moving target, Lassiter shot him twice. Blackshear came up suddenly on his toes, eyes in the bearded face looking blank. He leaned far forward as if to kiss the ground. Which he did, literally, falling onto his face.

Yelling encouragement to his men, Lassiter opened up on the remaining attackers. The remaining three members of his crew had taken cover behind the wagons, their fire so accurate that the attackers began to mill in confusion.

Bert Oliver shot Jody Marsh near the Adam's apple, which sent him tumbling backward off the rump of a roan. He struck the ground, arms and legs flopping as if barely fastened to his body. As he rolled, Oliver shot him a second time through the chest, just to make sure. Another attacker screamed and went down. That settled them. They went pounding back into the aspens that had given them their original cover.

As the sound of hoofbeats began to fade, Lassiter reloaded his Henry rifle. His mouth was dry as he looked down at Ed Kiley, whose blasted skull was nearly under an iron wheel rim of the first wagon. He seized Kiley by the heels and pulled him from under the wagon. It took the four of them to pull the dead gray horse off the road so they could get by.

Lassiter had skinned one knee when he made the fast dismount. He was limping slightly.

Blackshear suddenly regained consciousness and began to scream, rolling about in the road, trying to stem a flow of blood with his two hands. But it trickled through his fingers and down onto his belt buckle.

Marsh was dead, his mouth open. His eyes were also open. One of them was blotched by droppings from panicked birds still circling madly above the trees on either side of the road. A splattering bit of warmth that Marsh had never felt. There was no pity in Lassiter for any of the Farrell men. They had intended to murder his entire crew. As the last of the receding hoofbeats could no longer be heard and Blackshear had ceased to scream, there was a new sound arising in the eerie after-battle stillness.

Lassiter was aware of a wagon approaching from the direction of Bluegate. It was driven by a thinned-down, middle-aged man named Enos Cavendish, who ran a few head of cattle out of town. Beside him was his wife, wearing a sunbonnet, with a face browned from weather and seamed from years of hardship. Five children were standing up in the bed of the farm wagon, peering in awe at the bodies sprawled in the road or adjacent to it.

The fourth casualty and nearest the wagon, was a stranger on his back, arms outstretched as if napping on the fine spring day. A small round hole made a third eye in his forehead.

Lassiter ran down past the corpse, yelling at Cavendish to back the team up and get away, to spare the children the gory sight. But it was Mrs. Cavendish who began to scream, not the children. She pointed a bony finger. But her screeching seemed to be a signal for the children to join in. The sound in the still morning air was so horrendous that Lassiter's men looked at each other worriedly.

Never in his life had Lassiter felt more helpless than he did as the hysterical woman and her frightened children continued screaming.

Lassiter walked up to the halted wagon, arms spread wide from his body, as if that would make the woman and her brood understand. "They jumped us!" Lassiter shouted above the sounds of hysteria.

"A terrible sight for a woman to see!"

Cavendish said shakily. "We heard shootin', but never figured to run into nothin' like this."

Cavendish started to turn his wagon around in the narrow road. When Lassiter tried to help him, the white-faced rancher angrily waved him off.

"You want to blame somebody, blame Farrell!" Lassiter shouted. "They were his men!"

But by then Cavendish had his team at a gallop and he doubted if he was even heard above the pound of hooves and the rattle of wagon wheels. The children, still sobbing, clung to the low sideboards to keep from being thrown out. Soon they were hidden by a bend in the road.

Bert Oliver scrubbed a forearm across his sweated face. "Sets a man's teeth on edge to hear such caterwaulin' from a female an' her passel of younguns."

"She couldn't have lived out here long," said Steve Baronski in his accented voice, "to throw a fit over a few dead men."

"I guess it was seeing five dead that got to her," Lassiter said with a sad shake of the head.

They loaded the four bodies of attackers onto the tailgate of the lead wagon, then wrapped Hooper in a tarp and tied him on top of the load.

By the time they ground slowly up to the sheriff's office, the bodies had been spotted on the tailgate and a crowd had gathered.

The deputy, Rudy Kline, came out of the sheriff's office and gaped at the bodies.

Lassiter said sternly, "I'll pay for my man Hooper to have a decent burial. I don't care a damn what you do with the rest of 'em. Although you might ask Kane Farrell to contribute."

This startled the onlookers as well as the deputy. Rudy Kline had a knob of tobacco in one cheek and almost swallowed it. He fidgeted from one foot to the other as Lassiter and his men unloaded the bodies and placed them along the walk.

Just as Lassiter was about to drive on with Hooper's body, Bo Dancur came striding along the walk. When the overweight sheriff saw the crowd, he quickened his pace. He thrust his way through the circle of silent onlookers and stared at the bodies laid out on the walk.

"How'd it happen?" he demanded, but his meaty face was losing color as he saw that three of the dead were Farrell men, Kiley, Blackshear, and Marsh.

Lassiter told him about the attack five miles out of town, as he had explained to the deputy.

Dancur made no comment when Lassiter had finished, just shoved back his hat and gave a deep sigh. He looked troubled.

Lassiter drove to Miegs' furniture and undertaking establishment. Miegs came out to the alley, rubbing bony hands together as he anticipated business. When Hooper's body was lowered, Miegs said, "He's been shot. The sheriff know about this?"

"He does. I want Hooper to be buried in the graveyard."

"He got kin?"

"I don't know of any. He never talked much."

"It'll cost you twenty-five dollars includin' a plain pine coffin. Oak'll cost you forty."

"Make it pine. I'll spend the difference on some poor family that maybe hasn't had a decent meal in a spell."

"Reckon you're the only fella I've buried, then had a talk with, over six months later, about the price for another funeral." He gave a wry smile and held out his small hand, palm up.

Lassiter dropped two double eagles and a

315

five into his palm. They quickly disappeared into a pocket of his black pants.

Miegs had a helper carry Hooper's body into a shed, and laid out on planks a couple of sawhorses.

"You gonna be here for the services?" Miegs wanted to know.

"I don't know for sure." *I might not even be alive*, he almost added.

With that he mounted and led his wagons slowly to the big turn-around that adjoined the Mercantile. The attack had come at mid-morning. Now it was noon and they'd had nothing for a midday meal.

He told Oliver and the other two men that he'd watch the wagons while they ate at the cafe. "Bring me back a meat sandwich. I'll eat it on the way to the mine."

Roma saw him from the alley window of her hotel, standing beside one of the wagons, smoking a cigar and staring moodily off into the distance.

Slipping the veil over her head, she started for the alley door.

27

SHORTLY PAST TEN o'clock that morning, Rip Tolliver had come riding up to the Farrell house on a lathered horse. He had lost his hat and the loop of brown hair always tumbling across his forehead was nearly in one eye. Angrily he brushed it aside.

Farrell heard the hoofbeats and came to the door. Tolliver breathlessly told him about the failure of the attack on the Northguard wagons.

"Goddamn Ed Kiley rushed things when he shouldn't have an' give Lassiter time to get set."

Farrell's face was ashen. He told Tolliver to go get himself a drink at Shanagan's, that he'd join him soon. In the parlor he stood staring at the faint marks on the fireplace stones above the mantel where Lassiter's belt had been displayed. His mouth twisted.

Just last evening Lineus Swallow had arrived on the stage in answer to Farrell's letter. He was a dapper little man in a red vest with a pencil mustache above a mouth that looked thin enough to have been cut into his face with a razor.

Farrell had almost said, "You made the long trip for nothing. You didn't get here soon enough. My men will finish Lassiter in the morning."

But he had remained silent in the presence of the wiry gunfighter, who had earned his deadly reputation out in California and expanded on it in Colorado. He was thankful now that he had kept his mouth shut.

"Oh, goddamn you, Lassiter!" he cried, and shook his fist at the fireplace.

Roma heard Farrell shout her name. "I'm in my room," she called.

At first, she couldn't imagine a man wanting to sleep alone after he made love. That was the best part of it, the period she had so enjoyed with Lassiter. But after a few nights with Farrell, she welcomed being alone. He was a monster. She hadn't realized it because she had been so blinded with jealousy over Lassiter and that Vanderson woman.

Now that she had cooled down, she knew how foolish she had been. Lassiter had a right to his own life. Just because they had spent some weeks together didn't give her ownership. That came with one's family; a daughter betrothed by a father to the son of

318

a special friend. That was binding for life. Nothing else was.

Farrell stood in the doorway. "What the hell are you doing?" His face was livid.

She had been throwing things into a portmanteau on the bed. "I'm going back to my people."

"Take off your clothes."

Her eyes flashed as she spun around. "You don't yell at me like I'm a common whore!"

"Speaking of common whores, when I'm through with you I'll turn you over to my friend Blanche. She'll train you well."

"You try it." She bared her teeth. And when he reached out for her, she flipped up the skirt of a drab gray travelling dress, one loosely fitted so as not to show off her curves. A dress suitable for a woman travelling alone on a stage coach.

Her fingers brushed the hilt of a knife she wore in a scabbard at the top of a stocking. But Farrell was quick. He ripped the knife and stocking away, then flung her face down on the bed.

He tore her dress down the back, and ripped off her undergarments. He kicked the portmanteau onto the floor, then flung her over on her back and dropped his weight down hard between her knees.

She screamed and tried to sink her teeth into an earlobe but his weight pinned her and fighting was useless. She endured but her icy gaze was locked to his face the whole time.

And when finally he got off the bed and adjusted his clothing, he said, "Be gone by the time I get back."

"You go to hell, you filthy dog . . ."

He dealt her an open-handed smash. Her head rocked and she tasted blood. Then he hit her with the other hand. She tipped over on the bed. Seizing her by the hair, he jerked her face so that it was in range of his backhand. There were sodden sounds like slaps made with wet newspaper.

At last she lay back on the bed. Blood ran into the coverlet.

By then he was gone, the front door slammed so hard it seemed to rock the house. Somehow she crawled to where she could look into a mirror. Her ravaged face made her rush to a chamber pot where she vomited her late breakfast she had eaten in haste.

Then she gathered up her things and put on a fresh dress. She put a veil over her face, as if she were to do penance. Carrying the portmanteau, she finally ran into a boy. She gave him a dollar to carry the portmanteau to the hotel. There she paid for a room and signed her name. She asked for one on the ground floor.

Scrawny Del Watkins, who had been on duty as desk clerk, couldn't get the woman out of his mind. Later that morning he went to Shanagan's. A few drinks loosened his tongue. He told of glimpsing the woman's face when she partially lifted the veil so she could sign her name.

"Lordy, it was a terrible sight," Watkins said, shaking his head. "Somebody beat the livin' hell out of that poor female. Wonder who she is."

"What name'd she sign?" a man asked.

"R. Borjeau." Watkins spelled it and shivered. "If she's got a man friend, whoever done the beatin' on her better watch out."

The story spread. Kane Farrell yawned when he heard it. Bo Dancur got him aside. "I got a hunch she's the female you been keepin' out at your place. The one that come to town with that snake oil outfit."

"If it is, she got in some bad company since. She left me over a week ago."

"Kid that carried her trunk to the hotel was showin' off the dollar she give him. He said she was comin' from the direction of your place."

Farrell smiled. "You know as well as I do that there are any number of houses between my place and the hotel."

"Well, yeah . . ." Dancur rubbed his fleshy chin.

"I heard she took up with some drifter. He probably beat her up, then hit the trail."

"Well . . . mebby. . . ."

Dancur gave Farrell a long look, then walked out of the saloon.

As Dancur pushed his way through the double doors, Farrell was thinking of certain changes that would be made around here once Lassiter was dead, courtesy of Lineus Swallow. Dancur was one of them.

"Lassiter?"

He heard Roma's voice and turned quickly. She stood a few feet away near the freight wagons in the big lot next to the Bluegate Mercantile. She wore a blue dress and a heavy black veil over her head.

"I recognized the voice, so I know it's you behind that veil." He tried to smile, for he sensed she was troubled. When he stepped toward her, she backed up.

"Please, I don't want you to see me. I . . .

I tried to ride a bad horse. I was thrown. I look horrible."

Somehow it didn't ring true. Now that he looked closer he could see her black eyes through the veil and also faintly make out swellings on her face.

"I just wanted to say goodbye, Lassiter. And tell you I'm sorry and ashamed for losing my head and letting jealousy turn me to a man like Farrell. I . . . I don't blame you for being in love with that Vanderson woman. She . . . she's pretty . . ."

"What makes you think I'm in love with her?"

"You are. And she looks sweet. Sweeter than me. I've got a wildcat temper and I know it. . . ." Her voice broke and she knuckled tears through the veil.

Lassiter quickly stepped closer, took her in his arms. "I'm not in love with Melody Vanderson. She's just a friend. You came to say goodbye, so you said. Where are you going?"

"I'll find my people. My father had a husband picked for me. But I ran away and joined Doc and Rex. Now I'm going back. Because it's the only way I can live. I must marry and have children. I was wrong. I know it now."

Before she could stop him, Lassiter lifted a corner of the veil, saw the swollen cheek, the eye nearly closed. She jerked the veil down.

"Don't!" she cried.

"Farrell did that to you?"

"It . . . it doesn't matter. I'm going away and I . . . I just wanted to see you one more time. Because I'll never see you again."

She slipped out of his arms and ran toward the hotel.

He thought of going after her, but raw anger froze him where he stood. Of all the things Farrell had done, this was the most despicable. To beat a helpless woman. Although Roma hadn't told him it was Farrell, he knew as surely as if his name had been written across her forehead, where he had left his imprint in black and blue.

Once he made the delivery up at the Black Arrow Mine and before this day's sun dipped into night, he would kill Kane Farrell.

When Bert Oliver and the others came from the cafe where they had taken their noon meal, he had no appetite left for the sandwich they brought him.

"One of you eat it," he said, trying to keep the hatred he felt for Farrell out of his voice.

He didn't want to upset the men because they had a long, rough climb ahead of them.

FROM A GROVE of spindly aspen, not yet fully leafed out, Vance Vanderson watched the Northguard wagons begin the long haul up grade to the Black Arrow Mine. A slight breeze had come up to stir the cottonwoods that had been planted along Casitas Street, which was a block over from Center. On this street were located the Farrell stables and warehouse, which formerly had belonged to Melody. Due to her own foolishness, she had allowed Farrell to euchre her out of the property. And she hadn't asked his advice, even though he was her Uncle Herm's son. One thing he had learned early in life, was to never accept blame. It was always the fault of someone else.

If Melody had let him handle things from the start, the freight line could have retained the Bluegate property. Now she had done even worse by turning from him, her own husband, and taking up with that no-good Lassiter.

As Vanderson watched the wagons begin

their long, slow climb to the mine, he remembered Farrell's promise made yesterday. At the time, Farrell was certain that Lassiter would be dead by this morning. It hadn't worked out that way, according to Rip Tolliver, who'd had enough whiskey in Shanagan's to loosen his tongue.

"Lassiter won't be around to see the sun overhead at high noon tomorrow," Farrell had said yesterday, when Vanderson had been called out back of Shanagan's for a "conference."

"Why are you so sure about Lassiter after all this time?" Vanderson had asked.

Farrell only gave him a wise smile, but refused to divulge details. Instead, he launched into his grand plan. It was to be an act that would turn everyone against Northguard and against Brad Dingell, who had refused to do business with Farrell Freight Lines under any condition.

"The runaway will no doubt crash right into my warehouse, which is at the end of the mine road. Nobody will attach it to me because they know I wouldn't wreck my own property. There'll be some dead around, no doubt about that, the innocents. And such an act will turn all the venom against Northguard and the Black Arrow Mine, Northguard will go under and Dingell will be hounded out of the county. I shouldn't wonder if Black Arrow isn't put up for sale at a rather reasonable figure." A broad wink, a smile.

"I guess I don't follow you, Kane. What kind of an act are you talking about?"

Farrell peered down into the earnest face of the young hopeful. "A loaded freight wagon will get loose up at the mine and come streaking down the mine road like a projectile fired from a giant cannon."

"How in the world is the freighter going to get loose?"

"Whoever's in charge tomorrow after Lassiter's demise—Bert Oliver, I presume—will give the mules a rest after the long haul. So they'll be unhitched from the wagons. It's the rear wagon, the one nearest town, that I'm interested in. The rear wheels will be blocked. Unblock them."

"You mean . . . *me?*"

Farrell nodded. "I've planted a man in the mine crew. Sam Allard, you know him. He'll give you a hand if you need it."

"Why can't he do the job?"

"Because I'm paying *you*, Vance. I want a capable man so nothing goes wrong. You'll be in my organization, Vance. I'll make you a rich young man. Very rich."

Farrell went into more detail, then suggested he scout the area. And yesterday afternoon Vanderson had done just that, pretending to Dingell that he was interested in a claim some distance above Black Arrow.

Dingell was pleasant enough, but Vanderson doubted that he was fooled about his knowledge of mining. Several times Dingell caught him in discrepancies. But Vanderson had quickly glossed over them, so perhaps the mine owner hadn't noticed.

He saw Allard, the man Farrell had planted among the Dingell employees. He was a stocky man in his late thirties, with a ruddy face. When he got a chance, Vanderson whispered a word, "Farrell." Allard got the meaning and gave a slight dip of the head to show that he recognized a fellow Farrell man.

Vanderson felt he could count on Allard for any emergency which might arise, though he certainly wasn't expecting any. He had ridden down to Bluegate and reported to Farrell, who beamed and clapped him on the back like a benevolent uncle. Farrell took him to the hotel for a fine dinner and afterward drinks at Shanagan's.

And then this morning all hell had broken loose.

Lassiter was still alive and Farrell was meaner than a grizzly with a festering paw. Mean or not, he was more determined than ever to go ahead with his plan for the runaway freight wagon. So determined was he to bring down Northguard and Lassiter with it that he reinstated his original bonus of five thousand dollars. All Vanderson had to do was pull rocks from under the wheels of a wagon.

Just before leaving Shanagan's this noon, Miegs, the undertaker, had come limping in, saying he had finished with his preliminary business with five corpses, one to be buried with private money, the other four with county funds. Although no names had been mentioned, Vanderson had a feeling they were a result of the bungled attack on Lassiter's wagons.

Bo Dancur had sent a message to Kane Farrell, saying it was urgent they have a talk. Dancur waited in his office. He had sent his deputy out on county business. A discussion such as the one he wanted with Farrell could be overheard by too many ears at Shanagan's.

Farrell came swinging up the walk, his face tight. Dancur knew that his latest setback, trying to jump the Northguard wagons, had gotten under his skin.

Farrell flung himself into a chair. "You said you wanted words. All right, let's have them."

Farrell removed a cheroot from a case, bit off the end, spat it on the floor, and then lit it with a match he struck on the side of Dancur's rolltop desk. Dancur didn't comment. He put his feet up on the desk and began talking about Bluegate's future, how it was growing, ranches expanding, mines operating.

"Which adds up to exactly what?" Farrell said in a nasty voice.

"Some lady must've kicked you out of bed, the mood you're in." Dancur grinned slightly to take off the edge, then he recalled the woman with the beaten face and regarded Farrell soberly.

"Never mind about my ladies," Farrell snapped. "Get to the point." Farrell glanced at a slim gold watch he'd won at poker. "I've got a game in a few minutes."

"The point I'm making is this. Some people think there's business enough in this growing county for Farrell Freight Lines and also Northguard."

"And that means what?"

"You jumped Northguard this morning."

"*I* jumped Northguard."

"Your men did. You can't deny knowing Ed Kiley and Blackshear and Marsh and the other one whose name I don't know."

"So?"

"Cavendish and his family was coming in a wagon just after the shootin' this mornin'. Seein' them bodies layin' all over the road sent Mrs. Cavendish into a fit. It scared hell outa the kids, Cavendish says."

"Cavendish saw a little blood in the war, for crissakes."

"His wife didn't. Nor his kids." Dancur took his feet off the desk and sat up straight in the swivel chair. "I want you to get along with Northguard."

"I thought I had a sheriff who'd bark like a coyote when I pulled the string." Farrell gave him a rough smile. "Seems that I need a new one."

"New sheriff?"

"You heard me right."

"Anybody in mind?"

"Rip Tolliver."

Dancur almost laughed, then seeing the

set of Farrell's features, knew the man was serious. "Tolliver's a no-good son of a bitch, and you know it, Kane."

"He happens to be *my* no-good son of a bitch." Farrell got to his feet. "I'll spend the money to put Rip's picture on every third tree in the county. That all you wanted to talk about today, Bo?"

"Leave Northguard be. People are beginning to complain to me. They're afraid that one day there'll be a bad shootout here in town an' some kid'll git hit. Or a woman. This ain't Dodge City or Newton or Abilene. This is Bluegate an' we're on the way to bein' a city. Which means *civilized*."

"You're asking me to back away from Lassiter."

"Northguard, Lassiter. Same thing."

"That I'll never do." Lightning danced across Farrell's green eyes. "One of these days I'm going to take me a walk across a corral full of fresh droppings. Then I figure to get Lassiter on his back. He's going to lick every square inch of my boots till they're clean of every shred of manure."

"You'll have to kill him to do that."

"It's what I aim to do, after he gets through licking. Good day to you, Bo." Farrell went out. The etched glass in the door rattled when he swung it shut. Farrell strode off down the walk, trailing gray threads of cigar smoke.

Bo Dancur had a tautness in his gut. He felt helpless because he knew, as surely as he stood in his own office in Bluegate, that one day soon hell's hinges would never hold back the blast that would engulf the town.

Lineus Swallow had started out as boy and young man with a chip a yard wide riding his shoulder. It had to do with his names, first and last. There had been many broken jaws and teeth suffered by those who saw humor in Lineus . . . "what the hell kind of name is Lynn . . . ee . . . uss?" Or, "Swallow? You named after a bird or a swaller of warm hoss pizz?"

At fifteen when a man who insulted him lay dead at his feet, Lineus Swallow decided he had a talent with a gun. An old time gunfighter, T. J. Shaw, honed that talent.

For twelve years Swallow had traveled about the West, hired by those who wanted someone dead in a legal, standup gunfighting way. He never failed.

He and Farrell had done business before.

At first, Rip Tolliver was surprised and disappointed at seeing the man in Shanagan's. Swallow was short, with narrow shoulders and a waist that looked like a woman's under the binding of a corset.

"About as rugged as a boiled owl," was the way Rip Tolliver put it. "Or a boiled swallow."

Farrell shushed him. "For crissakes, don't make jokes about his name. He's killed for less than that."

Tolliver lost his laughter and took another look at Swallow, who was talking to the meaty Shanagan. There was something in Swallow's pale eyes that peeled the starch out of a man's backbone, Tolliver noticed. After a few drinks, Tolliver was recovering from his big scare that morning out on the Bluegate road.

Farrell took Swallow to a table and Shanagan brought a bottle of Colonel's Choice and two glasses. Farrell nodded and Shanagan walked back behind his crowded bar. "You remember Lassiter," Farrell said to Swallow.

"Do I remember my mother's name? Hell yes, I remember him. That time when you an' me . . ."

"Never mind about yesterdays, it's today that counts." Farrell poured for the two of them. "Can you take him?"

"Can I take him? Does ice melt in the summer?"

"Don't underestimate him. I want you two facing each other. Draw your guns and may the best man win. The better man," Farrell added with a tight smile, correcting himself.

"Yeah, I can take him."

"I want it where everyone can see it."

"Why?"

"If all goes well, Lassiter is going to be very disliked around here. But even so, I want him dead by a faster gun. And good riddance at long last."

"He step on your toes?"

Farrell took a sip of whiskey. "A spy tells me that certain businessmen are getting up a petition to hand to me, listing various reasons they want me out of the county. The one man they'll rally around is Lassiter. After today, he'll be disgraced. But even so, I want him dead also. In his grave at last. A grave for Lassiter."

"It'll cost you. No more partnerships like we had before. This time it's cash on the table."

"How does ten thousand dollars sound?"

"I could hear you better if you said fifteen," Swallow said, his razor cut of a mouth offering as much of a smile as he ever allowed.

Farrell didn't know whether he cared much for Swallow's brand of humor. But he did need the man, unless he himself decided to challenge Lassiter. But that he would never do. One thing his sojourn in Bluegate had taught him—you can buy a fast gun.

29

LASSITERS TWO WAGONS groaned and creaked behind him as they made the long ascent over the uneven road with its potholes and uncovered slabs of rock. In the past few days, Dingell and his crew had worked on the upper half of the road, dumping wheelbarrows full of dirt where the protruding rocks were higher than the roadway.

But the lower half was the way winter had left it, with deep ruts and rocks, some the size of small boxes, half-buried in the narrow dirt road.

They dipped into the creek where it crossed the road and flowed west, instead of continuing south, toward a basin at the foot of the mountains.

With a mounted Lassiter urging them on,

it was all the sturdy legs of the mule teams could manage to haul the first wagon out of the water and back to the dry road. The second wagon was even heavier. Water dripped off mules and wheels as a rest was called for.

A stiffening breeze had finally blown away a buildup of clouds above the Black Arrow Mine. Even at this altitude, where the air was crisp, Lassiter noticed that the mules were soaked in sweat, with froth at their muzzles.

When they were on the slow crawl again and Lassiter's gaze fell on the first wagon, where only one man was seated instead of two, he could see Kane Farrell in his mind's eye, with his superior smile. One more score to settle, he thought with a sudden flare of anger. Included in the burgeoning rage was Roma with her swollen face. He visualized stripping the hide off Farrell's bare back with a horse whip or calling him into the street and gunning him down. The latter part of it only if his luck held. But the moment the grim possibility started to lodge in his consciousness, he kicked it out. In a standup gunfight of course he'd triumph over Farrell. No doubt about it. Confidence had brought him through similar trials in the past and would not desert him now.

"Not much farther, Bert!" Lassiter sang out to Oliver and the lank southerner nodded his head.

Within minutes they ground up to the platform that had been lengthened since Lassiter's last visit, to accommodate two wagons at a time instead of one. They came to a halt, the mules with heads down, winded after the steep climb.

Rocks were wedged under the back wheels of the rear wagon which rested on the last three feet of level ground before the road dropped precipitiously.

Dingell came out of the mine, wiped his hands on canvas pants and offered one of them for Lassiter to shake. "Figured you might git here before noon," he said with a smile.

When Lassiter told him about the attack that had delayed them, the mine owner's face tightened.

"Thank God it wasn't any worse," Dingell said fervently. "You better spend the night up here an' rest up. Plenty of room to spread your blankets."

Lassiter shook his head. "Want to get

down to Bluegate before dark. Got business to tend to."

Dingell looked up into the grim face. "Farrell, you mean?"

But Lassiter stood staring at Bluegate below and didn't reply.

Dingell said, "I'll set my boys to unloading the first wagon. You fellas deserve a drink an' a chance to catch your breath."

Lassiter agreed. But first there were the teams to unhitch. They were driven to the creek, on the far side of the road, where it gushed down from springs at a higher elevation. Then grain was poured into the long canvas troughs so the weary animals could be fed.

By then the first wagon was half empty of steel rails and ore cars. Eventually they would have to unload the heavier second wagon, also carrying ore cars and rails but with the added weight of the big copper boiler.

"While you were gone," Dingell said over whiskey, "some of us in business here got together and made a list of things Farrell has done in these past few months. All of them bad."

"If you run out of ammunition," Lassiter said wryly, "I can supply plenty." Dingell nodded in appreciation. However, Lassiter intended to get the matter settled before the sun went down. He didn't tell Dingell, nor his men.

Dingell talked about a petition to present to Farrell, but Lassiter said they might as well forget it. "He'll only laugh at you," Lassiter put in.

"But if enough responsible citizens are behind it . . ."

"He'll still laugh. I'm sorry, but I know the hombre." Lassiter's lips whitened. "Either laugh or he'll bring in gunhands to cut you down, one by one."

Dingell seemed startled. "I thought he had a rep himself as a gunfighter. Or is he yellow at heart?"

"Never a coward, I guarantee that. But he's just a little more cautious these days. If it comes right down to it, he can still handle a gun. I'll bet on that. He earned his rep the hard way and he's not about to turn his back on it if he should draw a bad hand."

"I understand he's already sent for a gunhand," Dingell said, after taking a sip of the whiskey.

Lassiter leaned forward so that his dark face was in shadow. He was straddling a chair. Bert Oliver and the other two men

340

were seated on a bench. From the platform came the clank of steel rails being stacked.

"This gunhand have a name?" Lassiter asked softly.

"Lineus Swallow. I saw him in Shanagan's this morning. Not much to look at, to tell the truth."

"Lin Swallow. Well, well."

"You know him?" Dingell asked narrowly.

"Our trails have crossed. He worked with Farrell down south on a cattle swindle. They tried to get the last dollar out of a young widow. But they didn't quite make it."

"From the look in your eye," Dingell said, "I've got a hunch you had something to do with their failure to bilk the widow."

"Farrell and I have tangled before coming to Bluegate."

"Just be careful of him. And of this Swallow."

"Yeah, that's good advice. To be careful." Lassiter looked up at the higher peaks wreathed in clouds. His smile was hard. "Seems this isn't a year for being careful." It's a year for calling a man and getting it over with. Which I intend to do. He didn't voice it, however.

Sipping Dingell's good whiskey, eased the

raw weariness of Lassiter's muscles. The gunfight on the Bluegate road that morning had been fury in a capsule. Everything had happened so fast there had not been time to even think. Thank God his instincts were still good or they might all be dead. He had heard the sudden but faint throb of hoof-beats. Something twitched in his brain so that they were audible even above the patient plod of mule hooves, the creak and groan of the two heavily loaded wagons. He had looked to the left into a thick stand of trees and had seen the horsemen. Only split seconds before the firing started. But it was enough to give him an edge.

He stared out of the lean-to window. Bert Oliver and the two men had gone outside. Oliver, a rifle under his arm, was walking the length of the loading platform. Dingell's four miners were still unloading the lead wagon. One of them, stocky, with lank brown hair and a lazy eye, was loafing on the job. He seemed to be more interested in something at the far end of the platform that he was in the unloading. Well, a lazy worker was Dingell's problem, not his.

But on second thought he might speak to the mine owner before they left. Dingell was certainly entitled to a day's work from his

342

men. Maybe he hadn't noticed this one and might appreciate having it called to his attention. On the other hand, he might not. He didn't know Dingell all that well. Although he seemed pleasant, tough when necessary, there was no guarantee that he might not get his feathers ruffled if someone tried to point out a deficiency in one of his men. He remembered the man now, Sam Allard, a drifter who did odd jobs around town.

As this was going through Lassiter's mind, he heard a man's sudden scream of pain and then heard Bert Oliver shout something. He saw Oliver take aim with his rifle.

 30

VANCE VANDERSON HAD made it to the top of the grade, just below the mine entrance, without being observed by anyone who counted. The only one who saw him was Sam Allard, the man Farrell had planted with the Black Arrow crew as a spy. Allard gave him a quick nod of the head, a guarded smile. Then he picked up a heavy packing case from the lead wagon and carried it to the end of the loading platform where other crates and barrels were being stacked. Two of the men were unloading lengths of steel rail for the narrow gauge Dingell intended to run from the mine to the foot of the grade in Bluegate.

Watching his chance, Vanderson at a crouching run left some sheltering pines and ducked under the tailgate of the last wagon without being spotted.

A large rock was tucked under the rim of the right rear wheel, next to the loading platform. Vanderson was surprised how easily he was able to remove it. He tossed it aside without thinking. Immediately the rock bounded down the road, sometimes soaring five feet into the air when it struck one of the slabs that had been uncovered by winter storms. He held his breath, wondering if the sudden descent of the rock would have been heard. But it wasn't, because Allard was tugging another crate out of the wagon, this one making a squealing sound as it was dragged over nailheads on the platform.

Quickly Vanderson ducked to the left rear wheel of the wagon, which was within kicking distance of the trees where he would take instant shelter. Grunting, he tugged at the slab of rock that blocked the wheel. This wasn't going to be so easy. With his hands he dug into the soft ground under it, then tried again. It gave slightly and the wagon moved an inch or so. Looking the length of the wagon, he could see that the end of the tongue resting on the ground had indeed moved. He froze. Had anyone else noticed it? But he heard no outcry.

Scrubbing a forearm across his sweated face, he returned to the wheel block. By working it in short tugs he was able to loosen it considerably. Here the ground was level with a barely perceptible slant until it reached the end of the steep road. He reached up with both hands, intending to give one mighty wrench, then leap aside as the wagon began to move.

Then he thought of his gun. Better to have it handy if somebody jumped him. He drew the .45 from his holster. A nearly new weapon he had bought for a few dollars from a drifter. He'd paid to have his initials etched in the grips, just in case the drifter had stolen the weapon and somebody tried to claim it.

He laid the gun on the ground by his knee. Taking a deep breath, he reached up to tug the big rock aside. Then, before the wagon gained momentum, he would duck into the trees, mount his horse and be off. Near as he could tell, the only other saddled horse at the mine was the one Lassiter rode. A fine animal. After Lassiter was done for, Vanderson intended to talk to Farrell about letting him have it.

If Lassiter tried to chase after him in the dense coverage of the pines, he was a dead man. The prospect of finishing Lassiter off brought a nervous smile under the mustache he was so proud of.

He was tugging and working the large rock. It was gradually inching out from under the heavy steel rim of the wheel. Anxious to get the job done, he cupped the fingers of his left hand around the top of the rock, while exerting pressure at the base with his right.

The rock moved farther than anticipated, out from under the wheel rim, but not to one side as he had intended. His right hand slipped off the base of the rock at the last moment. Before he could jerk his left hand out of the way, his fingers were trapped between the wheel and the rock. Terrible pain shot through him, more intense than any he had ever experienced. Somehow he managed to jerk the hand free as he nudged the rock aside in a desperate move with his knee.

In shock he stared at his mangled fingers as the wagon moved slightly. They were smashed, the ends flat and spurting blood.

Dazedly he looked at the blood as great bursts of pain filled his mind. Then he realized he was screaming.

As the wagon began to move more freely he barely got his right leg out of the way before it was crushed by the heavy load.

Up on the platform, the screaming caused Bert Oliver to throw a rifle to his shoulder. Vanderson, still screaming hysterically, snatched up his revolver and fired up at the lanky Oliver. He never did know whether he hit the mark or missed, for at that moment something exploded in the brain. Mercifully his pain was suddenly gone with the flood of darkness that engulfed him.

Lassiter came pounding from the mine office, gun in hand. "What the hell happened?" he yelled at Oliver and then saw that all four wheels of the second wagon were turning as it reached the grade. It began to pick up speed.

Oliver was pointing at Vanderson crumpled near the loading platform. "Son of a bitch shot at me. I nailed him!"

Through the head, it looked like. "But that goddamn *wagon!*" Lassiter yelled.

"Too late, Lassiter," Oliver said in a strained voice. "He worked the blocks out from under them wheels. An' practically right under my nose. My gawd! What'll happen when that wagon gits to town?. . ."

"If I can help it, it won't. I'm going after it!"

"Boss, you'll bust your neck!"

Dingell came charging from the office just as Sam Allard fired a pistol as he fled toward the trees. But the bullet clanged off the stack of steel rails instead of into Dingell.

Dingell cut loose. Allard, at a dead run, collapsed in a tangle of arms and legs. "That one I been wondering about, to tell the truth. Lassiter, where you goin'? . . ."

But his voice barely carried above the sudden thunderous roar as the runaway wagon, going backward, picked up momentum. It was now fifty feet down the grade and picking up speed every second. Almost hidden now by a great gout of dust raised by the tongue dragging behind.

Without even stopping to consider the hazards, Lassiter leaped into the saddle of his black horse, rammed in the spurs. At reckless speed he began to chase the rumbling monster of a wagon.

Sparks flew in the dusty haze as wheel rims struck the stretches of bare rock. Down, down raced the speeding wagon, straight as the arrow for which the mine above had been named. The roadbed was in a natural depression all the way down, with the sparkling creek on one side and thick pines and aspens on the other. On the left side was a manmade bank, erected to minimize the chances of the road being completely washed out whenever the creek overflowed. Even so, most of the top soil had been washed away during last winter's storms. Raging waters had found a natural conduit in the roadway when hard rains struck higher elevations.

A gust of wind tore off Lassiter's hat, it went sailing through the air like a black, wingless bird. Ends of black hair whipped his face. Wind tore at his eyes so that he had to squint to keep the racing wagon in view. His horse at a gallant run was gradually closing the gap. But at any second the animal could slip on bare rock and send them both to disaster. Somehow in the mad rush down the mountain it kept its feet. Mane and tail streamed out by the wind generated in the mad race to catch up to the runaway.

Once he thought the wagon would solve his problems by destroying itself. The left wheels struck a ledge of rock that had been uncovered by hard rains. It bounded high into the air, tipped at a dangerous angle that

Lassiter was sure would send it crashing over the embankment and down into the creek. But somehow the speeding vehicle righted itself and continued the plunge down the mountain at dizzying speed.

When the wagon had tilted, Lassiter noticed the tongue fly high into the air as it struck an obstruction. Here a cacophony of sound beat at his eardrums as the wheels on the right side screamed along a stretch of rock and shale.

Wind sucked at his breath. Every muscle tense, he unhooked his catchrope that was bouncing to the great lunges of the galloping horse. Bent over in the saddle, he shook out a loop. If he could time it just right when the end of the tongue went flying into the air, he might be able to rope it. And then send his horse either to the left or the right. It would turn the front wheels just enough to send the careening load either into the creek or smashing through the border of trees.

Again the tongue bounced when striking a rock. He shot out a loop. He missed. His heart lurched. He could taste bile. His throat was dry, his lips tasting like warm paper.

He tried again. Again he missed and

hauled in his rope, being careful the speeding horse didn't trip on it.

Some distance ahead was the big dip in the road where the creek veered to the right. Pray to God that a wheel would be smashed on the rocks. Anything to break the deadly downward plunge that second by second was sending it hurtling toward the busy town.

Roma left the hotel by the alley door because she needed to stretch her legs. Tomorrow she would see the last of Bluegate. She wouldn't be sorry to leave. She had acted a fool over a man because of having fallen blindly in love. And when she thought he had spurned her for a slim blonde, she had turned to a man who was his enemy. Anything to disrupt his tranquil life with his new woman.

But she was the one who had paid the price for this folly. Lassiter had told her only an hour or so ago that the blonde meant nothing to him. Perhaps he was only trying to be kind. On the other hand, he had seemed sincere. Reaching the end of the alley, she hurried to cross the street so as not to be so conspicuous to the occasional passerby. As a veiled woman she was bound to cause comment, she well knew.

When she reached the west wall of the big warehouse, she began to slow and to relax. By the time she had walked clear around the big sprawling structure and returned to the hotel, she would have gotten the kinks out of her muscles. She had always been active and being cooped up in a small hotel room was like prison.

Her main objective in life now was to make peace with her father and her betrothed and get on with her life. For a time she had thought there might a different life for her with Lassiter but that had only been a very bad dream. Lassiter was lucky to be rid of such a jealous fool.

As she neared the end of the warehouse, she could hear the voices of young boys. Often on previous walks from Farrell's house, she had seen them there lagging pennies against the large back wall of the building. Here they were more or less inconspicuous from adults who might frown at the gambling of boys so young.

As she turned around the north wall of the warehouse, she started toward the boys at the far end. They were laughing wildly and an older boy was trying to hush them.

They saw her coming and stared. A strange lady who limped slightly and wore a heavy veil so her face didn't show. A lady of mystery.

She had taken no more than three or four steps when she heard a sudden sound. A great rumbling—a chilling sound. It came from the direction of the mountain. She turned so she could look up the scar that was the road, straight as a line drawn in sand between two posts.

Far up the road she saw dust and something that caused her to utter a small cry of fear. Out of the dust came the rear end of a wagon travelling at tremendous speed. It was heading directly for the dozen or so young boys gathered at the far end of the wall.

Picking up her skirts, she began to run and to scream at the boys of the approaching danger.

In Shanagan's there was also a sudden awareness of the strange and distant rumble.

"Sounds like thunder," Miegs the undertaker stated positively.

"No thunder like I ever heard," Shanagan said from behind his bar, round head cocked at the increasing roar.

Kane Farrell at the end of the bar with his bottle of Colonel's Choice, grabbed Rip Tolliver by the arm. Some of Tolliver's whiskey spilled. Farrell's green eyes bore a peculiar shine.

"If it's what I think it is," he said in a hoarse whisper.

He drew Tolliver out of the saloon. "Be ready to jump when I yell," Farrell said, and began to run toward Casitas Street and the warehouse.

Lineus Swallow, who had gone to the hotel to get a room, came out of the building and called to them. "What's that noise?" Everyone was turned now in the direction of the sound that seemed to be increasing by the second.

"Come along, Lin!" Farrell shouted. And Swallow came nimbly down the veranda steps and started running at Rip Tolliver's side. Farrell was slightly ahead, a tight grin stretched across his face.

From the sound, it seemed that Vanderson had fulfilled his mission. Bless him. And if Lassiter killed him, probably had, an indignant Swallow would say that Vanderson had been his friend, and demand satisfaction. Seconds later Lassiter would be dead in the dust.

31

AS LASSITER WATCHED, from the saddle of his speeding horse, he saw the roaring runaway crash into the creek where it crossed the road, throwing water in rainbow tints through bars of sunlight. Without losing a thumbswidth of speed, it rumbled up the far side and on down the road, always with the desperate horseman in pursuit. Shaking out a loop for another try, hoping the flying feet of the tiring horse didn't get entangled and bring them down.

Ahead he could see the north wall of the warehouse. And at street level were some figures, not much larger than ants at the distance. His heartbeat quickened. Human beings in the path of the runaway.

Cold sweat dampened Lassiter's body. Every nerve end screamed. He tried again with the rope as the tongue flew into the air. He missed. But this time it was closer. Very close. But dear God was there time enough to halt this plunging mountain of steel and wood.

At this speed, why didn't an axle snap or

a wheel spin off? He reeled in his dragging rope and got ready for another attempt.

Never had the north wall of the warehouse looked so formidable, like the flat side of a towering cliff. So it seemed in the dizzy moments as the hurtling behemoth narrowed the gap. At top speed, with the saddlehorn jolting against his breastbone, Lassiter, bent over on the back of his galloping horse, shook out another loop in his rope. He set it whirling above his head. Using all his strength to keep the tearing wind that rushed against him like a giant's breath from blowing it down. The loop formed, whirled, whirled and he made his cast.

Just as he let it go, following through so he was within kissing distance of the billowing mane, he saw Roma. Just a flash of her standing against the warehouse wall, motionless as an insect under glass. Her black eyes wide, the lips taut as bowstrings. And she was frantically tugging at the arm of a boy. A wisp of a little fellow probably no more than six or seven. The narrow little face seemed ashen, the eyes enormous. His mouth was wide open as if screaming. But due to the monumental din, the boy's voice was unheard.

For Lassiter to digest all this had taken

no longer than the twitch of an eyelid. Roma's veil had slipped off, revealing her swollen features. By brute force, she dislodged the frightened boy from the wall and sent him spinning toward Casitas Street. People in the street were scattering. Voices also beyond hearing because of the thundering runaway, the pound of hoofbeats from the lone horseman.

As the wagon tongue bounced high into the air after striking a half-buried stretch of flat rock, Lassiter felt as if his right arm was nearly wrenched from its socket. Even so, exultation swept through him as he realized his rope had snagged the roaring beast at last. Which way to turn this granite cliff on wheels hurtling down a mountainside? Lassiter started to wheel his horse to the left, but that would endanger Roma who was still running wildly. As was the young boy who had found his legs and was scurrying to escape the great wagon with its load of deadly metal.

Desperately Lassiter reined his horse to the right. Wheels screeched as it left the road and hurtled toward the warehouse wall. And then with a shudder the wagon began to break apart. It started to cartwheel. Added to the din was the clang of steel rails and the mammoth copper boiler being ejected into the air. What was left of the speeding wagon slammed into the warehouse wall, going through as if it were made of paper. Lumber splintered as well as glass and there were screams from inside the building.

"Roma!" Lassiter cried out as he saw the girl nearly out of danger. But a steel rail, flying through the air like a flung spear, found her. She went down beneath it. Lassiter groaned. His horse, running for so long, seemed unable to stop. It carried him through the great gap in the warehouse wall. Fifteen feet inside the shattered building, Lassiter managed to bring it to a halt. It stood with barrel heaving, slick with sweat. Foam dripped from its muzzle.

A dazed Lassiter stared at the chaos. The desk where he had first seen Melody, months before, was flattened under the copper boiler. Two men lay at the edge of what had been the arena the day of the fight. Another man was crumpled over a shattered chair. From his right arm was a length of white bone.

In the street there were cries and harsh voices. The sound of men running.

Lassiter got out of the saddle and stood on a stable section of flooring; much of it had been shattered by hurtling steel rails and ore cars. What was left of the wagon lay scattered, wheels and shattered body.

His catch rope, like a long dead snake, dangled from the end of the wagon tongue which had been torn loose and now lay propped against one of the ore cars.

With his breathing returning to normal, he was about to rush outside and see if Roma was badly injured when he heard a man's voice behind him.

". . . and you shot Vanderson down like a dog. He was my friend. Better than friend, he was shirt tail kin. Turn around, Lassiter and pull your gun while you're doin' it!"

"Who the hell are you?"

"Lineus Swallow. Turn around, damn you!"

Farrell's man, inventing a tale of relationship to that cowardly Vanderson, the cause of this chaos and responsible for Roma being smashed to earth by a steel rail.

He was in no mood to play games, with Roma lying out in the street, injured or dead.

He looked over his shoulder and saw Swallow with a confident grin, wearing a red vest decorated by a gold watch chain with large and impressive links. Swallow's right hand dangled like a rag in a breeze just above the grips of a holstered gun.

In the gaping hole that had been the north wall of the building were many faces, some frightened. As Swallow's challenge echoed throughout the wrecked end of the building, men began to push out of the way, some shouting their fear.

Lassiter made his turn quickly, dropping to one knee as he did so. Swallow wasn't going to give him a chance to turn clear around. That was evident. For when Lassiter sank to one knee in his turn, Swallow's gun crashed. Lassiter sensed rather than felt the puff of air against his left cheek as a bullet missed by inches where his heart should have been.

It was from a crouched position that Lassiter thumbed a shot. Swallow staggered, looked surprised as the front of his red vest began to darken. Light was leaving his shocked eyes even as he collapsed.

"He tried to trick you, Lassiter," Loland of the Mercantile shouted excitedly.

Lassiter pushed his way through the crowd, having no wish to see Swallow. He had seen more than his share of death in his lifetime.

He got outside and elbowed his way to

where Roma lay in the street. He thanked God because he could see that her eyes were open. Her breasts rose and fell evenly to show that she breathed normally.

Two men had bent down to lift a steel rail from her right leg.

"Let me," Lassiter said and took the rail into his own two hands. He threw off the heavy length of steel and heard it thud against the earth. A smear of blood stained the right side of her dark green skirt.

"My leg," she groaned.

Lassiter's rigid features melted into a smile of encouragement. "Doc will take care of your leg. I want a litter for this lady," he said to the crowd and there was a scurrying of men to carry out his request.

There was a man's sudden scream. "Farrell, you tromped my toes!"

Lassiter froze. He straightened up from Roma and saw Farrell walking purposely through the crowd, unmindful of the feet of other men. The one who had cried out was favouring his left foot and grimacing.

"You've been howling for a chance to meet me face to face," Farrell said in even tones. He halted. "Now's as good a time as any. You've wrecked my building, caused injuries to several of my employees, the deaths of two that I know of. Besides that, you shot my friend Lineus Swallow. No doubt by some sneak trick. You could never have beaten him in a standup gunfight."

"Liar!" Loland of the Mercantile cried, shaking his fist. "It was Swallow tried a trick. It didn't work. This town is fed up with you, Farrell . . ."

"This town has got me for keeps," Farrell said arrogantly.

He didn't even bother to look at the owner of the Bluegate Mercantile, but kept his eyes on Lassiter. A few women in the crowd began to whimper and push away because of the threat of danger.

"Hasn't there been enough killin' this day?" one of them cried out.

In the silence, nobody answered her question.

Lassiter gestured at Roma, who was clenching her teeth at the pain of her injury. "I want to get this girl to the doctor's. Then I'll face up to you, Farrell."

"Always got an excuse, ain't you, Lassiter?" It was Rip Tolliver standing a few feet from the elegantly tailored Farrell in a gray suit with small dark checks. His boots were black, with only a light coating of dust to mar the high polish.

Overhead a flock of brown birds swooped low over the street and then as if mystified by the insanity in the street below, whirled, chattering, and flew toward thick trees at the edge of the mountain.

People were crowding in close to peer down at Roma's bruised and swollen face, evidence that she had been beaten.

Lassiter pointed at Roma. "You marked her, Farrell. Your two hands did that."

"Of course," he admitted with surprising candor. "She's nothing but a fallen woman. She came to my ranch time and again and prostituted herself with my men . . ."

"No!" Roma screamed.

". . . so I decided to teach her a lesson."

"Liar!" Roma cried. "Filthy liar!"

"Listen, everybody," Lassiter said, fighting down his anger, for he knew it was Farrell's plan to get him in a rage so he'd make some stupid move. "Farrell's great friend, Vance Vanderson . . . he's the one brought tragedy to this town. He'll talk."

Farrell laughed. "Now who's the liar?"

"He'll tell the truth about who paid him to pull out wheel blocks and set that wagon on the loose."

"How can a dead man talk?" Farrell sneered.

"He's very much alive . . ."

"You'd never let him live, Lassiter. I know you. . ."

But there was indecision on Farrell's face. He stared hard at Lassiter, then his right hand whipped under his coat and withdrew with a gleaming .45. Above the screams of onlookers, the sudden shifting of feet, came the spiteful crack of the weapon.

But Lassiter had moved suddenly, hurling himself aside, to draw fire away from Roma. He landed on his right shoulder as the screaming from dozens of throats increased. Pain knifed through arm and shoulder as he drew his gun while rolling, rolling. A bullet slammed into the hard-packed street, showering him with dirt. Lassiter sprang to his feet, lunged to the left in order to give Roma more room. He felt as if punched in the stomach as a slug nicked a corner of his silver belt buckle and went screeching into the air.

In the turmoil, with everyone trying to reach safety, Lassiter spotted Farrell duck into the ruined building. Lassiter was after him at a crouching run.

A man yelled, "Lassiter . . . watch out . . . *Tolliver!*"

And Lassiter saw him just as he charged through the gaping hole in the warehouse wall. Tolliver loomed up amidst the wreckage and fired almost point blank. But somehow the bullet missed Lassiter, who was dodging at full speed through the ruins. He saw Tolliver's face, the ever-present curl of dark brown hair low on the firehead. Lassiter fired from the hip. Suddenly most of the curl disintegrated. Strands of it flew into the air. Tolliver's lips parted and all life was washed from the eyes. Blood mixed with a grimy gray matter appeared in what was left of the lock of hair. Tolliver crashed into a ruined chair and flopped over a scattering of steel rails.

"It's you and me now, Lassiter!"

Farrell was calling to him from behind a thick beam that dangled from part of the ceiling that had erupted when the runaway freighter crashed through the north wall.

Farrell stepped into view, hands lifted chest high.

"Let's go at it, man to man," Farrell taunted. "If you have the guts."

Lassiter carefully straightened up. "Who else have you got hidden out?"

"Nobody. Now it's just us, Lassiter. You and me."

Harsh laughter was Lassiter's answer.

"Holster your gun, Lassiter. We'll go at it even up."

Lassiter hesitated, trying to read Farrell's expression through streamers of dust and gunsmoke. There was just a trace of mockery on the full lips. A bank of strained faces crowded at the break in the wall and at the middle doors that had been slid open. Not a sound. The stillness was strange in Lassiter's ears, after the agonizing minutes of the thundering runaway wagon and the pounding rhythm of his own horse straining to the limit of its endurance.

"All right," Lassiter said in a tense voice. "We go at it even up."

He holstered his gun. And the very moment his gun touched leather, he knew he had been tricked. One thing he had forgotten, Farrell was ambidextrous. A faint gleam of steel was visible as a knife passed through a bar of sunlight shining down through a wide crack in the ruptured roof. A knife hurled expertly by the left hand. The point aimed straight for Lassiter's wide chest.

And in that shattered part of a second, Farrell drew his gun. As Lassiter drew his. Farrell's .45 boomed like a cannon. Sound waves whipped through the wreckage, making onlookers jump. But Lassiter had turned sideways to the oncoming knife in that splinter of time, so the bullet cut neatly through a bulge in his shirtfront. The long barrel of the .44 was clanging against the thrown knife, knocking it to the floor. As Farrell fired a second time, Lassiter was on the move. He leaped over Rip Tolliver's body and came up suddenly on Farrell's left side. Farrell was forced to swing around. His green eyes mirrored not only anxiety, but surprise. His teeth clenched as he let fall the hammer of his gun. But Lassiter in a zig zag run was nearly behind him then.

"Even up is it?" Lassiter shouted. "You and your goddamn knife!"

Almost in desperation, Farrell cried, "Stand still!"

He whirled, just as Lassiter aimed for the widest part of his body, and fired again. But the bullet tore up a shower of splinters where it struck that portion of the office floor that had not been caved in.

The impact of the .44 caliber bullet into the chest, knocked Farrell back on his heels. There he took a few staggering steps while staring at Lassiter in disbelief. Desperately he tried to bring up the .45 that dangled from the right hand, while Lassiter stood ready to shoot him again. But Farrell lacked the strength and his gun clattered to the floor. As Farrell sank to his knees, the shocked green eyes never left Lassiter's face.

"I shouldn't have been so cheap," he said in a hoarse whisper. "I should have paid ten men to come and kill you."

Then, with that note of regret in his voice, he fell forward on his face. Some men rushed forward and turned him over.

"Dead," Loland announced with a shake of his head.

At Doc Overmyer's small hospital, Lassiter found Roma. She was in bed and her leg had been splinted.

"I'm going to leave, broken leg or not," she said, her eyes wet.

"We'll talk about it later."

He patted her shoulder and went out. The Thursday northbound stage was just rolling in. Aboard it was Herm Falconer. Lassiter hardly recognized him. He had lost so much weight he seemed almost scrawny. He used a cane to help him walk with a peg leg.

"Took you long enough to get here, Herm," was Lassiter's greeting. But he gave the man a weary smile and shoved out his hand. They shook.

"For a time there I figured to let you an' Melody run things. I guess hearin' about my brother Josh, then losin' my leg, well . . . I just didn't give a damn. But you kept writin' an' I kept thinkin' . . ."

"You're here now and that's what counts. And just in time. You're the one going to help Melody run things."

"Where you think you're goin'?"

"I've got a date to take a lady home. She nursed me when I had a bullet in the back. Now I'll do the same for her with a broken leg."

"You an' my niece never hit it off, huh?"

"I wrote you she married Vance."

"Yeah. I'm sorry about that. I could've told her he wasn't much good."

"He's dead, Herm."

Herm Falconer blew out his cheeks, leaned on his cane and reached for a bandanna. He wiped his eyes. "I feel bad on account of his ma, my poor wife. She loved him . . . too much, I reckon."

Three days later, after a tearful farewell with Melody, Lassiter left with Roma in a wagon. He would stay with her till her leg healed and she found her family.

He turned to look back at Melody, seeing Brad Dingell standing at her side. They both lifted their hands to him. He waved back. Nearby was Melody's Uncle Herm, leaning on his cane. She would be in good hands between the two men. And if she found marriage for a second time in her young lifetime, he hoped it would be better than the first. With Dingell it was certainly possible.

Roma called to him from the bed of the wagon. "I'll be with you all summer, Lassiter. I have a feeling my leg is going to take an awful long time to heal properly."

He smiled to himself. "We'll see."

"Can't we make an early camp tonight?"

"Maybe."

"The laudanum the doctor gave me killed the pain. I want you with me tonight."

"We've got to be careful of that leg."

"It won't be in the way. You'll see."

He looked back at her under the canvas top, black eyes shining mischievously.